Carissa Ann Lynch is the *USA Today* bestselling author of the *Flocksdale Files* trilogy, *Horror High* series, *Searching for Sullivan, 13, 13: Deja Vu, Grayson's Ridge, Shattered Time, Things Only the Darkness Knows, Shades and Shadows*, and *This Is Not About Love*. She resides in Floyds Knobs, Indiana with her husband, children, and collection of books. Besides her family, her greatest love in life is books. Reading them, writing them, holding them, smelling them... well, you get the idea. She's always loved to read and never considered herself a 'writer' until a few years ago when she couldn't find a book to read and decided to try writing her own story. With a background in psychology, she's always been a little obsessed with the darker areas of the mind and social problems.

 /CarissaAnnLynchauthor
 /carissaannlynch
www.carissaannlynch.com

My Sister Is Missing

CARISSA ANN LYNCH

A division of HarperCollins*Publishers*
www.harpercollins.co.uk

KillerReads
an imprint of HarperCollinsPublishers Ltd
1 London Bridge Street
London SE1 9GF

www.harpercollins.co.uk

This paperback edition 2019

First published in Great Britain in ebook format by HarperCollins*Publishers* 2019

A catalogue record for this book
is available from the British Library

ISBN: 9780008324490

This novel is entirely a work of fiction.
The names, characters and incidents portrayed in it are
the work of the author's imagination. Any resemblance to
actual persons, living or dead, events or localities is
entirely coincidental.

Set in Minion by
Palimpsest Book Production Limited, Falkirk, Stirlingshire

Printed and bound in the UK by CPI Group (UK) Ltd, Croydon CR0 4YY

To my children

Monsters are real, and ghosts are real too.
They live inside us, and sometimes, they win.
Stephen King

CHAPTER ONE

That old saying, *you can never go home again*, tickled the edges of my memory and floated on the back of my tongue as I accelerated through the Bare Border welcome sign in my rented Honda Civic. The car was supposed to be the 'luxury option'. Stupid me – I'd actually expected something fancy, like a Rolls Royce. The Honda wasn't bad looking, but as soon as it hit 45 mph, the doors had begun to rattle and shake, the wheels threatening to tumble loose, and the peppery must of cigarette smoke from the previous driver was making my temples ache. In truth, I longed for a cigarette myself, but the last time I'd smoked was, well … it was the last time I came back home.

Nine years ago, I'd come to Bare Border for my sister's wedding, but even then, I'd only stayed for the ceremony and reception. I didn't visit with family. I didn't stay overnight. I'd shared the champagne toast, made a clumsy congratulations speech, then ducked out before the clock struck midnight, Cinderella-style.

I didn't want to stay in Bare Border then, and I don't want to be here now.

But Madeline had asked me to come; not just for a visit, but to 'stay for a while', however long 'a while' meant. She wanted to talk to me about something, but not over the phone. My big sister had never been the mysterious type; in fact, she was pretty terrible at keeping secrets, or at least the old version of her used to be, the one I remembered from my childhood.

What do I really know about her now, besides the fact that's she a mother, and happily married?

I don't know what I was expecting when I passed through the entrance to my hometown – storm clouds and thunder? An ominous feeling in the pit of my stomach? The theme song to *Stranger Things* prickling my subconscious? What I found instead was a scene from a movie script, but not the creepy, menacing variety. The afternoon sky was a silk-screen blue, the sidewalk teeming with children on bikes, and tiny mazes of houses puckered out between the only buildings in town— Maggie's Mart, the elementary school, the library, the post office, and a couple of fast food joints. It looked downright charming and quaint.

As I passed through the town square, I spied the bingo hall that also functioned as a church, creeping up ahead on my left – where my sister was married. From this vantage point, everything about my hometown looked the same as it always had, how I remembered it…

Maybe you can *go home again*, an annoying voice tickled my ear.

I think the expression means that you can go home, but it will never be the home you remember. Nothing is static; everything looks different through a child's eyes. But in my twenty-nine-year-old periphery—nothing about Bare Border had changed.

But, then again, this was as far as I'd been in just under a decade.

Rundown storefronts and residential houses faded away as I navigated up the steepest hill I'd ever climbed in my life. Even though it had been a long time, I knew I had to speed up, or else risk rolling backwards.

I punched the pedal to the floor, revving the engine up the

twisty incline, instantly shifting around the once familiar curves from my past. The Honda rattled dangerously as I gripped the wheel with both hands.

It's not until I reached the top of 'Star Mountain', as the locals called it, that I realized I'd been holding my breath. I hadn't tackled this hill since I was twenty years old, and when you're twenty, nothing seems scary. But now it wasn't the climb itself that gave me a jolt, but the drop off on either side of it. There was nowhere to go but down, down, down if you fell … *and what's at the bottom?* I wondered. I'd never really cared to ask when I was a teen.

Thankfully, the road flattened out again, and right away, I was back on autopilot, taking a right on Painter's Creek Road and then a sharp left on Knobby Pine. There were no more children on bikes, the old farm roads abandoned. Population: nobody cares. There were just too few to count, although that number had probably grown since I'd last come back.

A thousand times I'd made these turns—making the drive back and forth from my first job at Maggie's Mart, driving myself to junior prom after Paul Templeton had stood me up, and my first wreck, when I'd T-boned Mrs Roselle. For the record, the accident wasn't my fault – that woman always ran the stop sign on Lowell's Lane, which intersected with Painter's Creek Road.

My sister's house, and the place where I grew up, was right up ahead, exactly where I left it all those years ago…

The trees opened up and there it was: the crooked old sign for the 'Bare Border Inn'. It whistled back and forth in the wind as I turned down my sister's driveway. The 'inn' was nothing more than a two-story, eight-room house that my grandparents used to run as a bed and breakfast back in the Fifties. To me, it had always just been our house, but my mom and dad had never taken down the sign.

This place has character. History. You can't get rid of that, my mother had told me.

The bubbly vibrations of gravel beneath my tires welcomed me home for the first time in years.

I'd ripped and roared through town, but now all I wanted to do was slow down. I wasn't ready for this reunion – the one between my sister and I or the one with my own childhood. Going back was like returning to the scene of a crime when you were guilty: it wasn't advisable.

But I'm not a criminal. I have nothing to run from, right?

The house itself loomed like a ghoulish shadow, a black silhouette against a backdrop of crisp summer sun. Only, the sun was fading now, a gloomy dull film settling over the rickety inn...

The driveway was longer than I remembered, and the further I got down it, the foggier the air around the Civic became.

The inn was set back from the road in a clearing, thick woods surrounding it on two sides. Almost like an appendage, like it was a part of the woods, not the other way around. I could sense movement beyond the trees ... barefoot children scurrying through the branches, keeping beat with the sluggish pace of the rental car.

These were the children of summer. Bees zipping, bird wings flapping, the rolling water of the creek – all part of their never-ending summer soundtrack. In reality, there wasn't anyone moving through the trees, only ghosts of the children my sister and I once were. The sticky taste of cherry Kool-Aid still clung to my upper lip, mixed with the sweat and dirt from running in that muggy, marshy forest...

There was a pang in my chest – the concept of *family* was something I hadn't thought about in a long time. *There are crevices inside me, yearning to be filled,* I thought, and then I shuddered at the memories and laughed at my own silly thoughts.

Off to my right was a flat field, and in the distance, despite the fog, I could just make out the shape of the Tennors' cottage, and beyond that, Goins Farm. I looked left and right, from the woods and back to the field, and now I had no other choice but to face the giant looming before me. Here it was—*home*. For such a simple, monosyllabic word, it contained so much meaning. So much memory.

I wish I could say that the house looked different, older like the sign. I half-expected it to look more modern, new paint or shingles, at least. But the two-story inn looked just the same. Pale blue shutters, faded windows, blood-red flowers, and overgrown plants licking up the sides of it. In the low-setting fog, it was almost like a house from a storybook. *Memories.* It held almost all of mine, and so many of those weren't good...

A chill ran up my spine as I parked the Civic next to, what I could only guess, was my sister's khaki-colored Jeep. After putting the car in gear, I closed my eyes and counted to ten. *Am I ready for whatever it is my sister has to say?*

Who was I kidding? I already knew why she asked me here; the only real question was: *why now?*

She was pissed off at me, for not coming home for our father's funeral, but that was nearly a year ago. *If she was going to say something, why didn't she say it then?*

Although we had been estranged—besides the wedding nine years ago—we still talked occasionally via text. Neither one of us had ever been fond of phone calls, but lately, even the texts had come fewer and farther between.

I know she's sore at me about the funeral, but I thought she'd get over it after a while. Maybe that was it ... maybe she called me here to ream me out and get it over and done with, I considered. You're supposed to come home for funerals; you're supposed to mourn people when they die. *It's just what you do,* I could imagine my mother saying, if she were still alive. But on the days leading up to my father's funeral, I couldn't force myself to pack my things. I couldn't force myself to pretend I wasn't angry, to pretend that he was this upstanding man who didn't break my mother's heart...

'Emily?' I jerked at the sound of my sister's voice. She was bent down next to the driver's window, her own face inches from mine. Stunned back to reality, I rolled the window down.

She was already talking to me through the glass, her words warbled and low. 'Wow. What were you thinking about, Em? That was one hell of a daze you were just in.'

I could make up some sort of stupid lie, but I won't. This was my sister – sisters don't lie to each other, even if they're not as close as they once were.

'I'm sorry. It's creepy being back here, to tell ya the truth. I'm excited to see you, but also worried about what this thing is you want to talk to me about. Before you say anything, I – I should have been here for you, for dad … the funeral…' As the words tumbled out, they were strangled, like I was trying to say them from under water.

But before I could utter one more misshapen word, Madeline yanked the car door open and scooped me into a hug. I was surprised to find myself shaking with relief, my eyes brimming with tears I didn't know I had. I hadn't seen my sister in so long, yet her arms were warm and soothing, the way a real *home* should feel. *I'd missed her so much.*

Promise me, her voice whispered through the trees. *Promise me we'll be more than sisters.* It was another memory, but one I hadn't remembered until now: Madeline using mom's kitchen shears to draw blood from both of our fingers. Summer sisters, she had called us.

'I'm not mad at you about the funeral, Em. I'm really not.'

'You're not?' We were still holding onto each other, and I whispered the words into her hair, relief flushing over me. Her sandy blonde hair still smelled like that stupid coconut cream shampoo she'd been using since we were teens. She nearly broke my finger once, yanking that prized bottle of shampoo from my hands as I teasingly threatened to pour it down the drain after she made fun of me about a boy.

'I'm not mad, I swear.' Madeline stood up from where she was crouched beside me. She dusted her hands off on her jeans and then worked tangles out of her hair with her fingers.

Her hair was still wavy and unkempt, just the way I remembered, but her face was creased with age. There were tiny little crinkles around her mouth, and even the lines around her eyes had deepened. For the first time, I realized how much she resembled our mother.

'I knew you probably wouldn't go to the funeral, anyway. Things with dad and you, and dad and me … well, we aren't all the same. I can't blame you for handling your grief in your own way. I was a little miffed at first, I admit, but that's not why I asked you here.'

Gathering my purse and keys from the passenger seat, I wiped my eyes and stepped out of the car. I stood there, gripping my purse like a shield, waiting for her to explain. When she didn't, I said, 'Okay, can we cut the suspense now? Why did you ask me to come?'

'All in good time, little sister. The kids are inside waiting to meet their Aunty Emily they've heard so much about … so c'mon! I can't wait for you to see the inside of the place. I know the outside looks the same, but I've replaced all of the furniture, obviously. Well, just wait, you'll see.'

My duffel bag was still wedged inside the trunk, but I chose to ignore it for now.

Now that I was here, standing in front of the old place, and I knew Madeline wasn't angry, I was eager to go inside and check it out.

There was a manic bounce in my sister's step as she led me toward the house, and I couldn't help noticing that she was thicker now, her hips wider since giving birth to my niece and nephew. I sort of liked this filled-out version of her. She looked glowing and healthy, like Mom when she was in her thirties.

'You look really good. I can't believe how long it's been since I saw you. Everything about you is still the same.' My sister looked back at me from over her shoulder, rolling her eyes. She pointed at her soft belly. She was wearing loose-fitting mom jeans and a Green Day T-shirt that I was pretty sure used to be mine. I couldn't help but smile.

'I don't look great, you don't have to lie to me.'

Before I could argue, she pushed the front door open.

The first thing that hit me when she opened the door was the smell. It wasn't unpleasant, but it wasn't flowery either. In fact, it reeked of sweet, dusty old fruit—until now, I hadn't realized that my childhood had a smell, but it did. The past came rushing back to me ... Madi and I, racing through the front door as kids, shoving each other down the driveway to get there first. Madi in her overalls, one long strap swinging wildly behind her. And then, when she was older, she wore low-slung jeans and cropped T-shirts. I always admired her style, and the way she could outrun me every time...

As I stepped in behind her, it took me a minute to clear the fog of confusion.

What used to be the front living room was now some sort of office-playroom. The only thing that seemed the same was the heart pine flooring. I stared at the entryway beneath my feet; it was covered by a fuzzy, polka dotted rug, but I knew without thinking that if I peeled it back, I would find a horseshoe-shaped groove below it, from the time dad tried to lug that steel safe over the threshold. Mom damn near killed him for buying it.

The right half of the living room was a chaotic scene of toys: a rocking horse, a chalkboard on wheels, and buckets of Legos and dolls. But on the left side of the room was a neat yellow desk with, what I guessed, was my sister's computer and stack of work papers.

'Just ignore this room. It's a mess. I've given up on trying to sort those toys. Follow me. The kids are in the kitchen.'

Suddenly, it seemed so quiet I was overcome with a strange sensation – the air in the room was too thick, like there was some sort of tension swirling around us. I couldn't help feeling like I'd walked into some sort of tomb.

'They're being awfully quiet,' I remarked, trailing my sister as she led me through the familiar arch from the living room to the dining room, and then onto the kitchen.

I am the worst aunt in the universe. Ben was eight and Shelley was three, and I'd never laid eyes on them. Not really. Sure, I'd liked their pictures on Madeline's Facebook and Instagram accounts, but that didn't really count for much, did it? We had planned nearly a dozen meet-ups over the years, but I'd always used my work as an excuse not to come. It wasn't that I didn't want to meet my niece and nephew … I just didn't want to come to Bare Border to see them. Madi had never shown any anger about my absence from their lives, but I suspected that my failure to be a decent aunt, and not showing up for my father's funeral, were the reasons for her becoming more distant with me over the phone lately.

'Here they are!' My sister was standing in the middle of the kitchen with her arms spread wide, and all I could think was: *This is where my mother should be standing.*

An image of my mother in her stained cooking apron, tapping her foot impatiently as she waited for her famous lasagna to finish baking in the oven, sprung up from my memories.

'Where are the kids?' I brought myself back into focus.

There was no one in the kitchen, besides my sister and me.

I walked around the empty space, taking my time. The wood cabinets were still painted white, just like mom used to keep them, but these were newer, not the same … yes, there were shiny new handles on the cabinet doors. I opened one of the drawers and closed it back. I could feel my sister watching me.

The sink had also been replaced by one of those modern vessels I'd only seen on TV. Tenderly, I ran my hands over the navy-blue countertops, my nose recognizing the green dish soap mom used to use. What was it called … Palmolive?

9

'Are they hiding?' I glanced back at my sister.

I was surprised to see that her expression had changed. Her lips were curled down, her eyes hard and serious, like two little black beads. Her initial excitement to see me had morphed into a mask I knew too well … she was worried about something.

'I don't have any children. I made all that up. The pictures, the stories…everything was a lie.'

'Huh?' I tilted my head to the side, waiting for the punchline. But she still looked strange, her eyes floaty and her voice flat. *Is my sister capable of telling such a massive lie? It's not like I would know the difference—after all, I've never actually seen Shelley or Ben in person…* My heart was thumping in my chest as I waited for Madi to explain.

'Ahhh!' I jumped back in surprise as the cabinet doors beneath the sink sprung open with a sharp bang. One at a time, two small children popped out and ran straight for me. I chuckled at my niece and nephew, surprised.

Behind me, Madeline was cackling now, just like she used to when she drank too much Seagram's when we were teens. After all these years, I'd almost forgotten how much she loved to play pranks.

'I see you haven't lost your sense of humor,' I said, rolling my eyes, and then I mouthed the word, *bitch*, over my shoulder, so only she could see it.

I knelt, taking both children in my arms.

The smaller of the two, my niece Shelley, lifted her feet in the air as she hung on my left arm. Ben was excited to meet me too and wrapped both arms around me. With the weight of them both, I had to steady myself.

'So, you must be Shelley and Ben. I'm excited to finally meet you guys. I'm your Aunt Emily.'

'We know that already, silly woman,' said Ben. He let go of me, pacing back and forth next to little Shelley, while making a high-pitched squeal that set my teeth on edge.

10

His strange squealing didn't surprise me much – Madeline had told me that he struggled with hyperactivity, and recently, a doctor had told her that he might be on the autism spectrum.

Shelley was more subdued, and keen to stay in my arms. I stood back up on my feet, lifting the tiny girl onto my right hip, then shifting her to my left in an awkward pose. I was surprised at how heavy she felt. I'd held a baby once or twice, but I'd never held up a toddler with one arm like this. Again, I felt my eyes welling up, as I stared into the face of my sweet little niece. She had my sister's pointy chin and big smile, but those eyes ... those bright blue eyes matched mine. I swallowed down a lump in my throat, trying to hold the tears at bay. It felt so good meeting these children – these extensions of my sister and I – for the first time. Suddenly, it seemed so ridiculous that I had waited this long to be in their lives.

'And your imaginary husband ... did you make him up, too? Where is John this lovely evening?' I teased, glancing over at my sister.

Madeline's bright red cheeks and toothy smile faded almost immediately. The worried look returned. I was half-expecting another stupid joke to follow, but when my sister pursed her lips and changed the subject, I knew something was wrong.

'Let's show Aunt Emily the bedrooms, shall we?'

Shelley and Ben wanted to show me their rooms first, of course. Overcome with nostalgia, I let Ben give me the tour of his bedroom, the same room where my sister had slept when we were kids. The Debbie Gibson posters and purple speckled paint were gone, replaced by neat brown and blue wallpaper, pictures of boats and trains on the borders.

'Mom's going to let me paint it soon. I don't want these baby pictures no more. I want *Five Nights at Freddy's* covering my walls.' Ben raced back and forth in front of his TV set, running the tips of his fingers along the wall. There was a clear wear pattern in the carpet where I suspected he paced a lot.

11

'Do you know the game *Five Nights at Freddy's*? Want to play it with me?' Ben asked, his words loud and strung together.

'He's obsessed with it,' Shelley whispered, squeezing her tiny hand in mine.

Before I could answer Ben's question, Madeline replied, 'I'm sure Aunt Emily would love to, but not right now. We're going to finish showing her around the house first.' Ben made that high-pitched squeal again and saddled up to a laptop that set on his desk.

We left him there, already focused intently on his game, while we moved on with the tour.

Next was Shelley's room. It was only one door down from Ben's, but this room was smaller. This was the one I was most excited to see because Shelley's room used to be mine.

Expecting to see a huge change in décor, I was shocked to see the same pink plaster, with tiny unicorn paintings on its surface. I'd painted those unicorns myself when I was only eleven years old.

'You didn't paint over them...' I reached out to touch one of the unicorns. With its blue-black eyes and a long golden horn, it was sneering in a way that now almost seemed grotesque.

'Of course not,' my sister said.

'I thought Mom would kill me when she saw what I'd done,' I whispered, still running my fingertips over the bumpy paint.

'Oh, I didn't. I knew she'd love your little masterpiece,' Madeline said, quietly. I didn't have to see her face to know there was a trace of resentment there.

While she was always my father's favorite, I was my mother's baby. So, it was no surprise that when they split, we both took separate sides...

You let her get away with everything! I could still hear my sister's startling screams echoing through the hallway. She loved me to death when we were kids, but our teenage years were strained.

The bedroom closet had white pocket doors that also looked

the same. They were pushed halfway open, and without thinking, I reached for the handles, eager to see inside it.

'I did paint over your stuff in the closet, though.'

My hands froze on the handles. 'I'm glad,' I mumbled as I turned away from the closet.

'I love your bedrooms!' I was trying to be one of those perky aunts, with overdone enthusiasm, like the ones you read about in wholesome novels, but in truth, this whole situation felt awkward and strange. I wasn't used to being around kids, and even though I was thrilled to meet them, I couldn't help feeling like an actress playing the part of 'Aunty Em'. I should have come home when Ben was born, and then Shelley, and there were plenty of chances in between too – birthday parties, and the funeral – but I wasn't ready to face this place, not yet, at least.

'Shelley, why don't you go play with Ben? Or take some of your dolls out of the trunk? Your aunt and I are going to have some coffee and a little chat. Please don't fight with your brother. I would hate for Aunt Emily to see you guys get in trouble.'

Ben had drifted back into the hallway and he was clinging to Madeline's leg. 'Go on now, you two.' She gently nudged them. They galloped toward Ben's room, pushing and shoving one another in a race to see who could get there first. I smiled at them, overcome by my own memories of sibling rivalry.

Grateful to have a moment to speak alone with my sister, I followed her back down the hallway toward the kitchen. I hadn't seen the rest of the house yet, and I was eager to see which bedroom Madeline had chosen for her and John, and which bedroom she'd put me up in for my stay.

'The kids are beautiful. I wish I could have met them sooner,' I said to her backside as she walked.

As soon as we were back in the kitchen, she set to work pulling out coffee mugs and plugging in her Keurig machine.

'John left me for another woman.' Her back was still to me

when she blurted out these words, and I saw her hunch down in a defeated posture.

I took a seat at the table, flinching as the chair squealed loudly across the tile floors. I wasn't sure what to say. I was shocked, to say the least.

Mournfully, I watched my big sister glide around the kitchen, taking a package of cookies down from the cabinet and choosing a coffee blend for both of us.

This was the thing about Madeline and me – we were comfortable in our silence together, even after all this time. I could tell her I was sorry and ask a million questions, but I knew she would tell me when she was ready.

After the cookies and coffee were on the table, she told me, in a hushed whisper, that John had been having an affair.

'Did you know?'

Madeline shook her head. 'I had no idea. He told me two Saturdays ago, out of the clear blue, that he was leaving me for his secretary. Her name is Starla. What kind of stupid name is that?'

'Pretty freaking stupid,' I agreed. 'I'm so sorry. Have you filed for divorce?'

She took a sip of her coffee, and said, 'Not yet, but I'm going to. I haven't even told the kids. I covered for his sorry ass. Told them he was going on a business trip for a while. I thought maybe he would change his mind … but he hasn't even called or come by once since his little crude announcement.'

'He hasn't even come around to call on the kids?' I was shocked. I didn't know John well. Sure, he'd seemed pleasant at the wedding, but that didn't mean much. I tried to remember what I knew about him but it wasn't much. He was essentially a stranger to me. Madeline rarely talked about him in her texts. There was one time she called me … what was it that he said in the background? I couldn't remember. He'd been irritated about something, shouting about one of the kids. But she'd always given the impression that things were good between them.

Madeline shook her head in disgust. 'He took a duffel bag of clothes and his bottle of cologne, and then told me he was staying at Starla's for a while.'

What an asshole, I thought, clenching my teeth as I thought about those sweet little kids and my sister struggling to work and take care of both of them.

'What can I do? Tell me how I can help.' I took her hand in mine, my jaw still tight with anger.

'Well, I could use your emotional support, for one. But most of all ... the kids go back to school next week. I need more time – time to figure out what I'm going to do. Time to plan my next move. Also, I have to sell this house, Em. I can't afford the utilities or the property taxes, not on my income.'

'But the mortgage is already paid for.'

Madeline stuck up a hand to stop me. 'I still can't afford it. Well, I could if...'

'If...?' I pressed.

'If I had a roommate. Or, I was thinking I could open it up again, like Grandma and Grandpa used to do...'

My heart filled with dread as I realized what she was asking.

'I can't move back here. I can't. There are too many bad memories here, Madi, you know that...'

'But there are good memories, too, aren't there?'

I nodded slightly, unsure if there really were...

My sister's eyes were filmy again. She was staring at an old-fashioned cat clock on the wall. Following her gaze, I suddenly realized that it was the same one that had always hung there. *You can never go home again* – those words pinged around my head like ping pong balls, but I quickly shook them off.

'I can stay for a while. I'll need an internet connection for work.'

'Already have one,' my sister gushed. Her face was red and cheery again, like a heavy load had just been lifted from her shoulders. I didn't want to get her hopes up too much – I couldn't stay *that* long.

'Thank you, Em. I knew I could count on you.' My sister threw her arms around me for the second time today, nearly knocking over the coffee between us in the process.

I rested my chin on her shoulder, staring out the kitchen window behind her. The sun shone brightly again, and through the trees, I could see a sparkle of water glistening between them. Those woods held nothing but horror for me, memories of the time I got hurt out there circling back for the first time in years…

Even though I was sitting here now, doing the right thing, I wanted to grab my own duffel bag and run from this place.

Maybe the saying means you *can* go home, you just shouldn't.

CHAPTER TWO

The night trickled into the early morning hours, my sister and I chatting on the couch in the den. We chatted for hours after the kids went to bed, about John, about my lackluster love life. My sister asked me questions about work and college. *Has your life turned out the way you thought it would?*

It was strange how even after all this time, and distance, things between us felt the same. My sister was the only person who could pluck a thought, just like that, from my brain. The night had taken on a dreamlike quality, the wine she kept pouring making me fuzzy and strange.

By the time I stumbled back out to the car to retrieve my bag, I was overcome with sleepiness. The long drive to Bare Border and the hours of catching up had gone straight to my head. A rush of wind ripped through the trees surrounding the property, creating a thousand tiny whispers in the night air…

Like a timid child, I yanked my bag out of the trunk and ran back inside with my head tucked down to my chest.

Madeline was waiting for me in the doorway. She looked tired too, and she pointed down the east hallway as she rubbed sleep from her eyes.

'I put you up in the guest room. The Mello Yellow Room.'

I nearly choked when she said that – either from tears or laughter, I didn't know. I'd forgotten we called it that because it was so yellow, like our favorite citrusy drink when we were kids. Mom had painted the room herself, and she'd chosen this god-awful mustard-colored paint that gave the room its name today.

Well, it's my sewing room. So, it doesn't matter if you girls like it or not, my mother had huffed. She would sit back there for hours some days, her posture perfect and stiff as the machine whirred and droned out its own methodical beat.

There was a pang in my chest as I dragged my bulky bag down the dark hallway, which was on the other side of the house as Madeline and the kids.

With the kids asleep and my talk with Madeline over, the house resumed its crypt-like silence. The door to the old sewing room creaked open and I felt around for a light switch.

When the lights popped on, I gasped. Mello-Yellow was no more; the walls had been repainted a soft petal pink.

As I tossed my heavy bag on the full-sized bed in the middle of the room, my chest thickened with fury. *How could you, Madeline?*

The room was mostly bare. It was obvious that it was rarely used anymore.

Besides the bed, there were a small heart-shaped nightstand and a stout chest of drawers in the corner. I walked around the room, eyeing the pale pink walls.

My mother had painted this room yellow. With her *own* hands.

Now she was dead, and her hands would never create, paint, cook, sew, or hold me again.

And you just had to paint over it, didn't you, Madi?

It had been a long time since I'd felt this sort of anger toward my sister. I'd nearly forgotten how easy it was to dislike her sometimes…

It was now, in this moment, that I realized I'd never gotten over the fact that it was her and Dad on one side, and Mom and

18

I on the other. After twenty-five years of marriage, Mom had found out he was cheating. Instead of kicking my father out of the house that they had raised their children in, she had packed up her own belongings and left town. Madeline and I were adults by then, but still – their divorce had shaken me to the core. I was furious with my father; I wouldn't even speak to him for months. But my sister, on the other hand, shamelessly defended his actions.

He deserves to be happy. You know he's never been happy with her, Emily! This is good for both of them, don't you see that? My sister tried to reason with me, but she always made it sound like Dad was doing Mom a favor by cheating on her, or that Mom was somehow responsible for his misdeeds. She took his side and I took Mom's. We drew our lines in the sand and tossed handfuls of nasty words across the middle…

But it turned out Mom didn't need me to defend her because six months after moving into her own apartment, she suffered a massive heart attack. I would never say this to my sister, but I'm certain she died of a broken heart. Losing my father killed her – literally. And even though, deep down, I knew it was completely irrational, I blamed that man for her death. *I blame him still.*

Now he's gone too, and there's no one left to blame.

Is that why I stayed away so long … because of him? I wondered. There were always excuses – visiting Madi and the kids was that one thing on my to-do list that always got carried over to the next week, the next month, the next year. I didn't want to see my father, but it wasn't only him, it was the ghosts of my past – old friends, old boyfriends, and … the woods. I hated those damn woods.

Shuddering, I thought about my sister's current situation with her own husband, John. He was cheating on her, just like Dad did to Mom.

Deep down, there was this niggly, nasty part of me that wanted to say, *It's your fault. You didn't make him happy, Madeline. This is better for everyone; don't you see that?* Give her a taste of her own medicine.

But those sorts of vicious thoughts made me instantly feel ashamed. I wanted my sister to be happy, and despite what happened with Mom and Dad, she didn't deserve to be treated that way by her husband.

I yanked the duvet off the bed and crawled beneath the sheets. My new silk pajamas were folded away in my bag, and I casually considered getting back up to slide them on, but then my thoughts were still muddled, my feelings toward my sister unclear…

Maybe Dad had painted over Mom's walls. He lived here up until last year when he died, after all. But with my eyes closed, I could still see that pretty shade of pink. It was something Madi would choose.

Should I ask her about it tomorrow? Or am I just being petty and overly nostalgic about Mom? Before I could give it a second thought, there was a soft tap on the door.

I pulled the covers up to my chin, strangely afraid. 'Who's there?'

'It's your sister, silly.'

The door was unlocked, and a moment later, Madeline pushed it open a crack and looked in at me. 'You got everything you need? What time do you want me to wake you up?'

My mind was still angry over the paint and mom, but I said, 'I'm fine, and I'll set my alarm myself.'

'Thanks again for coming, Em. And thanks for staying a while. You have no idea how much this means to me.'

I nodded, still unable to meet her eyes. I wanted to cry about the paint on the walls. I wanted to cry over my mother's death. Hell, maybe I wanted to cry about dad, too. I wanted to be left alone.

Mom doesn't live in the layers of paint on the walls, Emily, I reminded myself. But this was exactly why I didn't want to come home. When I was away, I could push it out of my mind. I could forget. *But here, there's no avoiding the past…*

'Goodnight,' Madeline said, pulling the door back closed.

'Madi? Wait. Why didn't you just tell me over the phone? I don't understand why it was such a big deal, why this thing with John was some sort of secret?'

My sister peered back in through the crack. Her mouth looked droopy and strained, her eyes getting that far off look in them again...

'That's not the only reason I asked you here. There's more. But we'll talk about that tomorrow.'

The door clicked shut. I listened to the soft tapping sounds of my sister's footsteps moving down the hallway. *What the hell does that mean? Why is she being so vague and mysterious?*

I slipped back out of bed and flipped out the lights. Before getting back in, I tiptoed over to the window and peeked out through the blinds.

The backyard was dark, but I could see billowy shadows dancing in the distance – the trees in the forest never went to sleep.

They were always there, watching me, haunting me, even when I lived far away ... those creepy woods were the one thing I hadn't been able to forget. Sometimes, I still dreamed of *falling, falling, falling...*

I wonder if it senses me, if it knows I've come back home. Again, I scoffed at my own childish notions. Maybe my sister wasn't the only one acting strangely. Being here was bringing out the worst in me already. *Those slender crevices are splitting open—waiting to be filled with memories ... memories I've lost forever.*

What my sister didn't know was that I had a secret too. Mine wasn't as cryptic as hers, but it was equally important.

She'd been asking me to come back home for so long. And I'd never planned on actually coming, but there were events that had occurred over the last few weeks that made the timing just right for a trip back home.

I'd lost my job at the paper. I hadn't told Madi yet, although she'd given me plenty of opportunities to bring it up earlier this evening. But I would. *I'll tell her tomorrow,* I decided.

So, even though I could stay and help out with the kids for a while, I couldn't help much with bills until I found a new job. There wasn't much work to be had in this town, and even if I did find a job, I didn't want to stay here long enough to need one anyway.

I crawled back into bed and pinched my eyes shut, desperate to sleep away the worries. I thought it would take hours to drift off, but my mind turned cloudy and wild, and within minutes, I was dreaming of the trees.

CHAPTER THREE

When I woke up, the house was shaking, the *tat tat tat* of heavy rain pounding the windows and rooftop like a gangster from a black-and-white mobster movie. Startled, I sat up straight in bed. Mom's old sewing room drifted back into focus.

Coming back to Bare Border hadn't been a dream after all. Too bad.

As though my movements were their own version of an alarm, someone rapped on the door.

'I'm up, Madi,' I grumbled.

'It's Ben.' The door creaked open and one big brown eye peered in at me through the crack.

'It's storming. Can I get in bed with you?'

I was surprised but tried not to show it. I'd only met my nephew yesterday. 'Yes, of course.'

I pushed the covers back and motioned for him to crawl in beside me. He bounded toward me like a Saint Bernard minus the slobber. He jumped up and down on the bed, to the count of eight, then wriggled like a worm beneath the blankets.

I wrapped an arm around him and sniffed his soft brown hair. It was too long, scruffy around his ears and hanging too low in his eyes, but it felt soft like feathers and it smelled like the same shampoo Madeline used.

Stealing a glance at my cell phone on the nightstand, I was surprised to see it was nearly eleven in the morning. Sleeping this late wasn't all that unusual for me, but I was surprised Madeline wasn't up making breakfast, or whatever motherly things she did on Saturday mornings.

'Where's your sister?' I asked, stroking my fingers through his hair. He shied away from me now, skirting closer to the edge of the bed.

'She's been up for hours, too. She's watching *Teen Titans Go*. I turned it on for her and poured her a cup of juice. I did spill some on the floor though...'

'Where's your mom?'

'Where's your mom?' he repeated my words.

Madeline told me he liked to do this too – repeat words and phrases, and sometimes echo back what he'd just heard. I wasn't sure if I should repeat my question or move on.

'Okay, buddy. Let's just get up. When I was your age, I liked to watch cartoons on Saturday. What is your favorite cartoon?'

'I don't watch cartoons. I play *Five Nights at Freddy's*. Maybe they will turn it into a cartoon. Want to play it with me?'

I assured him that I would soon and listened as he described every level of the game while I pulled on cotton shorts and my favorite morning hoodie.

Ben told me more about the game as I padded down the hallway and made my way to the kitchen. *Coffee. Why hasn't Madi made coffee yet?*

'Is your mom sleeping in, too?' I fiddled with the fifteen buttons on the coffee machine before I realized it wasn't plugged in. Ben didn't answer me, just stared up at the swooshing black tail on the cat clock, hypnotized. As I scavenged through the cupboard for coffee cups, my foot landed in a puddle of juice.

'Okay,' I said, flustered, switching my focus to finding paper towels.

After I cleaned up the spill, I made my way toward my sister's room. On the way, I passed Shelley. She was sitting pretzel-style on the floor in her room. She was indeed watching *Teen Titans Go* and her lips were stained purple from the juice drink.

The door to my sister's bedroom was closed.

'Does Mommy normally sleep this late? I don't want to wake her up...'

Shelley noticed me, finally, and waddled out into the hall.

'No, Mom's an early bird. Early birds eat worms.'

I smiled. I might have been my mother's favorite, but she and Madeline had a lot in common; they both liked to get up early – too early for my tastes.

'Well, your mom and I were up pretty late last night. I probably wore her out.'

Softly, I knocked on my sister's bedroom door, then waited. Ben clung to my legs now, squeezing my thighs like a vice grip, as he rambled on about that game.

Shelley tiptoed up beside me, gave me a knowing look, and tapped the door with her pointer finger. She was right—it wasn't closed all the way, and when she jabbed it, the door wobbled forward.

'Madeline, are you still asleep?' But even from here, I could see that she wasn't.

The bed was perfectly made, the corners tucked in tightly, military-style the way she liked them. I pushed the door all the way open. My sister wasn't in her room.

'Madi?' I called out again. I'd almost forgotten, there was a master bathroom attached. I jiggled Ben off my legs and walked toward the bathroom.

But one glance inside the open door revealed she wasn't in there either. The bathroom was pristine, clean white counters with bottles of perfume perfectly aligned.

It almost looked like she never slept in the bed or used the bathroom at all.

'Maybe she got up early and went to the grocery store.' I

25

shrugged. A quick glance out the front curtains revealed I was right – the tan Jeep was gone, only the rented Civic remained in the driveway.

'While we wait for her to get back, why don't I make you guys a late breakfast?' The idea of me cooking was ridiculous, but I felt like I had to do something. If I couldn't help Madi out financially, I could at least pitch in for a little while, with housekeeping and cooking chores.

I opened the fridge and peered inside. There was plenty of food, and I thought it was unlikely that Madeline had gone out to get groceries after all.

'How do you guys like your eggs?' They were standing in the middle of the kitchen, looking up at me like eager puppies.

'We don't do eggs,' Shelley said.

'Ew,' Ben concurred.

'Okay, well, then what do you guys want to eat?' I asked, exasperated.

'Mac and cheese?' Shelley suggested, with a hopeful smile.

Mac and cheese actually sounded good to me, too, and it's one of the few things I knew how to make. In fact, pasta from a box was about all I ate myself anymore.

It took me a minute to find the macaroni, pot, and spoon. And then another few minutes to figure out how to light Madeline's gas stove.

While I boiled the water and softened the noodles, Ben told me more about his favorite game. Shelley was intent on helping me. At first, I was worried about letting her stir, afraid she would get burned, but she seemed to know what she was doing, and she was eager to mix in the cheese and milk when it was done.

'I'm going to be a chef,' she told me, but it sounded more like 'seff' when she said it with her tiny baby voice.

I watched the children eat, my own appetite gone. Moving to the kitchen window, I looked out at the backyard from my childhood. Water shimmered on the trees in the forest, and from here, they seemed to be covered in tiny wet diamonds. But other than that, there were no traces of the storm I'd heard when I first woke up.

I wondered where Madeline had gone, and why she didn't tell me first. What if the kids had gotten hurt and I hadn't heard them? Would she leave me alone with the kids all the time now that I was staying here? I didn't mind helping out, but I was definitely not equipped to be a babysitter. I didn't have the experience, or the patience…

After lunch, Ben showed me his game and insisted I play it, too. Shelley watched and cheered us on, lining up Barbies as spectators. Finally, Ben was ready for a break, so he and Shelley played with their toys and chalkboard in the living room, while I checked the windows often, waiting for Madeline to get back.

When Shelley stood up from playing, I noticed a dark, circular stain on her pajama pants. She saw me looking, and said, 'I peed my pants.' Her lip trembled, and my heart lurched.

While Ben shouted for Shelley to come back and play, I scooped my hands under her armpits and carried her to the bathroom, careful to keep her urine-laden clothes from touching mine. My biceps burned as I lowered her onto the bathroom floor. Struggling, I peeled the wet bottoms off as I tried to coax Ben. 'She'll be right back!' I huffed.

By the time I'd located clean shorts for Shelley and got her changed, it was nearly five o'clock.

I was starting to get annoyed. It wasn't that I minded spending time with my niece and nephew, but I was still wondering why Madeline hadn't at least bothered telling me she had somewhere to go. Shelley seemed fine without her mother here, but Ben was getting more and more restless, causing my own panic level to rise.

'Where is my mommy?' he asked, for nearly the tenth time. Like me, he paced in front of the living room window, looking out often.

'Out shopping, I guess. I don't know,' I mumbled, wringing my hands.

I texted her again, and when she still didn't answer, I called. Her phone rang and rang, finally reaching her voicemail. I left another shaky, awkward message, trying to hide my indignation. It was the fourth or fifth message I'd left so far, and I was starting to feel resentful that she hadn't, in the very least, called back to tell me where she was or what she was doing...

'What's for dinner?' Shelley squeaked. Tiredly, I rubbed the back of my neck. *Do these kids ever stop eating or playing?* An image popped up of one of those battery commercials ... *they keep going and going...*

I wanted to take a shower and relax in my room, but the kids kept me moving. My own stomach was rumbling now, too, and I wondered briefly if there was a pizza place that delivered nearby. But I already knew the answer to that. There was nothing much around here. The closest pizzeria was twenty miles south of Bare Border. You want pizza around here, you either drive to get it or you settle for the waxy crap they sell at the store.

My mouth watered as I thought of the Chinese carryout store near my apartment. *Takeout sounds so good right now ... the peaceful silence of my apartment sounds good, too.*

My phone rung and I jumped up from the couch, eager to talk to Madi. I was disappointed when I saw that the caller wasn't her.

I recognized the number – it was my landlord, Jin. He knew I'd lost my job, and he was probably calling to see if I'd made arrangements to move out yet. I wasn't sure if that's what I wanted to do, but without a job, I wouldn't have much choice. I silenced the call. Shelley and Ben were still staring at me, waiting for me to say something.

'Not your mom. But I'm sure she'll be here soon.' They didn't look convinced, my own voice shaky, unsure.

I tried one more time to call her, reaching her voicemail again. *Damn you, Madi. Where did you go?*

'Alright,' I said, sighing, 'So, what do you guys want for dinner? Chicken noodle soup, hotdogs...?'

'It's time to go to the woods!' Ben leapt up from the floor where he'd been playing and ran for the door. Shoes were piled on top of each other next to the front door and Ben struggled into a cute pair of green Chucks.

'Ben, let's wait on that. We need to eat, and your mom will be home soon...'

'Mom always lets us go play in the woods before dinner. Ben will get mad if we don't go. He likes to do things at the same time every day,' Shelley warned.

'She lets you go by yourself?' I asked, bewildered.

'No. I won't go by myself,' Ben answered, his eyes widening in fear. He paced back and forth in the front of the door, like a puppy waiting to be let out.

My stomach turned as I thought about going down to those woods. I took a deep breath in through my mouth and blew it out my nose, like a mad bull preparing for battle. *I can't do it.*

Just the *thought* of going into those woods was enough to trigger a panic attack. I couldn't imagine what would happen if I actually took them down there...

Ben rocked back and forth, the shrill screech of that squeal ripping through my head in waves. *Where are you Madi? I can't deal with these kids right now!*

'Okay. Shelley, do you know how to put on your shoes? Let me get mine on, too. But only for a few minutes, guys – you all need to eat dinner, and I'm getting hungry, too...' It was like someone else was saying the words, some puppet master pulling my strings. *Could I really face those woods again, after what happened down there?*

But therein lies the problem – what *did* happen down there? I'd played in those woods all my life and then one day something had gone seriously wrong. The details leading up to that day were not only sketchy, they didn't exist at all. Flashes come and go sometimes, but I haven't thought about it for a while. I could remember going down there to play after school. I could remember the pain and the *red, red, red,* and the hospital room after ... but other than that, my accident was a gray, smudgy speck on the part of my brain that controlled my memories.

'I want to go now! It's after five! We should be down there already.' Ben was tugging at the door handle now, impervious to the fact that it was locked.

'I can't get it open. Open up, door!' He smacked the door with an open, frustrated palm.

'Ben, chill out! I'm getting my shoes on.' *What the hell does my sister do when he acts like this? And where is she, anyway?*

My sandals were lined up next to the random shoe pile, my sister's blue Nikes sitting next to mine. She was wearing those yesterday when I arrived. *Did she wear a different pair of shoes to the store?*

I decided then that there was no store in this scenario – the chances of her grocery shopping for five hours were pretty slim. She must have put on different shoes, but where the heck had she gone? She hadn't said anything about having to work today, and surely, the kids went to daycare while she worked…

I considered the possibility that maybe my sister had gone to speak to John. That was probably it. She probably used the opportunity of having me here, to go and try to rekindle things with him.

Ben reached for my right hand and yanked on it. Shelley pulled on the other. As I thought about going down to those woods, my face felt hot and tingly.

I stared at my sister's sneakers. This strange thought was taking shape, that if I wore her shoes, the answers to all my questions would seep into my skin, like where she went and what this mysterious thing was she needed to talk to me about…

I did, in fact, put her sneakers on. My sandals wouldn't hold up well in the woods, anyway.

'Alright, let's go … oh, hold on. Wait, guys.' I rushed back into the kitchen and pulled out a pad of paper and pen from the junk drawer. With shaky hands, I scrawled a short, sloppy note on the paper: *Took the kids to the woods. BRB.*

We went out the front door, Shelley leading the way and Ben marching behind her. Together, we circled around the inn, and both children made a beeline for the woods.

There was a narrow path at the center of the forest, the same path I'd followed as a kid…

I stopped walking, the world around me tilting left, then right, and then forward and back. I tried to steady myself, breathing in through my nose.

From here, the path appeared to be moving like a twisted snake. The mouth of the woods the snake's gaping, waiting mouth … waiting to devour me whole.

'I can't.' I choked the words out, bending at the waist and closing my eyes to stop the dizzy spell. Ben and Shelley were running straight for the snake's mouth, much to my dismay.

'Stop! Stop now!' I screamed. At my wild cry, they both halted immediately.

'Back in the house. Back in now! Please,' I whispered, motioning them to come back toward me. Reluctantly, they shuffled back.

'Let's go inside. It's going to rain,' I rested my hand on their backs, practically pushing them back toward the inn.

'No, it's not! Look at the sun!' Ben shouted. 'I want to go now.' The words came out strangled through his clenched teeth.

'Now,' he repeated, stomping his foot as he turned back toward the woods. Shelley hunkered down, looking as though she might cry.

'It's okay. We can come back later. We'll play pretend inside,' Shelley tried to coax her brother. Ben rocked back and forth, finally dropping down to the ground.

'But Mommy takes me every day,' he moaned, anxiously rubbing his own cheeks until they looked red and splotchy.

'I'll bring you later, I promise. I just … not right now, okay? I want to go inside and wait for your mom.'

'I'm staying here,' Ben huffed. He crossed his arms over his chest.

What am I going to do with this kid? My eyes travelled back to the woods. The path looked normal now, just a dirt-trodden trail I'd followed a million times as a kid, but as I considered going, the path turned wavy again.

I need to get inside now. As I bent down to pick up Ben, I forgot about that whole 'lift with your knees' bit. Lifting him from the ground, I let out a painful groan. To make matters worse, he started to kick and twist in my arms.

'No! I'm staying out here!' He threw his head back, nearly slamming against my teeth as I whipped my own head back to get out of his way. I trudged back up the hill, Shelley in my shadow and Ben flopping doggedly in my arms.

Back inside, I released him from my arms, panting. Worried he might try to run back out, I collapsed on the living room carpet beside him. Shelley sat down too, giving herself distance from Ben.

'I'm sorry if I disappointed you. I know your mommy and you have a routine. But, when I was a kid, I fell down and hurt my head in those woods. Now, every time I think about going down there, I get really sick and nervous. Do you know what it feels like to be nervous, Ben?'

Ben looked exhausted now, curling up in a ball on the floor. The tantrum had sucked the life right out of both of us. *I need Madi here to help me*, I thought, dejectedly.

'I get nervous a lot,' Ben whispered. He surprised me by scooting close to me, and the next thing I knew, he was curled up on my lap.

***

We ate dinner at the table. Noodles again. My sister didn't come home, and she didn't call back either.

Ben loved the noodles, although by the time he was finished, there was more pasta covering his lap and chair, than he could have possibly consumed. Shelley, on the other hand, was nice and neat, wiping her mouth more than necessary, and tucking her napkin onto her lap like a fancy lady. They couldn't be any more different from each other, but they were hooked at the hip, despite their age difference.

Ben seemed fine now, the temper tantrum temporarily forgotten. *What will happen tomorrow when he wants to go again?* I wondered. But then I thought, *Madeline will be back by then. I'll let her take him.*

After dinner, I gave them both a bath. They insisted on taking one together, assuring me that it was okay, and they always did that. It felt strange, being around children like this, and being the one in charge. I couldn't help feeling as though I was one of them, just playing the part of grown-up in our own made-up play.

Ben and Shelley didn't wash much; they splashed around, squirting each other with green and pink rubber duckies, until the other screamed and got mad. By the time they were through, the tile floor in the bathroom was covered with a thin coat of water. I sighed, drying up the floor before lifting their bodies, like slippery noodles, out of the tub. Madi and I used to be the same way, fighting constantly but loving every minute of it. My heart ached as I thought about my sister – where in the hell was she?

My anger and frustration were becoming something else – *concern.* Why would Madi leave without telling me? Did she go talk to John, did they get into a fight?

Again, I realized that I barely knew him. *Hell, I barely know her anymore.* We'd been close when we were kids, but whatever sort of bond we'd once had had come untethered over the years.

When your relationship consists mostly of monthly texts and Facebook updates, it loses its fortitude.

I tucked the kids into bed around ten o'clock. Shelley wanted to watch Elmo on her Tinkerbell TV set, but Ben insisted on me reading to him. I turned the DVD on for Shelley, and then I chose a book from one of the bookshelves in the family room for Ben. It was a tattered, old book called *Where's Goldie?* The fading sticker on the front said it cost only sixty-nine cents. Sure enough, when I opened the cover, I found my own name inside, scrawled in sloppy cursive.

Peering at the shelves, I realized most of the books were either mine or Mom's. I used to be territorial with my books. Well, I still was, actually, but back then, I used to scribble my name on everything. I took the book back to Ben's room, relieved to see that Shelley was already asleep as I passed by. The tune to *Elmo's World* rang out through the speakers.

Ben was pleased with my book choice and bragged that he always knew where to find Goldie, the naughty little yellow bird that hid from her perpetually perplexed owner, Maggie.

I had to do three full read-throughs before he even closed his eyes. I lay beside him for nearly a half hour, listening to the sounds of his soft breathing, like the purr of a happy cat. That tantrum today had sucked the life out of me, but Ben seemed perfectly fine now.

I listened for sounds outside, hoping I'd hear the Jeep pulling up in the driveway. My stomach churned as I realized I was alone again. With the kids asleep and Madi gone, I wasn't sure what to do with myself. Something was wrong, I could feel it.

I might not know my sister as well as I once did, but she still wouldn't leave me, of all people, in charge of her kids without saying something first.

Finally, I pushed myself out of bed, careful not to wake up Ben. I crept down the hallway, and walked through the house, turning off excess lights. Back in the living room, I flipped on the porch light for Madeline. All those late nights I'd waited up for her, so eager to hear stories about her night – parties with alcohol and boys who knew how to kiss ... it wasn't until later, in our twenties, that she confessed her stories weren't true. Some of them, yes. But mostly, they were embellished. She wanted to impress me, but more than anything, she *wanted* the stories to be true. As a teenager, Madi could be a liar and a fantasist sometimes. Was that what was going on now? Would she show up at the door, like she did all those years ago, with some wild story to explain her absence today?

Sitting down in her office chair, I spun around in circles, feeling childish. I held my phone in my lap, staring down at the blank screen. My landlord had left a voicemail earlier, but I didn't feel like hearing his wheezy voice right now.

I thought about calling my sister again, but then I thought better of it. I was acting like one of those babysitters that call every twenty minutes and ruin the parents' night out.

But I'm not the babysitter. She didn't even ask me to watch them. For the first time all day, I wondered if I should be seriously worried. If I should perhaps phone the police.

I considered the possibility that something really was wrong, some sort of desperate emergency. But I knew it wasn't family related – Mom and Dad were both dead, the few aunts and cousins we had lived thousands of miles away, and we barely spoke to them anyway.

It must be something to do with John, I decided. *But what if she got into an accident or got hurt somehow...?*

Slowly, I strolled up and down the hallway, looking at our family photographs. Last night, it'd been too dark to see them all, but now the hall was lit, old photographs of my mother and father illuminated on its walls. There were so many pictures of the four of us – Mom, Dad, Madeline, and I. There were a couple of our grandparents, too, and toward the end of the stretch were pictures of my sister and John, and baby pictures of Shelley and Ben.

In their wedding photo, John and Madeline stood behind a giant white cake, John holding a silver knife as he prepared to make the ceremonial cut. A crazy thought flashed through my head – *what if John had taken my sister? What if he'd hurt her?*

'I've really freaking lost it now,' I muttered. I'd been watching too many of those true crime mystery shows on the Discovery channel. I was up late every night, and there wasn't much else on besides those types of shows and info commercials.

I pulled my eyes away from the happy couple and headed for my own room to change my clothes. I passed Dad's office on the way. Last night, I hadn't paid it much attention, but now it sat stark and empty, even his old desk was gone. Instead the room seemed to be used for storage; boxes of books and paint supplies were stacked in one corner of the room and several see-through plastic tubs of old clothes.

I sniffed the air, half-expecting to smell my father's aftershave and pungent cigar smoke floating in the room. *He's gone. Every last trace of him is gone. And I didn't even go to the funeral to say goodbye...*

Guilt festered inside me, but, like always, I pushed myself to move forward, to forget what I had or hadn't done.

In the guest room, I gathered a change of clothes and then went back down the hallway to the bathroom. I was worried about being able to hear the kids if they woke up and needed something, so I left the door open a crack as I showered.

After scrubbing the dirt and sweat from my face and hair, I went back out to the living room, giving the driveway one last, wistful look, hoping my sister would return. It was nearly midnight by now. This was getting ridiculous.

Torn between irritation and concern, I fought the urge to text or call again. Finally, I made my way to her bedroom. It seemed wrong to sleep in her room, but the Mello Yellow room was too far from the kids. I didn't trust myself to wake up if one of them cried out in the night or got sick. *What would I even do if they got sick or hurt?* I wondered.

As happy as I was to meet my niece and nephew, I didn't know much about kids. And I definitely didn't feel comfortable being in charge of them for this long.

My sister's room was still pristine, and it smelled like some sort of cleanser – bleach, maybe? Turning on the fan to battle the fumes, I folded down her strawberry quilt, and climbed beneath the sheets. The bed was cold, like lying in an ice cube tray. Tucking the covers up to my chin, I flipped onto my left side like I always do. From this angle, I had a straight-on view of my sister's closet. It was pulled most of the way shut, but there was a small gap in the white pocket doors. I could see a box labeled 'Pictures' sitting on the closet floor.

I flipped to my right side, staring at my sister's billowy red curtains instead. Then it hit me – the balcony my parents used to go out on to smoke was off the master bedroom. Sliding the covers down, I emerged from the bed and pushed the curtains apart. Sure enough, the white door to the balcony was still there.

It wasn't really a balcony since it was on the ground floor, but that's what we always called it. My parents used to sneak out there and smoke cigarettes as though Madeline and I didn't know what they were doing. The house would reek of it every night after we went to bed, but I never really minded. I always liked to imagine them out there kissing, like secret, star-crossed lovers, and the smoky fumes were almost a reminder, that my parents were truly in love.

But that wasn't the case, was it? Their love was as fake as these loose-fitting curtains covering the door. It wasn't real, none of it was.

The bolt on the door was stiff, as though Madeline hadn't used the balcony in years. I gripped the metal latch and pulled on it until my hands burned. Finally, it snapped over, pinching the tender spot between my thumb and pointer finger.

The gold knob twisted easily, and I pushed the double doors out, the cool night air hitting me with such force that my nightgown blew up above my waist. It was black as a raven out here, but I stepped out onto the balcony anyway, breathing in the cool lilac summer air. The balcony wasn't very wide, just enough to stand at the wrought iron railing and catch a breath of air, or lean over it, puffing on a cigarette with your spouse...

A streak of moonlight constellated edges of the tree line, the path I'd feared earlier coming into focus. A sudden chill trickled up my spine as I remembered my flashback near the ominous entrance of the woods. *Why couldn't I remember that day?*

Bits and pieces came back, every so often, but most of my memories from that summer day were of the crisp white hospital room where machines whistled and whirred, a small team of doctors bandaging up my head. They didn't let me go to sleep, I had to fight through the concussion as they stitched my head back together.

My eyes sought truth in the darkness. 'Why was it so traumatic? It's not like I hadn't got hurt while playing before.' The words were whispered, a plea to the forest gods: *tell me why.*

My eyes scanned the tree line, for animals or man. A strange smell filled my nostrils – like something charring over an open fire.

My neck prickled as I tried to shake away the sudden sensation that someone was watching me from out there. *Waiting. Watching.*

All these years, I'd assumed it was just a freak accident – that I'd tripped and hit my head so hard that I couldn't remember the fall. But if that was truly the case, then why was I so scared to go back? It was just an accident, an incident that could have happened to any kid ... kids get hurt all the time. But there was something so scary about the not knowing, the fear of memories lost ... what happened in those moments leading up to the fall? *Why did those memories never come back?* I wondered.

I'm going to have to face those woods and face my fears sooner or later, I decided.

Childishly, I rushed back in, slamming the heavy door behind me. I whipped the curtains closed, covering the door completely.

What I needed to do was get some sleep, but I felt wide awake. Plus, part of me felt like I needed to stay up. I needed to wait for Madi to come home.

My gaze wandered back over to the closet doors. Trembling, I slid the pocket doors apart. Then I slid the cardboard box labelled 'Pictures' out onto the carpet next to the bed. There were stacks and stacks of photo albums, some plain and generic, others flowery and neat. I lifted the first album from the top and gently, I flipped through its pages.

These were more photos of my sister and John. I could tell the difference immediately, the before and after children photos. Before, there were pictures of John and Madeline, smiling over plates of fancy food, low-lit smiles in the corner of some bar. There were pictures of them at a rock concert, Madeline flashing a peace sign at the cameraman, who I presumed was John. He, too, looked young and silly in his pictures, sticking his tongue out at my sister.

The after-children photos looked happy, too, but they were of zoo trips and family portraits –a more subdued life. I wondered what happened between them. Why did it all fall apart?

You need to come in here. I can't deal with these fucking kids. John's words in the background came floating back to me. Was that what he really said, or was my mind just filling in the blanks?

He seemed normal at the wedding, but what did I really know about him? Maybe having kids changed him … maybe he couldn't handle Ben with his schedules and quirks? Whatever led to the affair wasn't any of my business, but I sincerely hoped my sister hadn't gone after him, trying to get him to come back home. The thought of her doing that, of seeming so desperate, made my stomach curl. But where else could she be? I remembered that worried mask she wore last night … something heavy was on her mind. Was it just about John, or something else?

I sat that album aside and reached for the next. Instantly, I recognized myself in one of the photos. It was my first-grade class photo, and next to it was Madeline's fourth-grade photo. We almost looked alike at that age.

I kept flipping, past photos of Madeline in cheerleading and me in band, and both of us in our prom dresses. Madeline was asked to the prom by several boys, but she coyly told them all no. I'd almost forgotten until now how tied to the hip Madi was with her two best friends in high school. Right on cue, the next photo was of Madi, her arms looped around Jessica Feeler and Rhonda Sheckles. Oh, how I loathed those girls…

The three of them couldn't have been any more different from each other, Jessica with her bone-straight blonde hair, Rhonda with swirly red curls and freckles, and Madi in the middle, with her blondish brown hair cut in a jagged bob. But, in this particular picture, Madeline's hair was dyed platinum blonde. I remembered her begging Mom to buy the dye, to let her change her hair. Rhonda and Jessica stayed over that night, helping her apply the malodorous color to her hair.

At that point, Madeline had moved upstairs to the bonus rooms, to get away from the rest of us. I could remember creeping up those steps, slithering on my belly, as I tried to catch a glimpse of what she and the older girls were up to…

I held the album up, studying the contours of my sister's face. She was pretty then, and still so pretty now. A little triangle of film poked out from behind the picture of the girls. Gripping it between my nails, I slid another photo out from behind theirs.

I gasped, staring down at the small school photo in my hand. It was a picture of a girl named Sarah Goins. She was probably in fourth grade in this picture. She and I were in the same class, but we may as well have been from different planets.

While most kids spent their free time playing on the swings

or chasing each other in a game of tag, Sarah spent her time in the dirt. She liked to make up stories and talk to herself, sometimes even pouring bits of loose gravel and dirt over her own head. Her hair was greasy and limp, her lips and eyes the color of dust balls and slate. I stared at the picture, mesmerized by the girl looking back at me. She was less of a girl, and more like a ghost.

Sarah Goins looked haunted, but wasn't that what they always said about pictures of dead girls?

Sarah had disappeared in sixth grade. Everyone suspected that she either drowned in Moon Lake by accident or went crazy and ran off. She wasn't a happy child. Maybe she did run away, but, deep down, I knew she had to be dead. Why else wouldn't she have come back home?

But, then, I thought about myself … I hadn't been back home either. Until now.

I didn't really know Sarah well, none of us did. But a memory was rising – *didn't she give me this picture?* I remembered now … Sarah, in her dirt-stained overalls, racing around the playground, a toothy smile on her face. She was handing out these photos of herself; she wanted to trade pictures with the other kids. She came from a poor family; her father dead and her mom left to run the farm on her own. 'Mom bought my school pictures this year. Here, I want you to have one!' She looked so happy as she thrust one of the photos into my hand. I told her thank you, and feeling self-conscious, tucked it quickly away in my jeans pocket. Next Sarah approached a group of girls by the jungle gym. 'Here, please take one,' she told a girl I didn't recognize. Sneering, the girl accepted the photo and then promptly, ripped it to pieces. In a flash, she had yanked the rest of the stack from Sarah's hands. One by one, she shredded the pictures to pieces and then, in a final dramatic gesture, she threw them up in the air. Tiny white flakes of photo paper caught in the air and floated around the playground like a miniature snowstorm.

'How could you?!' Sarah screamed, clawing at her own cheeks. Her face was so red, so angry in that moment … and who could really blame her?

'She can't even spell her own last name!' someone shouted. 'G-o-i-n! Do you know what that spells, Sarah! Go in! Go in! We don't want you on this playground!' And just like that, the other kids were chanting, their fists pumping the air, their giggles high and cruel. 'Go in!' they sang in chorus.

I squeezed my eyes shut at the memory, trying to keep the tears at bay. Finally, I opened my eyes and slammed the album closed, but not before stuffing Sarah's picture back inside.

I climbed back into my sister's bed and pulled the covers up over my head. I tried to force myself to sleep, but those chants wouldn't go away. Like a broken record, or a song stuck in my head, the voices called out, 'Go in! Go in!'

And one of those voices was mine.

CHAPTER FOUR

Golden sunlight burned my cheeks, the cool bed sheets like salve on an open wound. I curled up into a protective ball, slipping further down beneath the blankets. It was way too early on a Sunday to get out of bed yet.

'Where is my mommy?' Ben's voice was so close to my ear that it made my cheek vibrate. I pushed the covers up with my knees like a tent and watched him crawl inside it.

'I don't know, buddy.'

'I don't know, buddy. Wait, how can you not know?' His eyes were red and raw, as though he'd been crying, and his mouth was twisted up with worry. I shouldn't have told the truth. Sometimes it's better to lie.

'I think she had some stuff to take care of, but please don't worry, Ben. I'm here now. I'll take care of you until she gets back.'

'Promise?' He nuzzled his head into the crook of my arm and curled his legs around my own. My sister used to do the same thing, sometimes digging her feet into the back of my calves until they ached. The realization that he was a mini-version of her was like a bowling ball in my chest. *Where is my sister? Why isn't she back yet?*

'Promise. Now go wake up Shelley and get dressed, please. We're going to Bed and More.'

'What about breakfast?'

'We'll get something on the way.' I threw the covers aside and slithered out of bed. Ben took off across the hall, shouting for Shelley to 'rise and shine'.

My sister had worked at Bed and More since the summer she turned seventeen. While I went off to college and the 'big city', as she called it – for the record, Charleston, South Carolina was nothing like the 'big city', in my eyes – she stayed behind, graduating from stocker to cashier, and then finally to part-time manager. I used to tease her a little bit about it. Then one time, she said, 'Well, someone had to stay behind with Mom and Dad. I guess that someone is me.' She always seemed to like working there; Madeline loved talking to people and was good at selling things, apparently.

I padded down the hallway, poking my head into Ben's room. Shelley was in there, helping him pull on a pair of sweatpants. She was a good little sister, staying patient as she fought the material over his toes.

I went into the guest room. The bed was still unmade from where I'd slept in it yesterday, my duffel bag sprawled open on the floor. At some point, I knew I should probably hang up my clothes. I remembered my promise to stay for a while. Was Madi in some sort of trouble? Was that why she hadn't come home?

Digging out a pair of jeans and a tank top, I quickly got dressed and went out to the living room, peeking back out through the curtains, hopeful that Madi had returned. The Jeep was still gone.

I checked my phone for missed calls; there were none. I tried to call Madi again, but this time, her phone went straight to voicemail. *Did she turn her phone off, or did her battery die?*

I tried to keep my fear at bay, but it was fruitless – something was seriously wrong here, and today, I had to do something about it.

It took another half hour to get the kids' teeth brushed and they screamed and complained when I accidentally put Crest instead of the kid-flavored paste on their brushes.

It seemed like a lot of work just to drive a few miles outside of town and check to see if Madi was at work, but I had to do something. I had to know if she was okay.

By the time we were loaded in, it felt like the end of the trip instead of the beginning, and when I looked at my reflection in the rearview mirror, I was shocked by how hollow my cheeks and eyes looked. Without make-up, I looked sad and pale. My mossy brown hair was greasy, despite last night's shower.

It wasn't until I'd put the car in gear, that I realized my mistake. Neither Shelley nor Ben were old enough to travel without car seats. Ben could have gotten by with a booster, maybe, but Shelley was small for her age and needed a rear-facing seat. *What was I thinking?* I adjusted my mirror so that I could see them in the backseat. They were so short, and the seatbelt straps practically covered their faces.

'Dammit!' I covered my face with my hands. All this work, getting them ready, for nothing.

I took a deep breath and turned around to look at Ben. 'Do you know where your mom keeps your car seats? You do use car seats, yes?'

'Yes?' Ben echoed back, staring out the side window. I gnashed my teeth in frustration.

'They're in the Jeep,' Shelley told me. 'Mom took them with her. Why would she do that?'

'She must have forgotten.' The words trailed off as I stared out my own window. 'Come on, guys.' I got out of the Civic and opened the back door. Huffing and puffing, Ben climbed out, Shelley following behind him.

'We're going to see the neighbor.' I took their little hands in mine and we crossed the field together, toward the Tennors' cottage, though I was unsure if the Tennors even still lived there.

The cottage was smaller than I remembered, a soft, slow curl of smoke floating up from the chimney. It was way too hot for a fire, but to each their own, I guess.

A ball of nervousness rose inside me, but I forced myself to step up on the porch and knock. I held my breath, praying someone was home.

Ben and Shelley were distracted, chasing each other in circles while I waited.

I was about to give up when the door creaked open. A stooped man with white hair and a beard stood in the doorway. He was dressed in too-tight sweatpants and a canary yellow T-shirt. He looked to be about seventy years old.

'May I help you?' He peered past me, taking in Shelley and Ben.

'Hi. I'm Emily Ashburn. My sister lives next door…'

'Well, hello, Emily. I thought these were your sister's kids. Long time no see.' His eyes twinkled. So, it was Mr Tennors. He'd aged quite a bit since the last time I saw him, but that had to be what? Ten years ago?

'Nice to see you, Mr Tennors. How is Mrs Tennors?'

'I'm sorry to say she passed a couple years ago.'

'Oh, I'm so sorry.' I cringed, wishing my sister had thought to mention that. But, why would she? I didn't go to dad's funeral, so why would she think I'd care about some old neighbor's passing? And it wasn't like she told me anything anyway. She didn't even tell me where she was going!

'It's quite alright. I miss her, but I'm glad she's no longer in pain. She had cancer, you see.'

'I'm sorry,' I said again, feeling terrible and awkward.

'Would you like to come in?'

'No. I was just wondering – have you seen my sister? Outside, or anywhere in town this weekend?' I lowered my voice, glancing back at the kids. 'I don't really know where she is,' I whispered.

'Oh dear. I'm sorry, but no, I haven't seen her. Have you checked her place of employment? I was sure sorry to hear about John moving out…' I was shocked that he already knew about John, but then I remembered how small this town really was. Compared to the 'big city' I came from, Bare Border, Indiana was like a village. Nothing stays secret for long, not when you live in a bubble. That was one reason I moved away in the first place.

'Well, that's where we were headed. I was going to drive up to Bed and More, to see if maybe she went into work. But then I realized that I don't even have the kids' car seats. I'm feeling a little stranded here … and I was hoping maybe you'd seen her.'

Mr Tennors cleared his throat. 'Well, I could drive up there for you. Or, if you'd like, I can keep an eye on these two, just until you get back.'

Chewing on my lip, I didn't know what to say. Leaving the kids with him would be a major convenience, plus I could buy a couple car seats while I was out. But I'd seen so many scary movies and crime shows, about creepy old neighbors taking advantage of small children…

But this was Mr Tennors. He'd lived next door to me all my life. I played in the field by his house, and he'd never tried to kidnap or hurt me.

'Do you guys mind staying here with Mr Tennors?' I asked Shelley and Ben, tentatively.

Shelley shrugged. 'Can we play checkers again?' she asked Mr Tennors.

'You bet,' he said to her, grinning. 'It will be nice to have some company.' He directed this to me.

'Ben? Is that okay? I won't be gone longer than an hour.'

Ben nodded, chewing on his lower lip. His face was still thoughtful and worried.

'Will you bring my mommy home, please?' The shaky 'please' threatened to make me come undone. It broke my heart to see him without her. Between the two children, Ben relied on my sister the most, apparently.

'I don't know, Ben. I don't want to make a promise I can't keep. But I promise that I'll try to find out more while I'm in town. I'll also buy you guys some breakfast while I'm out.'

'Don't worry about breakfast. I got waffles inside,' Mr Tennors offered. I felt so grateful, like I should reach out and give him a hug. I thanked him over and over, then took off running across the field, eager to get to the bottom of my sister's strange disappearance, and secretly relieved to catch a break from the kids.

CHAPTER FIVE

The parking lot of Bed and More was deserted, but that's what I'd expected. Ten miles south of Bare Border, the town of Merrimont wasn't much bigger. Bed and More and Sam's were the only two stores around.

A woman in a blue apron greeted me at the door. I fought the urge to ask her if she knew my sister. I needed to go straight to the manager; I needed to know if they'd seen or heard from Madeline.

It had been years since I'd shopped at Bed and More. Once, Mom and Dad and I stopped by to see Madeline while she was working. Mom pushed our cart up and down the aisles while dad complained about the smell. 'It smells like potpourri. And not the good kind,' he'd whispered, whatever the hell that meant.

Today the store looked larger, like they'd done some renovations over the years.

There was furniture and lots of odds and ends – candles, bath towels, rolling pins, scented soap. Everything home-related you could ever need, all displayed in one cramped, stuffy building.

I walked through a library – rich oak cabinets filled with dummy books lining its shelves, and then drifted through pretend kitchens and living rooms. Couches and chairs were placed on top of rugs and angled around plastic TV sets, displayed on fancy entertainment centers. I fought the urge to plop down on one of the cushy sofas. An imitation of a better life sounded pretty good right now.

The checkout counters were on the other side of the store and I scanned the aisles as I went, wishing and hoping I'd find Madeline stocking shelves or sweeping.

There were nearly a dozen registers, but only one girl was working. I stood in line behind a heavyset woman with a cart full of plastic flowers and what looked like cardboard plant vases.

I tapped my foot, trying to feign patience. Madeline was always the patient one. Anytime Mom or Dad would take us out to eat or to the mall, she seemed perfectly content to stand in line, or wait an hour for food to arrive. Old habits die hard – I chewed on a jagged fingernail and gnawed on my inner cheek as I skimmed the store again for signs of Madi.

Finally, when the woman in front of me finished paying, I scurried up to the girl at the register. She looked leery of me, probably because I didn't have a cart.

'Hi, there. I'm Emily, Madeline's sister? I'm trying to find her, and I was wondering if she was working today.'

The girl couldn't be much older than eighteen. She had shiny black hair and dark, devilish make-up that made her look extra white and waxy in the light. 'Haven't seen Madi since ... well, let me think. It was Tuesday ... yeah, I think it was ... Misti!' I flinched as she shouted for another girl, and then suddenly a young blonde appeared. She, too, looked like a teenager. Did any adults, besides my sister, work here?

I was surprised to see the blonde was wearing a name badge: *Misti, Store Manager.*

'Have you guys seen or heard from Madeline?' I asked. Misti had young, pretty features – smooth hair and bright blue eyes – but her nose was misshapen, her two front teeth a little crooked. Her flaws made me like her more for some reason.

'Madi took off a couple days because her – well, you – were

coming to town. But she was due to work the 10 to 6 shift today, and she still hasn't shown up.' Misti looked down at her watch. From here, I couldn't see what time it was, but I guessed it was well past noon.

My heart felt heavy in my chest, like a lump of food was stuck between my wind pipe and stomach.

'Is Madi okay? She's our best employee. I'd really hate to lose her ... in fact, she would be the manager now, if it wasn't for her kids. She couldn't handle all the hours. I really need her help around here though.'

Before I could respond, the girl with the dark make-up chimed in, 'Maybe it has something to do with that husband of hers. He was a real piece of work. One of the grumpiest men I've ever met. And he was cheating on her. Did you know that?'

I tried to swallow, forcing the lump to dissolve, but it wouldn't go away. Chances of this being a simple misunderstanding were looking pretty slim. Madeline was *missing*. No-showing at work was not something she would do.

'I know about John already, and I'm not sure where Madi is. But I am sure it must have been something important if she missed work because of it. You won't fire her, will you?' I tried to give Misti my best imitation of puppy dog eyes.

'We won't, as long as she comes back soon. But if she doesn't ... well, I can only cover for her for so long...'

'I understand. Hey, do you guys know where that woman, Starla, lives? The one John's been seeing?'

'Mm-hmm. That I do know,' said make-up girl. 'She lives in Bare Border, right in the center of town. That old house across from the bingo hall, you know it?'

I do. I nodded and thanked them both, eager to escape the stale rush of air-conditioning in the store, and the cold chill running down my spine all of a sudden.

My sister wouldn't leave her kids and miss work for no reason. Either something had happened, and she'd had to leave town, or someone took her against her will. *Something is seriously wrong. It must be.*

My thoughts darkened. What if John did something to her after all? Things like that happened every day in the news. When a woman goes missing, it's almost always the husband or boyfriend. I didn't know him very well, but what I did know wasn't good. He was grumpy and impatient, and he was unfaithful.

The first thing I wanted to do when I climbed back in the Honda was race to Starla's house and confront my sister's soon-to-be ex-husband. But that seemed a little rash. What if John and Madi fought over custody when they got divorced? If she showed up in a day or two, he could use this incident to claim she's irresponsible…

Again, I realized that I'd been watching too much court TV. I didn't want to reach out to John yet, but I had to do something…

I debated my next move as I pulled into the parking lot at Sam's. Like a blur, I drifted up and down the aisles, picking out two car seats for Shelley and Ben – I wasn't even sure if they were the right size – and picking up some basic food items I wasn't sure my sister needed: eggs, milk, bread, bacon. In the fresh meats section, I tried to conjure up some sort of plan for dinner. But finally, I took my few items and the seats up to the check out, then loaded them into my trunk.

I called and ordered a pizza from Rosita's, and I sat in my car in their parking lot waiting for them to finish cooking it, while my brain raced with ideas. We did have distant cousins, but they didn't live anywhere nearby. Most of our family was in Montana or Tennessee. Even if something was wrong with an extended family member, my sister wouldn't just pick up and leave, and she wouldn't leave her kids like that. *Would she?*

My mind was still fuzzy as I roared up Star Mountain. I was eager to get back to Shelley and Ben. Some illogical part of me was wondering if they'd be gone too when I got back…

But when I pulled up to the driveway at the Bare Border Inn,

I could see them chasing one another in the field. Mr Tennors was smoking, white puffy clouds circling his head as he laughed at the children's game of tag.

I ran the milk and other items inside but left the car seats in the trunk. They were expensive. When Madeline got back, I'd make her pay me back. Or better yet, I'd save my receipt and return them on my way out of town.

The pizza box was steaming, and it burned the tips of my fingers through the cardboard as I sloshed through the field, carrying it out in front of me like a present.

'Pizza!' Ben and Shelley squealed in unison.

They followed the pizza into Mr Tennors' cottage like two kittens chasing laser lights.

Mr Tennors was surprised I wanted to eat with him, but he looked happy to have the company. His cheeks were downright rosy as he took down plates from the cupboard and laid them on the scarred kitchen table.

'I only have three plates,' he told us, setting out a plate for everyone except himself. 'I don't get much company these days.'

I offered to eat my pizza off a napkin, but he insisted I take a plate. We huddled around the small dinette table, quietly sharing our hot, gooey pizza.

Finally, Mr Tennors wiped his mouth and said, 'Any luck finding your sister?'

I could see Ben watching me from the corner of my eye, but I focused on my slice of pizza, worry bubbling up inside my chest like a hot tea kettle. I shook my head at Mr Tennors. 'I'm sure she'll be back soon though.'

The pizza was tasteless now, my thoughts rushing with what could have happened to Madi. If it was just Madi to consider, this wouldn't be so troublesome. But those kids needed her, and I wasn't fit to care for them myself…

A few minutes later, with the pizza all gone and the kids back outside chasing an old tomcat in the yard, Mr Tennors said quietly:

'Have you considered calling the police, Emily? Leaving those kids … especially that boy of hers, well, that's just not something your sister would do.'

I was inclined to agree. But contacting the police, like contacting John, seemed like a big move. My sister would kill me if she showed up tomorrow and I'd turned her whole world upside down.

'Maybe I will. If she doesn't come home soon, I will.' I said it more to myself than to him, watching Ben fall to his knees, and then bounce back up as he chased the cat. Shelley was running with her palms outstretched, dead set on petting the animal. They looked so joyous, so innocent.

I'd never considered having children myself. Well, I had *considered* it, but it wasn't in the cards for me. Standing here now, though, in my sister's shoes – literally and figuratively – I could see why she liked being a mother. Sure, her husband was a douchebag, but these kids were kind and good, minus the tantrums. My chest ached with worry for them. If it felt this good to be an aunt, I couldn't imagine how it felt to be their mother. My sister adored them. There was no way in hell she would just take off and leave like that – not for any reason, not for anyone.

'I'll call the police department this evening after the kids go to bed,' I said, firmly.

Mr Tennors nodded, tucking his hands in the pockets of his sweatpants. Like me, he was watching the children, a strained look on his face. 'Will you let me know how it turns out? And if you need anything, please don't hesitate to come ask.'

I thanked him again for watching the kids for me, then I prompted the kids to thank him too. We walked back across the spongy field, still wet from last night's rain, and headed back to the Bare Border Inn.

I gave the children baths again, this time taking more care to actually clean them. I washed Shelley's hair and then Ben's, my hands slippery and unsure. Shelley seemed to like the sudsy bubbles on her head, but Ben screamed. The sound of his shouting was so loud my ears were throbbing, but I forced myself to stay calm. *I have to stay in control until Madi gets back.*

'It's okay, Ben. Almost done, baby. Almost done,' I soothed, rushing to wash the soap out with a big plastic cup. Shelley was sitting in the back of the tub, and she stroked Ben's back until I was done, and until he had calmed down completely.

The nighttime routine was exhausting – bathing and brushing, then getting both children dressed and ready for bed. Shelley, again, seemed to like the brushing, and she pulled her pajama bottoms on with ease. Ben was more work, yelling in frustration as his pants got caught around his feet and ankles, and then once the pajamas were on, we had to take them back off because the tags were rubbing against his skin.

By the time I climbed in bed beside him, I was ready for sleep myself. It was barely even nine o'clock, but it felt like it was way past midnight.

'Let me go find a book,' I offered.

'No, wait.' Ben grasped my hand and I could feel his own shaking in mine.

'Can we just talk tonight?'

'Sure.' I gave his hand a little squeeze, worry fluttering in my chest.

'When is my mommy coming home?'

'I don't know, Ben.'

'School starts in two days. She wouldn't leave before school starts. She knows I need her, and Shelley needs her too.'

My heart skipped a beat at the mention of school. I knew summer was ending, but did the kids really go back this early? It was the beginning of August for god's sake. It seemed too soon. But Madi did mention that school was starting…

'Are you sure it starts in two days?' I grimaced.

'It starts on the ninth. I'm sure.' He let go of my hand and started chewing on his fingers, nervously. This nervous act reminded me of myself, and for some reason, I had to fight off the urge to cry. He was so scared, and so was I – but I didn't know what to do.

I took a deep breath. 'Even if she's not back by the time school starts, I want you to try not to worry. You know how DNA works right?'

Ben gave me a strange, sideways look. I must admit, I didn't even know where I was headed with this line of thought.

'I know you rely on your mommy for a lot of things. You guys are very close. But, if you think about it, I'm the next best thing because I'm your mommy's sister. We share very similar DNA, which means me and her are a lot alike. If your mom can help you, then so can I. She left you in my care for a reason. You trust her, don't you?'

Ben nodded, his eyes lighting up. 'So, you all have the same blood inside your bones, right?'

'Right. Well, sort of. It's not in the bones exactly, and it's not just the same, but we are a lot alike. If your mom couldn't be here, then at least you have her sister, right?'

Ben nodded again, the trace of a smile teasing up the corners of his lips. Suddenly, he rolled onto his side, away from me, and shut his eyes. His hair was so soft as I rubbed it, and he smelled just like Madi with that shampoo. When I leaned down to kiss him, I realized he was already asleep, snoring softly.

Shelley was asleep too. I went in her room and turned off the TV, then pulled her blanket up to her chin. With her eyes closed and mouth open, softly purring, she reminded me so much of Madeline when she was young.

It was so strange to be back home, but it wasn't the same anymore. It was an evolved version of it, and my sister and I were no longer the children of summer.

Thankful to have them both to sleep, I could have curled up and went to bed myself. But it was time to do what I'd promised Mr Tennors I would. I had to contact the police and report my sister as missing.

CHAPTER SIX

Water rolled down in hot soothing waves, but I couldn't stay in the shower for long. I washed my hair and scrubbed the dirt from my face, then toweled off quickly. By the time I'd slipped into my thin cotton pajamas, there was nothing left to do but call.

I sat down on the couch, my hands shaking, and tried to call Madeline one more time. Her phone was still going straight to voicemail.

'Damn you for making me do this, Madi.' I didn't have the Bare Border police on speed dial – why would I? So, I pulled it up on Google and found the number in under a minute.

My hands were shaking as the phone started to ring.

'Bare Border Sheriff's department,' said a croaky female voice on the other end.

I cleared my throat, nervously. 'Um. Hi. I'm calling from 316 Myrtle ... basically, I'm at the Bare Border Inn. You know where that is, right?'

'Sure do. Are you having some sort of trouble out there, Madeline?'

I shook my head. I don't know why I was surprised they knew exactly where I was calling from and who lived here. 'Actually, this isn't Madeline. It's her sister, Emily. Emily Ashburn. Everything is okay ... well, no it's not. My sister has gone missing. Can you send an officer out? I'd like to make a formal report.'

'What do you mean by missing?' the woman asked, a suspicious tone to her voice. And before I could answer, she added, 'I heard about her and John splitting up.'

I sighed so loudly that I'm sure she heard it on the other end. 'This has nothing to do with John. At least I don't think it does ... my sister asked me to come, she wanted to talk to me about something. Less than twenty-four hours after getting here, she disappeared without a trace. I went up to her work today, and it turns out she was scheduled to work and didn't come in. My sister wouldn't just leave her kids and forfeit her job. I'm afraid something bad has happened to her, possibly something violent...' Those last words surprised even me. *Do I really believe that?* It sounded so ridiculous, hearing myself say it out aloud.

'Okay. I'm sending an officer over to the inn now. He'll take it from there.'

I thanked the woman repeatedly and hung up, pacing back and forth in the living room. My heart was racing. Unsure what to do with this energy, I checked on the kids again. Ben and Shelley were still sound asleep, snuggly and purring in their beds.

My heart steadied at the sight of them.

In the bathroom, I brushed my teeth so hard that my gums bled. When I caught sight of myself in the mirror, my head still damp, and in my pajamas, I decided to walk back down to the guest bedroom and put on jeans and a button-down shirt. After changing, I finger-combed my hair as I went outside on the front porch to wait.

The last thing I wanted was for the kids to wake up and see me talking to a police officer. Then they would be even more worried than they already were...

The third step on the front porch still creaked. I sat down on it, the wind whistling through my damp hair and making me shiver. In the dark, the gravel driveway was long and endless, like a tunnel to another world. Off to the left was Mr Tennors' cottage, the lights all out; the only sign of life was the smoke trickling out of his chimney.

The trees to my right danced in the wind, and I got the strangest feeling that they were mocking me somehow. I kept watching the trees for shadows, but everything melted together in the dark.

Finally, two headlights rose in the distance, like two yellow cat's eyes growing bigger and wider...

The police cruiser was moving slowly, almost too slowly...

Getting to my feet, I wrung my hands together, my heart pounding in my ears. What was I so worried about? It wasn't like I'd committed a crime.

The cruiser ground to a halt behind my rented Civic. The headlights popped off, the door swung open, and a familiar face stepped out into the soft moonlight. My breath was sucked from my chest. *Oh my god.*

The last person I expected to see at this moment was Paul Templeton. When he stepped out of the cruiser, I recognized him immediately. He was taller, and his shoulders were broader, but he still had that chiseled jaw and off-center nose he'd had ten years ago. His bold blue eyes connected with mine, and a rush of electricity ran right through me, from my head to my toes.

'What are you doing here?' I sputtered, astounded. Paul Templeton was many things – my first boyfriend, my first kiss, my first date – but he was also my first heart break, and the one boy I'd never truly been able to get over. Sure, I'd dated guys in Charleston, but none of them had ever felt as passionate, as *electric* as Paul. Sometimes, although I'd never admit this to anyone, when I fantasized about men, it was his face I saw.

'I heard you were in town.' His eyes were wide, just as shell-shocked as me. *Of course, he'd already heard. There were no secrets in this town.*

'You're a cop now?' It was hard to believe that the same Paul I knew – the one who drove too fast on dirt roads in his dad's truck, threw kegger parties when he was underage, and was known to smoke the occasional joint behind the old concession stands – could possibly work as a police officer. *Why didn't Madi warn me? Surely, she knew.*

'I am.' Paul stood up straighter and stuck his chin out defiantly. 'I'm not the same guy I once was.'

'You're a man now, right?' It came out nastier than I intended and instantly, there was a rush of heat to my cheeks.

'I'm sorry for being such an asshole when we were younger.' Paul moved closer, reaching out. 'It's so good to see you again. When I heard you were back...' The tips of his fingers grazed my elbow. Immediately, I pulled away from him, studying his face. His eyes were the same – sparkling, and still a hint of that mischievous, joker-like smile. A memory flooded my brain – me standing on the front porch in my violet prom dress, shaking from the cold as I waited for him to pick me up. I kept closing my eyes and counting to ten, hoping each time that when I opened them, I'd get a different result, that I'd see his dad's truck pulling up the drive ... but he never came. He never did.

Still an asshole, I decided.

'I didn't call you here to catch up on old times. My sister is missing, and I need your help.'

'Okay, then let me help. Tell me exactly what happened.' His face was serious now as he crossed his arms over his uniformed chest. I still felt dizzy from seeing him after all these years...

I cleared my throat and started from the beginning. When I got to the part about me going up to Bed and More to see if Madi was working, his eyes grew wide.

'Wait. Are you telling me you left the kids with Albert Tennors today?'

I raised my eyebrows at him.

'Yeah. Is that okay with you? I didn't have car seats for them. I guess you'd prefer I ride them around town illegally?'

Paul rubbed his chin, glancing nervously across the field.

60

'What is it?' I asked, my stomach clenching.

'I just thought you knew. I thought everyone in Bare Border knew...'

'Knew what?' I was starting to feel nauseous now.

'Albert Tennors is on the sex offender registry. I mean, he's basically harmless, but still I wouldn't—'

'Harmless?!' I screamed. Bending over at the waist, I held my breath, fighting off the urge to vomit on my sister's shoes.

My sister was going to kill me when she found out. What if he did something to them while they were in his care?! Would the kids even tell me if he did?

The day played back in my mind. The kids were outside when I left and when I got back ... but he could have taken them inside. *He could have hurt them or taken advantage of them...*

But this was Mr Tennors we were talking about. If he was a creep, I would have known that. Wouldn't I?

'Oh, god...' I moaned. I couldn't fight the urge any longer. Vomit sprung from my mouth and Paul jumped back in surprise.

'It's okay, Emily. You didn't know.'

'Wait. Did my sister know this? Did my mother and father know?' The memory tape in my mind rolled back farther – my mom let us play outside, sometimes in the field, but never once did we go inside Mr Tennors' house or up to his door. An image of my mother on the porch, watching us run up and down the drive, her face cautious...

'Yes. I'm pretty sure they knew, and your sister too. But like I said, that was a long time ago and most people in this town think he got a bad rap. Mr Tennors is a nice old man.'

'A nice old man?! I'm sure that's what they say about all the creeps on the registry...' Reaching out, I punched him in the chest, instantly stiffening as I realized he was a police officer now.

'I could arrest you for that,' he grumbled, but there was a hint of a smile in his eyes. He moved closer, resting his hands on my shoulders. He'd always been taller than me, but now my face lined up with his chest. I fought the urge to lean in, to let him hold me...

There were other men in Charleston. Rewind nine years ... there'd been three apartments, two jobs, and dozens of crappy dates. Sometimes they'd get to the first date, the second, the third ... but eventually, the light in their eyes would fade. In a crowded restaurant, I watched their eyes – previously, fixed on me – start roaming the room. It was almost like a game to me. How long, how many dates, until the glimmer in their eyes died out? But Paul, his eyes were always drawn to me. That spark we used to have, it was still there. Even after he stood me up for prom, I could see it in his eyes as we passed in the halls – that want, that desire...

I stared up at him, unable to move but unable to let him hold me. *He hurt me, that I can't forget...*

'Let me take you in. I think there's vomit on your shirt.'

'Ugh. So gross.' He was right. I could smell my own puke permeating the night air. Mixed with the earthy smell of wet grass and clover, the aroma was unbearably putrid. 'We have to be quiet. I don't want to wake the kids. They're really shook up about all this and I don't want them to think something's happened to their mom when they see you.'

Paul placed a finger to his lips then pointed toward the door. I could feel him staring at my backside as I led him up the porch steps. Suddenly self-conscious, I smoothed my still-wet hair down and silently cursed myself for not wearing make-up. *Paul Templeton. He's the last person I expected to see right now.* I'd always assumed he left town, like his older brothers did. *This town is too small for the likes of me,* I could remember him saying one night when we were drunk on Zimas.

There was nowhere to sit in the living room, with only toys and my sister's one desk chair to choose from. I led him back through the kitchen and out to the family room. It was further away from the kids, too, so this seemed like a good place to talk.

As we reached the family room, his expression changed again. He was looking around my sister's house, taking it all in. His eyes drifted from the carpets to the walls, and even up to the ceiling.

'Looking for clues, Sherlock Holmes?' I asked, keeping my voice down.

'Something like that.' He walked along the wall with the bookshelves and ran his fingers over the dusty spines. 'Listen. I know you don't want to hear this, but maybe Madi just skipped town. The simplest explanation is usually the right one.'

I shook my head. 'Why would she tell me that she had a secret, or something important to tell me, and then sneak off during the night without ever telling me what it was? She hasn't called to check on the kids. She didn't show up for work. It doesn't seem like her.'

'Well, maybe she was trying to lure you back home. Maybe she wanted someone to watch the kids, so she could have her space. I heard about what happened between her and John.'

'*Lure* me? You make it sound like she's some sort of criminal!'

Paul put a finger to his lips again, reminding me to be quiet. Again, a memory returned —Paul and I meeting in the woods well after dark, his finger pressed to my lips as he pushed me up against a tree...

Shh. We have to be quiet. Don't want anyone to know you're out here with me, do ya?

I tried to focus on his face and forget the past, but my eyes kept drifting down to his lips. *Our first kiss – he tasted like spearmint and salt. He was nervous and sweating, but even his sweat tasted good on my tongue...*

'She wouldn't lure me here,' I shout-whispered again. 'Why would she?'

'Maybe she couldn't take it anymore. She needed an excuse to get you here, and then she ditched you with the kids. She might show back up in a day or two.'

Narrowing my eyes at him, I fought the urge to punch him

again. 'No way. I'm the last person she'd leave to take care of her kids. I'm not even close with them. Why pick me if she wanted to leave?'

'Besides their father, you're their last blood relative, aren't you? Or at least the closest thing...'

I gnawed on my lip. He was right about that. The rest of our family members were distant or dead. But still, Madi loved her kids. She wouldn't just leave them with me without asking first.

'Everyone knows she's been having a hard time. With your mama dying, and then your daddy ... and then finding out John left her for a younger woman. And I know that boy of her has something – autism, isn't it?'

'His name is Ben,' I growled, feeling strangely protective of him suddenly. 'He's different, but nothing is wrong with him. And you're wrong about my sister too. Yes, she was upset about John. In fact, she was planning to divorce his ass. But she seemed happy to see me, she seemed to be doing okay.' But again, I remembered the worried look on her face. When she didn't know I was watching, the mask slipped...

'Sometimes people get happy before ... well, before they make big decisions. Does Madeline own a gun, by any chance? She wouldn't hurt herself, would she?'

'You're unbelievable.' I stepped closer, pushing my face into his defiantly. 'Thanks for wasting my time, Paul. But that's what you're good at, isn't it? Not showing up when I need you.' Never in a million years would I talk this way to a cop, but this was Paul Templeton. *He crushed me. And now he was only making my sister's disappearance worse.*

'Emily, I'm trying to help. Any other cop would be asking the same questions I am. And, if it makes this any easier for you, let me just say that I'm sorry about the time I stood you up...'

I shook my head and pointed in the direction of the front door. 'Just go,' I tried to say, but my voice cracked. I was thinking about my sister and Ben and Shelley, and about how I screwed up and left them with a supposed pedophile today, apparently. *Mr Tennors, really?* I still couldn't shake that thought. He'd seemed so nice, so helpful today.

My eyes were burning as I turned away from Paul. I didn't want him to see me cry. *Not again.*

'Did she give you any hint what this secret was, by any chance?' Paul asked, looking away from me to save me some pride.

I swiped at my cheeks, focusing on a dent in the wood-paneled walls in the family room. I'd wanted the cops to help me, but now I just wanted him to leave...

'No, Paul. She asked me if I could stay for a while and help her out with the kids, but she said there was more to it than that...'

Paul raised an eyebrow, his lips twisting to one side. Hearing myself say it out loud, I could see where his theory about her leaving me in charge of the kids made even more sense now. *She did ask me to stay...*

'And then she was just gone the next morning? Any signs of foul play, or some sort of struggle? Anything off or unusual?'

I tried to think back to yesterday. 'The door to her bedroom was closed. Her bed was made up like she never went to sleep. Her Jeep was gone.' I tried to remember every detail of that morning when Ben woke me up...

'Her shoes were still here,' I added, suddenly remembering that. 'I'm wearing them now actually.' I sniffled as I stared at my feet.

'Does she have more than one pair of shoes?' Paul pressed, gently.

I nodded. 'What woman has only one pair of shoes?'

'Anything else? What about the bedrooms upstairs?'

I froze. *Stupid me.* Never once had I even gone upstairs.

Those rooms were guest rooms and storage, she'd said. *Why didn't it occur to me to at least check them?* I chastised myself.

'Oh god, she could have fallen up there and I never even

checked!' I took off through the kitchen. Paul followed behind me, to where the door to the staircase was closed tight, in an alcove off the dining room.

'Let me go up first,' Paul insisted, gently nudging me aside. Slowly, he opened the door to the stairs. An instant smell hit my nostrils – nothing sinister, only smells of dust and mold.

'I don't think they come up here too often,' I remarked.

Following him up the stairs, I prayed my sister wasn't up here. If she was, then something was deeply wrong.

The upstairs looked the same as I remembered – deep red, knotted carpet lined the main hallway. There were two rooms off to the right and one to the left.

We used to use these as play rooms when we were kids, as soon as we were old enough to go up the stairs on our own. And eventually, as a teen, Madi used one of them as her bedroom.

Paul went into the first room on the right and I followed. It was mostly empty, besides a few boxes of books and an arm chair. Upon closer inspection, I realized the chair belonged to my dad.

I touched the soft checkered fabric, remembering how he looked leaning back in it, his pipe tucked between his teeth.

'Nothing here,' Paul said, more to himself than to me. The next room was full of toy boxes. Some of the toys were old and broken; some still looked new, but I guessed she was trying to clear out space for the kids' rooms downstairs.

'Nothing here,' Paul said again. He was really starting to annoy me.

The largest upstairs room was across the hall, and I could tell immediately as we walked in that it was much fuller than the rest. An old twin bed sat in the sloped corner of the room. I instantly recognized it as my old bed.

'I remember that bed,' Paul said, reading my mind.

'No, you don't,' I snapped. It was mostly true; he'd only been in my room one time, one day after school when my parents weren't home. We'd sat on the bed, kissing feverishly, until we heard my sister come home.

I blushed at the memory and coughed loudly to break the tension.

'What are these?' He pointed at rows of plastic tubs on the floor and neatly labelled cardboard boxes.

Paul squatted down in front of the stack of tubs, and read, 'School Clothes for Ben – Fall.'

Underneath was another container, also for Ben, labelled for winter. Shelley's bin was under his, labelled 'Preschool Clothes for Shelley – Fall and Winter.'

The cardboard boxes were full of what looked to be brand new school supplies – packs of pencils and loose-leaf paper. Packs of glue sticks and erasers. I quickly discovered that they were labelled with each kid's name as well. Neatly folded school supply lists – with everything checked off – inside two of the boxes.

I started lifting more of them and setting them aside. One contained new shoes for both children, the tags still attached, and another contained their important documents – social security cards, birth certificates, shot records…

The only thing in the room that wasn't well organized was a stack of old blankets and a scattering of old mail and postal boxes in the corner.

'She was planning on leaving, Emily. I hate to say it, but doesn't this make it obvious? It looks like she left everything here the kids would need…'

I plopped down in the middle of the floor, tucking my legs up Indian-style.

'I don't know. Maybe she was just really organized? Madi was always anal about everything. This doesn't mean she had it all planned out …does it?'

I looked up at Paul, my eyes searching for something. I needed him, or someone, to provide me with some answers. I needed my sister here to answer them for me, more like it.

'I can't be in charge of these children, Paul. You know how I am.' Paul whipped around to look at me, locking in with those eyes again…

'I do know. And you're amazing, Emily. You always have been. They would be lucky to have you. You should give yourself a little more credit.'

I don't know why, but his words surprised me. His face was softer now, more vulnerable than it used to be. I directed my gaze away from him, quickly.

Lifting a package of markers out of the box, I turned them over and back. *What am I looking for? Some secretly coded message from my sister?*

'This still doesn't make sense. She would leave a note, or she'd call. She would do something, dammit. Not just leave.'

'Listen. I'm going to figure this out, okay? I'll go down to the bank tomorrow morning. I'll find out if she's been using her debit card, or if she took out a large cash withdrawal. Also, I'll keep an eye out for her Jeep. I'll do everything I can to help, Emily, I promise.'

Back on my feet now, I couldn't help myself – I reached for the boy I used to know, the one I'd once loved and coveted, and even hated at times. I wrapped my arms around his neck. Gently, his hands slipped around my waist and I pressed my face to his chest. A rush of familiar smells – heady cologne and the faint scent of diesel fuel embedded under his nails and in the cracks of his hands.

'I really missed you,' he whispered in my ear.

I pulled away without saying it back. My body was tingling, lighter than air, as I followed him back downstairs, then walked him to the front door.

For a moment, I wondered if he would kiss me goodbye, but then I realized that would be ridiculous. *Even if he tried, would I let him?* Thankfully – or maybe not – he didn't try to kiss me. 'I'll find out what I can for you. Trust me,' he said again.

I followed him outside and stood on the porch, watching the taillights of his cruiser grow smaller and fade away into the darkness. Katydids and cicadas were singing, the sound of them reassuring, like a reminder that the world would go on no matter what happened.

I couldn't shake off the daze – the buzz of excitement in the air. It'd been years since I felt this giddy. Somehow, it seemed so wrong. *Your sister is missing for god's sake and you're thinking about a boy!* I chastised myself.

A couple lights popped on from somewhere inside Mr Tennors' cottage. My thoughts grew dark again. How dare he volunteer to watch the children, knowing his history? Tomorrow I was going to give him a piece of my mind.

Staring at his house, I could have sworn that I saw someone moving behind the window, the curtains slowly shifting. He must have been watching. What if he'd done something to my sister? Anyone capable of hurting a child, could surely hurt an adult, too.

But did I really believe that? He'd been my neighbor most of my life, and he'd never harmed anyone. Well, not that I knew of until now...

Suddenly frightened, I scurried back inside, quickly turning the lock and fastening the deadbolt behind me. Was it him I was afraid of, or something else?

I peered through the curtains, watched the trees sway side to side, like some sort of grotesque dance they performed only for me.

Closing the curtains tight, I then went room to room, checking locks on all the windows and side doors that led to outside. Lastly, I checked the windows in my sister's room. I was surprised to find them unlocked. *How long had they been that way?* The fear of not knowing who I could trust bubbled deep in my belly.

CHAPTER SEVEN

I tossed and turned, struggling to find a position that was comfortable in my sister's bed. I was restless, still trying to sort through the details in my mind. The neatly prepared containers of school clothes and supplies. All the kids' documents stowed away – stowed away for me, perhaps? I rolled on my side, adjusting and readjusting the pillows. Madi's ghostly scent was still embedded in the fabric. I could almost imagine her lying here. I blinked, seeing my sister's face on the pillow beside me. Facing each other, our eyes interlocked. *Who are you? Do I know who you are anymore?* I whispered to her in the dark.

Finally, I drifted off to sleep sometime after midnight, but I woke back up around 3 a.m. At first, I was panicky – *was someone in the house? Were the children screaming? What woke me up at this hour?* But it only took a few moments to understand why – my temples were throbbing, shooting pains coursing up and down the back of my neck and behind my eyelids.

These headaches had been happening all my life, ever since I fell and hit my head in the woods and was knocked unconscious. Luckily, my mom and sister had found me and immediately rushed me to the hospital. I had a concussion, but no brain damage. Sometimes I wondered if the doctors had missed something – they must have because why else would I still have these debilitating headaches?

I struggled to get out of bed, wincing at the blinding hot white pain rushing through my skull. Opting not to turn on the lights – I didn't want to wake up the kids and the light would make the pain even worse – I stumbled down the hallway and into the bathroom. I rummaged through my sister's cabinets, relieved when I found a bottle of extra-strength Ibuprofen.

My doctor would prescribe me something stronger if I asked. But that was the problem – I hadn't asked. The fear of becoming addicted to pain pills was greater than the pain I endured from the headaches.

I tossed back four of the pills and used my hands to cup cold water from the faucet and into my mouth. I drank the water greedily then wandered out to the living room, massaging my temples.

Once again, I went straight to the front window, in search of my sister's Jeep. It was becoming a habit now. *What if she never comes back?* said a tiny, wriggling voice in my ear. I plopped down at my sister's desk.

Even if I was qualified to care for the kids – which I wasn't – I didn't have a job anymore to support them financially. My sister had taken off before I had a chance to tell her about the job I lost at the paper.

I'd worked so hard, going to college and earning my journalism degree. All I ever wanted was to write stories – to share facts about the world with the general public, or present someone's story in a fun, entertaining way.

When I got the job at the *Charleston Chronicle*, I thought: *This is it.* Finally, I had a real chance to prove myself. I had an amazing office with a view of the harbor. And a plate on the door with my name on it.

But my stories weren't good enough, simple as that. They were passed over, and even laughed at by some of my colleagues.

I thought bullying was something that only happened in high school, but I quickly learned I was wrong. I couldn't figure it out at first – the screwed-up lines in my stories, the clutter strewn across my desk, the rumors about me and a male colleague...

Why were these things happening to me? Was I just that unlikable?

Near the beginning of the end of my career in journalism, I learned something that shed some light. When my job opened, there was a girl slated for my position. One of my co-worker's sisters. When she was passed over and I got the job instead, that co-worker and her cronies made it their life goal to force me out. Well, it worked.

Finally, after less than six months at the paper, my boss told me that I should consider a different career. *You don't really fit in here,* he told me. Tears stung my eyes as those words repeated over and over in my mind, remembering that final moment in his office. *'You just don't fit, Emily. Your stories are too short, or not thorough enough. You screwed up on "your" and "you're" the other day. Your piece on the Charleston Circus was a mess. Speaking of messes, your desk is always a wreck. Personally, I'm a little embarrassed for you. Don't you have a journalism degree?'*

Madeline's disappearance had pushed my lost job and soon-to-be lost apartment from the forefront of my mind. But now everything came rushing back – each thought, each worry, like a serrated blade sawing straight through my skull.

I needed a new job, and fast. Sure, I had a thousand dollars in the bank, but if Madi didn't come back soon, and I had to take care of these children and her bills ... it would barely last the month. *Oh god.*

The pain in my head was surging now, like an angry, roaring lion clawing from the inside out. I laid my head down on my sister's desk, willing the pain to go away. Suddenly, there was a small click as my elbow bumped against the mouse pad. The computer screen lit up and I squinted at the white light of her computer screen. Madeline's screen saver was a pic of her, John, Ben, and Shelley. They were all wearing Mickey Mouse ears on their heads. *She never told me they went to Disney World.*

I had missed so much of my sister's life, and for what? Because I was angry at Dad and afraid of some stupid forest? It seemed so ridiculous now that I was here. If Madi was in some sort of trouble, I could have helped her sooner if I'd just come home...

My headache forgotten temporarily, I scooted up closer to the screen. I studied the swirl of my sister's eyes – green with tiny flecks of brownish gold – and I couldn't pull my own eyes away. I willed her to tell me something, to give me some sort of sign. *What happened Madi? Did you run away or did somebody hurt you? What are you hiding?*

My eyes flicked over to John. He was handsome in that country-club, pretty boy sort of way. He had a thinning, brushed over hairstyle, and straight, perfect white teeth. His smile reminded me of that of a used car salesman. *It's always the husband.* I don't know where I heard that. Maybe from some late-night crime TV show or a true crime novel I read. I wasn't even sure if she was hurt – or worse ... but if something bad had happened to Madi, it was most likely at the hands of John. I knew so little about him, but what I did know wasn't good. He'd cheated on her and had snapped at her when she was on the phone with me. Her co-workers called him grumpy; had he turned up at her work and snapped at her there, too? I should have asked them more questions when I was down there...

Madi never mentioned any violence or verbal abuse, but of everyone in my sister's life, John had the best motive to want her gone. Did he run her out of town? Did he ... hurt her?

He had a new, younger girlfriend. Maybe he wanted Madeline out of the way, so he and Starla could move into the house that Madeline inherited from our parents. Maybe there was life insurance to consider. Maybe he wanted the kids all to himself. Or, maybe he just hated her that much, and it was a combination of all three…

But there was also Albert Tennors to consider. I clicked on the internet and pulled up Google. All it took was typing in his name and 'Bare Border' to find him.

The face of my sister's jolly, seemingly harmless, neighbor popped up on the screen. I barely recognized him in the photo. His hair was wild, his eyes slanted. He might have been drunk when this picture was taken. His address was listed under his picture, and below that were the words: *Sexually Violent Predator.* My heart slammed against my chest. Beneath that were his initial arrest date – nearly thirty years ago, but still – and his charge: *Rape.* There were no other details. I tried to click on his picture to find out more, but nothing happened.

Tomorrow I would ask Paul more questions about Mr Tennors, I decided. He'd lived next to us our whole lives and never tried to harm us. But what if losing his wife last year made him snap?

It was hard for me to believe, but then again, I also couldn't believe my sister would just jump ship and leave town…

Closing out the sex offender registry, I had another thought. Maybe Madi left a note for me on her computer. I hadn't seen any written notes, but what if she left it here…?

I did a quick search of all word files. Unlike my laptop at home, which was full of documents from stories I was working on, Madeline had very little. There were only three documents saved in Word. Two of those were shopping lists and another was a letter to John.

I opened the letter, instantly feeling guilty, like I was violating Madi's trust by snooping around on her computer. But what choice did I have at this point?

The letter was recent, timestamped from only two weeks ago. It was only a couple of paragraphs and then it stopped midsentence, like she'd either been interrupted or given up on the letter completely. It read:

74

Dear John,

No words can explain how I feel right now. I never thought we would be one of those couples. You know, the ones who have to sleep with other people or sneak around to stay happy. I'm usually an observant person, but I had no idea. And for some reason it's that – the not knowing – that bothers me the most. When you told me about this woman, this Starla ... I didn't know how to respond. I'm sorry for slapping you. That wasn't right. But I was so hurt. John, how the hell could you do this? Not just to me, but to Ben and Shelley. Do you really think you can make a life with this woman? Is that why you've been so distant, so short, with us lately? Do you really think she can keep

The letter ended after that. An image floated up – my sister, perched in this very chair, her hands shaking with anger as she typed up the letter. She probably didn't finish it because she broke down in tears. I know I would have.

The throbbing in my head was coming back, but I tried to push it out of my mind and focus on finding out more. I closed down Word and got back on the internet, pulling up my sister's search history. 'Give me something, Madi,' I whispered.

But she didn't. The search had nothing of significance – articles on ADHD and autism. A few articles on what to do if your child was being bullied. I paused at that. *Was Ben being bullied at school?* It wasn't hard to imagine. Ben was different than other kids – high-strung, obsessive, anxious. Certain things that seemed easy for Shelley, even though she was five years younger, seemed difficult for Ben.

Poor Madi. She had so much shit to deal with already, and then she found out John was cheating.

She was also looking up sites that listed the symptoms of depression. 'Oh, Madi.' If I told Paul about this, he would point out that it was even more proof she'd left on her own. *Does*

Madeline own a gun? His words rang out in my mind. I didn't think she owned one, but I guess it was always possible...

Besides the articles, there were more hits for Amazon and shopping sites. A lot of visits to Facebook and occasional ones to Instagram.

I decided to pull up Facebook and try to analyze my sister's recent posts.

I typed it in and was surprised to find that Madi was still logged in. She hadn't posted to her page in weeks, but she wasn't a frequent poster anyway. There were two unread messages blinking back at me. For half a second, I felt guilty, but then I remembered why I was doing this. *I need to find out where Madi has gone.*

The first unread message was from Misti, the manager I'd met today at Bed and More. **Where are you? Why didn't you come into work today? Your phone is going straight to v-mail. Call me ASAP before Bryan finds out about you missing work! (smiley face).**

Next, I clicked on the other unread message. It was from Jessica Feeler. Even though she looked much older than when I saw her last, I recognized her immediately as my sister's friend from high school, the same girl that was in the photos with her the other day. My sister, Jessica, and Rhonda Sheckles had been inseparable as teenagers. It shouldn't surprise me that they kept in touch. When I pulled up the message, I expected something casual, or an update on Jessica's life, but what I got was one simple, ominous line: **You'd better keep your fucking mouth shut.**

Leaning back in the desk chair, I looked at the words until they turned blurry. *You'd better keep your fucking mouth shut.* If that wasn't a threat, what was?

'Or what, Jessica? She needed to keep her mouth shut, or what? Did you hurt my sister?' I glared at the tiny bubble with her face in it. Finally, I clicked off the message and pulled up Jessica's profile.

She didn't look scary or threatening in her photos. She was married and had a daughter named Chelsi. She still lived in Bare Border, less than two miles from here.

I'd have to pay good old Jessica a visit soon. And I had to tell Paul about this, too.

Yawning, I stood up from the chair and stretched. My headache was gone, now replaced with a worried ache in my stomach. *Oh, Madeline, where are you?*

Back in her room, I opened and closed drawers and sifted through her closet. Most of John's clothes were still there. Everything was folded or hung up neatly. Besides the box of photos on her closet floor, there were only shoes, belts, and old magazines in there.

'Nothing in here,' I murmured, just like Paul did earlier. In truth, I couldn't blame him for thinking what he did. If I didn't know my sister better, I'd probably think she'd run off too.

Remembering the first night, and that goofy trick with the kids under the sink, it crossed my mind that maybe all of this was a prank. *No way.* Maybe if it was just me, she would do something silly like that. But, again, there was no way she would do that to her kids. There was nothing funny about this, no reason to play games…

I crawled back into my sister's bed and slid beneath the covers, my teeth chattering, although I wasn't cold. The clock on the night stand read 05:13. The sun would be coming up soon, but for now, I needed a little more rest. My body was exhausted from filling in for my sister, and my brain was shot at this point.

CHAPTER EIGHT

My dreams were mottled and strange – me, sailing through the air, crashing down on a bed of rocks. My head splitting apart, voices bouncing back and forth through the trees...

When I opened my eyes, I half-expected my head to be pounding again. But I was pain-free, albeit still exhausted from my late-night snooping session on Madeline's computer.

Instantly, I remembered the menacing message from Jessica Feeler and the wild look in Mr Tennors' profile photo on the sex offender registry site.

Someone was breathing beside me. Expecting Ben, I was pleasantly surprised to see Shelley. She was wide awake, her eyes bright and energetic.

'The sky's awake, so I'm awake. It's time to play,' she crowed, reciting lines from the Disney movie, *Frozen*.

'What time is it?' I mumbled, blinking sleep from my eyes. Gone were the days of sleeping in and waking up on my own volition in my apartment.

'I can't tell time yet, silly. That's why I need to go to preschool.'

I glanced over at the clock on the bedside table. It wasn't even 9 a.m. yet. It felt so early, but then again, when I was working at the *Charleston Chronicle*, I had to be there at this time every day.

Ben leapt onto the bed with an 'oomph' and Shelley giggled as she bounced up from the bed, like a fluffy piece of popcorn.

'Don't mind me. I'm just practicing my cannon ball,' Ben hooted. He stood up and jumped again, his knees barely missing my belly.

'Are you guys excited about starting school tomorrow?'

'Yes!' Shelley squealed. She was due to start at Frontier Academy, the local pre-school that was located a few buildings over from Ben's elementary school.

'What about you?' I asked Ben softly. I thought about the articles on bullying I'd found on the computer.

Ben's face confirmed my suspicions. 'I don't want to go,' he said, shaking his head.

'You know you have to. It's the law.' I wasn't sure if it still was, but I couldn't think of anything else to say. 'I'll walk you in. It will be fun, I promise.'

'Okay.' Ben nodded, but he didn't look convinced.

I pushed the covers back and sat up, yawning again. 'Today is your last day of summer. What should we do?' Despite what was going on with Madeline, I was determined to keep the kids as mentally healthy as possible. They didn't need this sort of stress, not at the beginning of the school year, and I couldn't handle any more of Ben's meltdowns.

'Can we have a picnic?' Shelley looked hopeful, her eyes sparkling.

'Sounds good to me. Ben?' He nodded.

'But not too long, okay? I hate mosquitoes.' His face was grumpy again.

'We'll put on some bug spray,' I suggested. While I got dressed, they did too. Today, Ben was able to get on his shirt and shorts on his own.

In the kitchen, I fixed three turkey sandwiches and cut them up into little triangles like Mom used to do. Shelley came into the kitchen while I bagged them up, dragging a raggedy, yellow blanket in her hands. 'We can use this to eat on!'

'That's perfect.' I smiled at her as I tucked the mayonnaise and meat back into the fridge.

'No! I won't do it!' Ben was standing in the doorway of the kitchen now; his shoes were on, but they were on the wrong feet.

'Oh, I forgot.' Shelley stared down at the blanket, her mood deflated.

'Why not, Ben? Shelley has a blanket and I made sandwiches.'

'Not that blanket!' Ben crossed his arms over his chest and whipped his head back and forth.

'He hates yellow. He won't touch anything yellow.'

I didn't bother asking why not. I could remember my sister telling me something like this – he had nonsensical fears and strange obsessions, sometimes.

I stared at the bright yellow blanket, a thought taking shape. 'Is that why your mom painted the Mello Yellow Room?' From their confused expressions, I realized that Madeline had never called it that in front of them. 'The guestroom. The one that used to be yellow and now it's painted pink.'

Shelley nodded. 'Yep! Isn't it pretty? Mom didn't want to paint it. She even cried a little bit. But Ben was scared to go in it, so she painted over it. She's going to turn it into a playroom for us, pretty soon.'

My heart softened. To think, I was ready to yell at her that first night when I saw the paint. Sometimes I could be so selfish.

Remembering the old blankets upstairs, I said, 'Don't worry. I saw a blue blanket that will be perfect for our picnic.'

I told them to wait in the kitchen and then I climbed the stairs for the second day in a row. Not finding Madeline hurt up here yesterday was a relief.

As I reached the top step, my thoughts traveled to Paul – that teasing smile of his, the peppery smell of his cologne…

I entered the room with the school supplies. *I'll have to lay out their clothes tonight and put their supplies in their backpacks*, I mentally noted. The thought of it was overwhelming…

Bending down, I scooped up the blue blanket from the stack I'd noticed last night. Suddenly, a box in the corner caught my eye. I walked over to the haphazard pile of old bills and boxes. Most of the boxes were from UPS or the post office. Generally, they looked empty, as though Madi was just saving them in case she needed them later ... but one caught my eye. Shoving the rest of the mail aside, I stared at the small cardboard box.

There was no return address on it, but Madi was the addressee. It wasn't the box itself that made me freeze – it was the tiny bird sketched on the side of it. Brooding and dark, the bird had a large, morose eye and wild tufts of feathers sprouting from its head.

Someone had drawn the bird on the side of the package. I'd seen it before, but where? I closed my eyes and tried to focus – something from a cartoon, or something my sister used to draw? Some sort of logo? *No, that's not it.* It was an image from my childhood, but I couldn't place when or where I'd seen it – all I had was this fading spark that screamed: *You know what this is, Emily!*

After Jessica's cryptic message on Facebook last night, I expected to find a threatening letter, or something strange, in the box.

But it was empty, like all the others. It was just large enough to fit a book inside, or something similar in size.

'Aunt Em, where are you?' Ben yelled from the bottom of the stairs.

'Coming!' I glanced at the box for another moment, noting the postal date was from two weeks ago. It was addressed to my sister. Why did this feel important?

'I'm getting scared!' Ben shouted, a quiver in his voice.

Afraid he'd have another tantrum, I dropped the box and ran back downstairs with the blanket tucked under my arm.

***

81

At first, Ben and Shelley suggested we set up our picnic in the front yard. But, remembering Mr Tennors, I insisted we do it in the back. I spread the blanket out wide and then we took our seats. The weather was perfect. Even the leafy light of the forest looked serene, not menacing like the other day.

The blanket was smaller than it looked folded up, and our knees were touching each other as we ate our sandwiches from paper plates on our laps.

After we ate, the kids ran around the yard. Ben made up some outside version of *Five Nights at Freddy's*, and Shelley went along with it. They ducked behind bushes, pretending to hide from the creepy characters Ben liked in the game.

I kept a close eye on them while I made a couple of calls on my cell phone. First, I contacted someone in the office at Ben's school and then I called Shelley's pre-school. I wanted to double check the start time. Filling in for my sister was hard, but the last thing I wanted to do was take them to school late on their first day. Ben had to be there at eight o'clock and Shelley started at nine-thirty.

As nervous as they were, I was twice as worried. I didn't want to screw up something as important as school. Thank god Madeline was prepared, with the school supplies and new clothes…

'Let's go to the woods!' Ben was sweating profusely, his too long hair dipping into his eyes and sticking to the tops of his ears.

'I thought we did that at dinner time,' I said, trying to stall the inevitable as I kept my voice even and cool. The last thing I wanted to do was have another freak out, but how long could I avoid those woods?

'But it feels like dinner time! We just ate! Please…'

Shelley looked hopeful, too, puckering out her bottom lip.

'Fine.' Brushing crumbs from my lap and tucking my cell phone inside my back pocket, I headed across the yard to meet them. In the butter-yellow sunlight, the path looked a little less frightening today...

Holding my breath, I walked, hand-in-hand, with Shelley and Ben to the mouth of the woods. I don't know who was holding onto who – most likely, it was me who needed their support.

The path was steeper than I remembered, and suddenly, I was worried the kids would tumble down it, and into the brambles on the forest floor.

'Wait, don't let go of my hand!'

But they didn't listen. They pushed and tumbled their way down the hill, shouting back and forth at each other, their voices shrill and disturbing as they bounced off the trees.

'I won!' Shelley cheered.

'No, I won!' Ben's cheeks were red like shiny apples as he raced after his little sister. I was still standing at the entrance, at the top of the hill. My own feet slipped and wobbled as I forced myself to move.

I made my way down the steep incline. The ground was soupy and slick from recent rain. I grappled for branches and leaves, anything to slow me down, but there was no use – my feet swished out from under me, and suddenly, I was sledding down the hill on my backside.

'Guys, stay put there. Wait for me!' The back of my pants was soaked. I dug my fingers into the mud and pushed myself up to my feet. I expected the kids to be giggling by now, having a laugh at their silly, clumsy Aunt Em.

But they were running again, farther into the trees, with Ben taking the lead this time. 'No, no! Let me win!' Shelley screamed, her tiny legs pumping as she leapt over rocks and the remnants of someone's pulpy fast food cup.

Back on my feet, I took off after them, the trees closing in around me like a cocoon.

Ben was headed straight for the creek, but my vision was off – was that Ben or Shelley ducking behind those trees?

'Wait, please…' I moaned, trying to walk a straight line and will my eyes to focus and find the children.

I hadn't been down here in a long time, but I still remembered the layout. With the recent storms, the water in the creek would be up, high enough to whisk Ben or Shelley away, all the way to Moon Lake…

'Guys, please wait for me!' I was running now. Tree limbs looked like bony claws reaching out for me, roots like serpents twisting around my ankles. I ran with all my might, pure terror boiling up in the pit of my stomach as I lost sight of both of them. Madeline would kill me if anything happened to them, oh god!

'Shelley! Ben!' My screams were shrill and frightened, like tiny little needles in the air.

A branch poked me hard in the shin, more branches slapping my face as leaves cartwheeled around me through the thickening trees. I stopped, spinning around in circles. The sunlight from earlier was gone, replaced by a big black shadow hovering above the trees. Was it real, or was it my imagination?

'Where are you guys?' I shouted, frantically.

Instinctively, I walked in what I hoped was the direction of the creek. I heard it before I saw it, the bubbly sound of water rumbling over stones.

I stopped at the edge of it, staring down into the water. *Water will cool and calm me down.* I knelt down beside the creek, my head roaring with pain, every blink flashed with *red, red, red …* and that's when I saw the blood. Red swirls of it running down my leg. My own reflection stared back at me in the water – a wild stranger, bloody and crazed.

It's me. It's just me. Isn't it? I blinked once, twice, staring at my own grim face in the water's mirrored shine. There really was a streak of blood running down my face.

Suddenly, like a flash, I was falling. *My arms pinwheeling, my feet slicing through the air like scissors … I'm falling down, down, until my head collides with the edge of a jagged rock. Pain explodes from my head, radiating through the rest of my body. This must be what dying feels like … but the pain of the blow doesn't stop there. Again, and again, my head collides with the rock, the pain so real and brutal, so terrifying, that I no longer can even feel it … all I can see, and taste is dirt, thick chalky globs of it in my mouth … this is it: I'm dead.*

'Oh, god. No, no, no…' Holding my head down between my knees, I gasp for air. The flashback was so disorienting, so *real*, that I could feel the injury all over again. Most of all, I could taste the fear in my mouth.

Cool wet hands brushed my cheeks. 'Aunty Emmy, you okay?' Shelley was kneeling in front of me. She had this calm, motherly look about her, like she was thirty instead of three.

'Thank god you're okay. Where's Ben?' I rasped.

'I'm here.' Ben stepped out from where he'd been hiding behind a thick oak tree. His hair was ruffled and sweaty, sticking to the sides of his face and covering up one eye.

'Were you both hiding from me? Don't ever do that again.' My teeth clenched together – I was furious. *Why did they do that to me?* I swiped at the blood on my cheek; I must have gotten scratched by a branch while I was running.

'We always race down the hill and pick a tree to hide behind. Mom lets us.'

Before I could respond, he asked, 'Where's my mommy?' again. This time, I ignored him.

Shelley's inquisitive eyes were still fixated on me. 'What's wrong with you? You looked like you were going crazy. We were right here, but you were spinning and spinning, acting like a scary person.' She spun her finger around in a circle next to her own temple, and suddenly, my anger dissipated. Shelley was wise beyond her years, her face solemn.

'Help me up, please.' Shelley and Ben each gave me a hand, and I pushed myself up off the ground. I was shocked to see that there was blood on my knee and elbows. Touching my face, I discovered another thin cut below my eye. Tiny drops of blood seeped out from it, but they were only minor scratches; not the rushing, roar of blood I saw in my mind when I peered at myself in the water…

'What was wrong with you?' Shelley asked again. I pointed for both of them to go back up the path, still trying to catch my breath. It was time to go in.

I stared at my feet, one right after the other … forcing myself not to look at the trees again. *I just need to get out of here, and then I'll be okay again.*

Clearing my throat, I said, 'When I was little, I hurt myself in these woods. I had a concussion and was in the hospital for days afterwards. I know I told you guys about it already, but it was pretty serious. I was too scared to go in the woods again after it happened. Do you know what a concussion is?'

Shelley shrugged, but Ben nodded. His face was twisted up with worry again.

'You guys have to be careful in these woods. I know you were only playing, but one misstep, one wrong turn…' Another image flashed in my mind. *A tunnel of water all around me, and the milky green surface of the lake, only I was looking up at it from below. Lying on the rocky bottom of the lake bed…* But that memory made no sense. Where did that come from?

I shuddered, shaking off my coat of fear as the path widened and we found ourselves back in my sister's backyard. My breathing became normal again, my chest burning with relief.

'How about more pasta for dinner? Do you guys like fettucine?' They nodded enthusiastically, then took off again, racing each other back to the house. I let out a whoosh of breath, trying to still my shaky nerves. *I'd never gotten over what happened to me in those woods.* I was missing moments, but those moments – whatever occurred – must have been pretty traumatic. I thought I was going to die that day … how could a simple fall cause that much fear?

'Emily?' I was shocked to see John crossing the yard, walking toward us.

'What are you doing here?' As soon as I said it, I felt ridiculous. This was his house and his yard after all. Technically, he had more of a right to be here than me.

He seemed to be thinking the same thing as he scrunched his nose up at me.

'Daddy!' Ben and Shelley squealed. They lunged into their father's arms. He knelt on the ground in front of them, squeezing them tightly. *Maybe he missed them after all,* I considered.

'We just got back from the woods. Do you want to go back down there with us?' Ben pleaded.

John patted Ben's head. 'No, buddy. I came here to talk to your Aunt Emily. Let's go inside now. You two can find something to do while we have a chat, yes?'

Shelley and Ben's faces went limp with disappointment.

'What do you want to talk about, John?' His smiling demeanor melted away as he looked over at me.

'What happened to you?' he asked, staring at the scratches on my face, legs, and arms.

'I took a tumble down the hill. Didn't realize how steep it was. What do you want to talk about?' I repeated.

'We'll discuss that inside.' And just like that, he was walking toward the back door, the kids trotting after him. Feeling as though I had no other choice, I followed too.

John entered the house first, his hands tucked behind his back. He paced back and forth in the kitchen, looking it over as though he hadn't seen it before. *What a dick.*

Even though this was his house, I couldn't help feeling violated. It didn't feel like he belonged in this space, and simply put, I didn't trust him. He hadn't given me one reason to trust him yet, and I remembered my sister's letter to him...

The kids took off through the dining room, running to their rooms to play. Initially, they had been so excited to see their

87

father, but now the thrill had worn off as though the fact that their father had been gone for weeks was no big deal. I immediately got the sense that Madeline did everything for the children, and John did very little.

I leaned against the counter, feeling defensive. *What does this asshole want? Does he know where Madeline is?*

John stood in front of the refrigerator, his hands mashed down on his hips, staring at a flier that was tacked to the door. Swim lessons.

Finally, he turned around to face me, his eyes hard and mean. I tried to conjure up memories of him at the wedding ... John laughing and smiling, twirling Madeline around in circles. He had seemed pleased to meet me. I think he even kissed my hand when she introduced us for the first time. One word to describe John then – *charming*. He had seemed like the perfect husband. But now he seemed anything but, his expression and movements were arrogant, and frankly, they were a little intimidating.

'Where is she?' John hissed, smacking a hand down on the counter top.

Startled, I said nothing for several seconds.

'I have friends in the police department. So, of course they told me that my wife was missing. Why didn't you call me sooner?'

I shrugged, then said, 'Honestly, I didn't know how to get a hold of you. Or that you would even care. And I was hoping she would show back up in a day or two.'

'Did she say where she was going?'

'Of course not. If she had, she wouldn't be missing, would she? Do you have any idea where she might have gone?'

John's eyes narrowed. 'Why would I? I have a new girlfriend now.'

I shushed him, shocked at his loud announcement. The kids probably weren't listening in, but I would have thought he'd want to keep his new relationship to himself for a while.

'I just mean, I thought maybe she called you? Or she mentioned something to you – about taking a trip or needing some time without the kids…?'

John shook his head. 'No, she didn't. We haven't talked for weeks. But frankly, I'm not surprised. Madi doesn't handle stress well.'

'What does that mean?' My chest tightened in anger. *How dare he?*

'She doesn't handle the kids well. Look at all of the problems Ben has…'

'His condition isn't her fault,' I snapped.

'Condition,' John mimicked, using quotes in the air. 'Being spoiled isn't a condition.'

I was so furious, I couldn't speak. How could my sister have loved this man?

'And why are you here, anyway? You've never made any effort to spend time with my kids. Now all of a sudden, you come to visit like you're their favorite aunt. What's up with that?'

'Speaking of spending time with the kids, you haven't been too worried about them yourself lately. Madeline said you haven't been by to see them in weeks.'

For the first time, John smiled at me. All his teeth were showing and for some reason, I thought about a hungry lion in the jungle. 'Well, that's about to change.'

'What do you mean?'

'I'm coming back to pick them up tonight at seven. Starla and I will keep them with us until Madi returns. You're free to go on home, if you want.'

Stunned, I opened my mouth to speak. Nothing came out but a small huffing sound.

'But they start school tomorrow. Have you even thought about that?'

John's smile grew even wider. 'I'm sure Madi already bought their supplies. Pack those up for me. And get a couple weeks' worth of clothes together, too. I'll be back to get them tonight, so don't give me any trouble. Those kids need to stay with their father.'

CHAPTER NINE

The woods were all but forgotten. The kids were taking turns playing on the Wii, and I was frantically stuffing school supplies and school clothes into boxes. I tried to focus on the task at hand, but my eyes were filmy with tears and I couldn't stop shaking.

Finally, I sat back on my heels and stared at the supplies, feeling helpless. I was more convinced than ever that John was somehow responsible for Madeline's disappearance.

My sister said he hadn't come by in weeks, but maybe that was because he was biding his time and waiting for her to drop her guard. She'd disappeared during the middle of the night. Plus, John was the only person I knew of who had a key to the house. He could have easily just walked right in, incapacitated my sister, and carried her away somewhere.

A small whimper escaped through my lips as I thought about the possibilities.

'Aunty Emmy, are you okay?' I hadn't heard Shelley come upstairs behind me. She stood in the doorway, her head tilted to the side.

'I'm fine, sweetheart.' I opened my arms and Shelley climbed on my lap. I kissed her forehead and rosy cheeks, I pinched her tiny button nose. 'Your daddy is coming to get you tonight. He wants you guys to stay with him and his friend for a while, just until Mommy gets back.'

'Is she his girlfriend?' Shelley was so innocent-sounding, but the question shocked me.

'Have you met Daddy's friend, Starla, before?' *How could she possibly know of her already?*

Slowly, Shelley nodded. I could tell she was holding something back and it broke my heart. That bastard. It was bad enough to cheat, but it was even worse that his three-year-old daughter knew he was doing it.

'Daddy gets days off sometimes. When Mommy goes to work, and Ben goes to school, sometimes Starla comes over.'

I stared at my niece, shell-shocked. I'd nearly forgotten about the fact that Shelley hadn't gone to school up until this point.

'Weren't you at daycare on those days?'

'Not when Daddy is home. If he stays home from work, Mommy leaves me home with him. The babysitter is expletive.'

'You mean expensive,' I said, softly. My eyes were cloudy with tears and for the first time, I seriously considered what it would feel like to kill someone. If I was going to do it, I'd pick that asshole, John. *How could he?* Not only did he have the nerve to cheat, but he was bringing her back here on his days off – to the house he shared with my sister – while his daughter was home. *Disgusting.*

'Is Starla nice, honey? Have you ever spoken to her?'

Shelley shrugged. 'She's okay. Doesn't talk much. I think she is in love with my daddy.'

I held Shelley close, unsure how to answer that. I rubbed her head and fought back more tears that were threatening to come.

How could I let the kids go with him when he might have hurt my sister?

But the truth was, I had no other choice. I couldn't keep these kids from their father. I was only their aunt – an aunt they'd met for the first time just a couple of days ago. John was right. I was overstepping my bounds.

Ben came trotting up the steps, making that squealing noise he always made. I wondered if some of his repetitive behaviors brought him comfort, soothed him.

I tried to imagine Ben with his father – a father who didn't even believe he had autism or ADHD symptoms.

Ben plopped down on the floor beside us. I nudged him toward me, holding them both on my lap now. *I won't cry. I can't. I must be strong for Madi.*

The first thing I was going to do when they left was call Paul. I would tell him about my suspicions of John and what happened today and see if he could get a search warrant for the house John shared with Starla.

Starla. What did I even know about her? Grimly, I considered the possibility that maybe she'd done something to my sister. After all, she had the most to gain from getting her out of the picture…

CHAPTER TEN

With a brave face on, I carried the boxes of school supplies and the children's new clothes out onto the porch. At 7.05 p.m., there was still no sign of John. I started feeling hopeful, that maybe he'd had a change of heart.

But those hopes were dashed as a blue-black Mercedes rolled up the drive at seven-thirty on the dot. The windows were dark, but I could tell that the driver was a woman. John stepped out of the passenger side, opening his arms to the kids once more.

A little less enthusiastically, they gave their father a hug. 'Pop the trunk!' John barked through the passenger window. Suddenly, the trunk clicked open on its own. I began carrying boxes over, expecting John to come over and help me.

But he didn't. He smiled at me and chatted with the kids while I packed it all in. *Asshole.*

I didn't expect to meet Starla since she'd opted to stay in the car, but then, the driver's door swung open and a young, leggy brunette stepped out.

She was young – very young. I wondered if she was even twenty-one yet.

'Hi. I'm Starla,' she said, shyly.

I looked away, sickened. 'I'm Emily,' I mumbled.

Starla followed me up to the porch and helped me carry the last of the boxes. John looked pleased as he watched us, probably enjoying my discomfort.

Starla was pretty, in a classic sort of way. She was wearing jean shorts; they were so short that the pockets hung down through the bottom. She was lean and tan, and as I draped several of the kids' outfits over the boxes, I got a good look at her face. She was lovely, as much as it pained me to admit it.

As Starla pushed the trunk closed, I took a chance and asked, 'Do you know where my sister is?'

She looked startled by my question. 'No, of course not. I haven't seen her.'

I nodded, feeling disappointed. But even if Starla did know something, it wasn't a guarantee that she would tell me.

I kissed Ben and Shelley on their cheeks, trying to stay strong. My smile was strained as they were loaded into the car, with the car seats I'd bought only yesterday. I kept on smiling, so much so that my cheeks were beginning to ache.

'If you need anything or want me to pick them up from school…'

John snapped, 'I can handle it.' Starla gave me an apologetic look, getting back in the driver's seat. I watched the Mercedes reverse down the driveway, wondering if I'd ever see my niece and nephew again. I couldn't shake the feeling that I'd just made the biggest mistake of my life.

***

For the first time since returning to Bare Border, I cried – not just a few messy tears, but sobs. They wracked my body, making it difficult to breathe, and with my fists pressed against the closed door, I realized I was alone. I'd returned to the Bare Border Inn to be with my sister, niece, and nephew. But now it was only me here – *what was I going to do?*

94

I sat down next to the pile of toys, my eyes burning from the hot angry tears. There was a sharp rap on the front door. I lunged for it, praying it was John again, that he'd changed his mind. But instead, Albert Tennors stood on the porch.

'Are you okay?' He looked genuinely concerned. 'I saw some of what just happened.'

'Of course you did.' I no longer suspected him – John was suspect numero uno, in my mind. But I still wanted nothing to do with a man who had hurt another child. 'You need to get the hell off my sister's porch. Now.'

'Why?' he asked, his voice small, frightened.

'Because I know about your history. I know you raped a child. I don't think you did anything to my sister, but either way, don't come around here no more. Don't even look at those kids.' I let out a strange grunt then slammed the door.

'Screw him, too' I muttered beneath my breath, pushing away the guilt threatening to creep up inside me. *Why do you feel guilty – because he's an old man?! He's a pedophile, Emily!* I admonished myself. But I still couldn't wrap my brain around those charges; they didn't add up with the man I knew, or thought I knew…

I peeked through the front curtains to see if he was still there. His head hung low, Albert Tennors was walking slowly across the field, back the way he came. Why was he watching the house so intently, anyway? That in and of itself seemed odd. In Charleston, I didn't even know my neighbors' names. That was one reason I wanted to leave home – to become my own person, in a place where nobody knew my name. Or my past. Here, in Bare Border, I would always be the daughter of Robert and Lily Ashburn, the less attractive sister of Madeline Ashburn, and the girl who suffered that head injury in the woods. Oh, and don't forget my personal favorite – the girl who got dumped by Paul Templeton. Speaking of Paul…

I yanked my cell phone out of my pocket and redialed the Bare Border Sheriff's Department. I wouldn't swear to it, but the woman who answered sounded like the same croaky woman from before.

'Hi. It's Emily Ashburn again. I'm staying at—'

'Yes, I know who you are. Any word from your sister yet?'

'No. But I need to speak to Pa – Officer Templeton, please. Can you give me his cell phone number, or a direct line to his office?'

The woman shuffled papers on the other end, and for a moment, I wondered if she'd put me on hold. 'He isn't in the office right now. And we don't give out our officers' phone numbers to...'

Just say it. Ex-girlfriends. Everyone down at the station probably knew that little fact, too.

'This isn't some sort of social call. This pertains to my sister's disappearance. Please. I need to speak with him. It's urgent.'

'I'll let him know you called and have him phone you back as soon as possible.'

'Thank you,' I grumbled, shoving the phone back inside my pocket.

I looked around my sister's living room, at the scattering of toys on the carpet and her empty desk in the corner. The house had taken on a sad quality, something I couldn't define. I paced up and down the hallway; the pictures on the walls were dusty, forgotten. I closed my eyes, imagining the repetitive squeal of Ben's voice as he rocked back and forth and played *Five Nights at Freddy's*. The whirring and *clack clack clack* of Shelley's train set in her room. The grating sound of my sister's laughter in the kitchen as she joked about the kids. And then I could hear even more – the click of my father's pipe in his mouth and the sweet, heady smell of a Cuban cigar. The *chukka chukka chukka* of my mother on her sewing machine. The giggling of girls from my sister's room – Madeline and her two best friends, Jessica and Rhonda. Memories rise up, then they come dislodged...

I take soft steps on the carpet, my eyes still closed, trying to remember every detail, as though I'd never get them back again. But that's what happened when I had my injury; I lost some memories from that day. And there was something terrifying about forgetting, almost like a piece of me had died, or been wrenched away from me...

I opened my eyes. The sounds, the smells ... they were like pieces of old ghosts, ghosts I could never get rid of. *And where is my ghost? What sounds are indicative of me?*

Without even realizing it at first, I was wandering down the hallway and into Shelley's room. Her pajamas from this morning lay limply on the floor. I picked them up and walked over to her closet. Even though it was still early evening, her lights were off, and her curtains were drawn, cloaking the room in darkness.

Tentatively, I opened the pocket doors of her closet. There was one metal bar; her neat dresses and jeans hung stiffly on hangers. I tried to imagine my own clothes hanging in here so long ago ... it felt like a different closet, but it wasn't. I pushed the clothes on the rack apart, then tugged on the pull light string.

The closet lit up, casting an orange smoky glow over the back wall. Madeline was telling the truth – she did paint the inside of this closet. But even so, there were still traces in the paint of those big black ugly words ... I don't know if it was my imagination or not, but I could still see the bubbly outline of them under the paint – I HATE MYSELF. I WANT TO DIE.

I wrote those words – me. And at the time, I meant them. I even had scars to prove it.

Blame it on Paul Templeton or blame it on teenage hormones. I didn't know why I did it. Maybe, deep down, it was a cry for help. Depression ran on my mother's side of the family. When she died of her heart attack, she was only forty-eight, and the first thing my father and sister asked was if she took a fatal dose of pills or tried to off herself because of the divorce. She didn't – she had a bad heart, according to the doctor. Nearly every single artery was plugged up tight. But her worst demon – the depression – was the first thing they suspected. And if anything ever happened to me, they'd probably think the same…

My sister always acted like she was above it – that she never got depressed or anxious – but maybe it was all a façade. Was that why she'd ran away? What if she tried to hurt herself, just like I did all those years ago?

I slammed the closet door shut, the white scars on my wrists burning…

The scar tissue, the shiny white lumps and lines, were barely visible now. Like my past, they'd faded, making me doubt they were ever real.

My thoughts felt warbled and strange. I drifted from room to room again, feeling lost, until I finally focused on the bed in the Mello Yellow room. Slowly, I took my time making it up. The corners weren't perfect, the way Madi liked them, but they were damn near close, for me. After that, I made up the kids' beds and Madi's bed as well.

I gathered up clothes from the floor and carried them out to the stacked washer and dryer in the hallway closet. Keeping busy kept my mind clear; my only thought was that maybe if I cleaned up for Madi, she would come home. That didn't make any sense, but it helped motivate me.

I scrubbed the dishes in the sink and swept the kitchen floor. I vacuumed the rug in the dining room. I even went back outside, gathering up the picnic blanket and empty food bags from our sandwiches earlier. The sun was dipping down low beyond the horizon. I hadn't eaten all day except a few bites of my sandwich, but I wasn't feeling hungry anyway.

'Emily?' I turned around and let out a sigh of relief. It was Paul. *He will help me. He's the only one who can.*

'I've been trying to call, and I rang the doorbell a few times…'

'I'm sorry. I couldn't hear you from out here. And I think I left my phone in Shelley's room. Thank you for coming.' I don't

98

know why, but I reached out for him. I needed someone, something to hold on to…

He smelled so good again. Today it was Listerine and something fruity – cherries, maybe.

'Let's go in and talk.' We sat at the dining room table and I told him everything that had happened since last night – the strange Facebook message from Jessica Feeler, and John's suspicious behavior today.

'I don't know what Jessica's deal is, but I don't think we need to worry about her. Listen, Paul, John did something to my sister. I just know it. I mean, sure, it's possible that she just ran off. Maybe she was depressed or needed some time away … but I keep circling back to him. He has a new girlfriend, he wants the kids to himself, and he didn't even seem to give a damn that Madeline was missing…' Up until now, Paul had been listening to me, staying quiet. In fact, he hadn't said one word since he'd showed up.

For the first time, I realized the intense way he was looking at me. It wasn't desire this time, it was fear. 'You finally believe me, don't you?'

Paul gave some sort of half-nod, half-shake. 'I do. But I should tell you something. You won't like what I'm about to say.'

My stomach lurched and the air around me was suffocating all of a sudden. 'What is it, Paul?'

'We found your sister's Jeep today. There was blood inside it.'

CHAPTER ELEVEN

The room was spinning as Paul filled me in on the details, his voice tinny and far away, like his words were flowing out of a broken speaker instead of his mouth.

The Jeep was found near Henderson's Bluff. Although it was technically ten miles from here, it seemed closer than that – you could see the edge of its jagged cliff poking out if you stood in the right spot in the woods behind my sister's house. *But what was she doing up there?*

At first, they wondered if she'd jumped from the edge, Paul told me.

But he and two other officers searched the rocky stones below – my sister wasn't there. The keys were in the ignition. Madi's purse was on the seat. There were no signs of a struggle. But there was a red halo of blood on the headrest of the driver's seat.

'Enough blood to indicate she was killed?' I asked him, the words coming from someone's else mouth, not mine, it seemed…

Paul shook his head. 'I'm not sure. I don't think so. But one thing is clear – your sister didn't simply leave town. Either she hurt herself, or someone else did the hurting.'

'You have to look into John. He was so heartless today, so mean, when I told him about Madi … and he has a motive.'

Paul grimaced. 'John has a lot of friends in the police department. In fact, he already came by today.'

'What for?'

'He wanted to file another report on his wife. Wanted us to know she's missing.'

I rolled my eyes. 'He took the kids. They're with him now. What if he's abusive, Paul? I have to get them back somehow. At least until we know what happened to my sister.'

'I don't think you can do that. You're not their legal guardian. He has every right to keep them with him. In fact, he said something along the lines of, "I don't know her sister, Emily, very well. I don't think she would hurt Madeline, but it's possible. All I know is that when she came to town, my wife left it. She was always jealous of Madeline. Madeline brought that up a few times…"'

I pinched my eyes shut. 'He's a liar. I would never hurt my sister. You know that.' Although the jealousy remark … I could see Madeline saying that. She was always a little arrogant. She probably liked to brag to her husband about how popular she used to be, how I was always in her shadow…

'I know you wouldn't,' Paul said, his voice tiny as a whisper. *He believed me, didn't he?*

'Will you at least go check on the kids? I need to know they're okay. You guys could keep him under surveillance or do forensic testing on the inside of Starla's house!'

'This isn't *Forensic Files*, Emily. This is a small town, with limited resources. But I will do everything in my power to find out what happened, I promise. We dusted for prints in the Jeep, and we're going to try to compare them to your sister's and see if we can get a match with someone else. And as soon as I find out more, about John, their financial situation, and if he has an alibi for the night she disappeared … I'll let you know.'

'You'll let me know?! So, that's it?'

'Emily, I'm sorry. I wish I could tell you more, but I don't know anything yet. I'm waiting to hear back from the bank about your sister's debit card. She and John apparently had separate accounts. I should know by tomorrow whether or not she's used her card. John is the obvious suspect, but besides him, and this Jessica Feeler woman, is there anyone else who would want to cause your sister harm?'

I tried to think back to every single conversation I'd had with Madi over the last few months. We mostly talked via text messages, and she hadn't been texting me much at all lately. I'd assumed it was because she was mad over the funeral, but something more was going on. Obviously.

'I still think it could be John, but we can't forget about Mr Tennors. He's the only other person I can think of. The window in my sister's room was unlocked. He easily could have crossed the field and taken her. Although, I just can't see it…' I tried to picture Albert Tennors, squeezing through my sister's bedroom window – it was a ludicrous visual image.

'I brought my fingerprint kit. If there's a chance somebody left their fingerprints on the glass, or around the window … well, it will be worth a shot. But I don't think you have anything to worry about when it comes to Mr Tennors.'

'You keep saying that, but I looked him up. He might be a nice old man, but he was charged with rape, Paul. How can that not be of any concern to you?'

'Albert used to be a truck driver. You probably don't remember this, because you were so young, but he used to be gone from his wife for long periods of time. Well, Albert made the mistake of picking up a hooker, and they had sex. As it turns out, the girl was only seventeen. Afterwards, she threatened to turn him in if he didn't give her money.'

'Did he give it to her?'

'No. He went straight home and told Lisa what he'd done, then they drove to the police department together. He turned himself in and the judge at the time took leniency on him. The court-appointed psychiatrist didn't think he was attracted to children. Albert was guilty of being a bad husband. He cheated on his wife with what he thought was another woman. He got five years' probation and a statutory rape charge on his record because of it. He lost his job permanently. That's why Lisa went back to work at the school. I'm not saying he's not a bad guy, but I don't think it makes him a kidnapper.'

'Why did Lisa stay with him after he cheated on her?'

Paul shrugged. 'I guess she loved him enough to keep him. I'm not sure. But I do know that he hasn't caused any trouble in this town for twenty-five years. He pays his taxes and comes down to the police station every six months to get his updated picture for the registry. I hate to say it, but I kind of feel sorry for the guy. As it turns out, he wasn't that girl's only victim. She did the same thing to other men, too.'

'She must have had problems. I can't help feeling sorry for her, too. Seventeen might seem close to being an adult, but it's far from it. Can you remember yourself at seventeen? I know I was screwed up. I wasn't the same person I am now.' But my stomach fluttered with guilt as I thought about how I'd slammed the door in Mr Tennors' face. I'd jumped to conclusions, but who could really blame me? I was scared for my sister, and now, I was scared for Ben and Shelley too.

Paul was studying my features and I watched his eyes float down to my lips and then slowly inch their way back up. 'You haven't changed, Em. You've only gotten prettier. I'm so happy you're home.'

'Don't.'

'Don't what?'

'Suck me in again with your charming bullshit. I fell for it once and I won't do it again. Plus, you need to focus every ounce of your attention on finding out where my sister is.'

'What makes you think it was bullshit?'

'You stood me up for the fucking prom, Paul! You broke my heart.'

His face crumpled in on itself, as though he was the one who got hurt and not the other way around.

'What is the plan for finding my sister? Because I'm not home, I'm not back … I just want to find her and make sure my niece and nephew are safe.' Pushing back my chair, I winced as it let out a high-pitched squeak.

'If it's okay, I'm going to call the tech guys over here when they're finished with the Jeep. I've already contacted other nearby departments. We're on the lookout for a…' Paul stopped.

'A body,' I finished for him.

Paul nodded, his eyes calm and gray in the dim light. 'Hopefully not. But we have to consider that possibility. I won't disappoint you this time. I'll find your sister, if it's the last thing I do.'

CHAPTER TWELVE

I sucked my teeth and chewed on a jagged hangnail as I watched three different officers, all probably under the age of twenty, drift in and out of my sister's house. I stayed put in my sister's desk chair, watching Paul instruct them. First, they went in Madi's bedroom and back around the side of the house. Fingerprinting the window on both sides, no doubt.

Another officer was dusting for prints in the kitchen and bedrooms. I suggested they check out the upstairs, too.

Watching this scene, it was like I was in some sort of made-for-TV movie, or an episode of *CSI*. Only not. I didn't feel good about this. It wasn't until after half an hour of watching them skim the carpets and walls for any signs of blood or clues that I realized one important thing – John's prints were all over this place. As they should be – he'd lived here. If he was suspect number one, finding his prints didn't mean squat.

My mind kept circling back to John and his new girlfriend. They were the only ones with a motive, weren't they? Even though he seemed like a jerk, I couldn't imagine him waltzing in here, while we were sleeping, and hurting my sister. *I would have heard something, wouldn't I?*

'What if you find a foreign print? One that doesn't match up to my sister, John, me, or the kids?' I asked Paul.

His back was turned to me and he almost looked irritated by my question when he turned around. Then his face softened. 'Don't worry. John's prints are on file because of his gun permit. I think we can isolate some prints to determine which ones belong to your sister. And the small prints, of course, belong to the children. I will need to get your prints though, just to exclude them.'

My mind was still stuck on 'gun permit'. 'John owns a gun?' The blood in my veins would have turned to ice if it could have. I thought back to that morning – the loud shaking of thunder, the storms that lasted through the night. I didn't think I'd heard a gunshot, but even if there was one, it might have been blocked out by the sounds of thunder.

'Most people in this town own a gun, Emily.'

Ignoring him, I said, 'The bloody spot on the headrest. Could it have been from a gunshot wound to the head?' I pinched the bridge of my nose, trying not to picture my sister's familiar face being blown apart with a bullet.

'Well, that's what the tech guys are working on. If she was shot in the Jeep, there would be blood spatter and a bullet hole, most likely.' One of the young officers had stopped what he was doing on the floor and was watching Paul. Paul looked from him to me. 'I – I can't give you all the details yet, Emily. I'm sorry. But I don't think anyone was shot in the car. The blood didn't look like enough to be a fatal wound to me…'

But any sort of wound to the head could be deadly, I thought.

As they went back to work, I slipped out through the front door. It was almost dark, but it felt like a sauna out here. My eyes drifted across the field to Albert's cabin. Once again, his curtains were moving – either he was watching or there was an air vent right beneath his living room window. After hearing his story, I didn't consider him a suspect. And even if he was, Madi could have outrun him or fought him off…

My sister's driveway was full of cars, vehicles belonging to the other officers. A couple were police-issued cars, but the others were just their personal vehicles.

I walked around the house, skimming the yard for clues. It had been raining all that night and morning, right before she disappeared. If there were any significant clues on the ground, they'd probably be washed away by now.

Once I reached the backyard, I headed down to the woods. It was the last place I wanted to go to, but there could be clues down there. Nothing could be overlooked and there was no room for my silly, irrational fears right now...

I took my time going down the steep dirt path, careful not to slip this time. Finally, the land bottomed out, and I was able to skim the ground for clues. I focused on the ground, instead of the trees, breathing deeply through my nose.

I felt jumpy though, my skin crawling. There were a million tiny noises that filled the silence of the woods – the rustling of leaves, the cracking of oak, the scurrying of squirrels on the ground and birds above...

I followed the sounds of the creek, retracing my steps from earlier, but then I stopped, staring at a small pile of garbage on the ground I hadn't noticed earlier. An empty can of RC Cola – I hadn't seen this brand in years, but the can looked fresh. Beside it was an empty granola bar wrapper and a flattened spot in the leaves. *Was someone camped out down here recently?*

I picked up the can and turned it over and back. It looked shiny, not dull and rusted like other old cans. This came from someone who was down here recently, I was sure of it.

I squatted down on the ground beside it and looked up toward my sister's house. Gasping, I realized there was a direct line of sight – a gap between two trees, that offered a perfect view of my sister's kitchen window. The curtains to the kitchen were parted and from here, I could see two of the officers talking in front of the window.

Was somebody watching my sister's house? Immediately, my thoughts strayed back to John. But why would he sit in the woods and spy on his own family? That didn't make much sense either.

My fingers fluttered, teasing their way up to the scar on my head … I'd always assumed what happened in these woods had just been an accident, but what if it wasn't? For the first time, I seriously considered the possibility that my injury could have been caused by someone else. *But who? The same person who was watching Madi and her family?*

I stared down at the can and wrapper, my hands still shaking. I would give them to Paul. Maybe he could fingerprint them or do some sort of DNA testing…

But before I touched them, I wanted to explore the woods more. I needed to.

This time, I followed the flow of the creek, counting back from one hundred to keep myself calm. Delving deeper into the rocky ups and downs, I was careful to watch my step this time, and maintain a sense of reality. *My sister is my only focus.*

I didn't remember where I fell, or how it happened in the first place. My dreams were so cloudy and strange, and who knew if any of the flashes were accurate, or if I'd just filled in the blanks over the years. I remembered the story from my sister's point of view; Mom shouting for me to come in for dinner. When I didn't respond, she'd sent my sister out to get me. She'd found me flat on my back, a thick pool of blood beneath my head. I was unconscious, but breathing, my pulse thready. Madi had screamed for my mom, who'd then screamed for my dad. They'd lifted me from the ground and they took me to the nearest hospital. I'd woken up in a bright white room, my parents and sister surrounding me. The last memory I have of that day was riding the bus home from school – everything else after that was gone or buried too deep inside myself to recall.

The doctor said it was normal. Trauma victims often experience short-term memory loss. They called it post-traumatic amnesia. All I knew was that I'd suffered from severe headaches ever since and beneath my hair, there was an ugly, crescent-moon gash that ran from one side of my scalp to the other, horizontally. If I ever went bald, I would look like the bride of Frankenstein. I'd never told anyone this – but when I touched the scar, I couldn't even feel it. It was as if that part of my head had lost all feeling completely.

I kept my eye out for more garbage, or clues of some kind. There were some grotty Styrofoam cups, spongy old packs of cigarettes, a smear of rotten meat from an old food can where animals had scavenged for it. But these all looked old, like something washed up by the creek or dragged around by animals.

I knew I should go back, get Paul, and show him the can and wrapper. But my feet betrayed me, pressing forward, zeroing in on some unknown goal. I followed the gentle rise and fall of the forest floor, batting away branches and careful to avoid poison ivy. I walked until I could see the shimmer of Moon Lake. And finally, standing at its edge, I stared down into the murky black water.

Moon Lake was less of a lake, and more of a pond. I hadn't been here since I was a kid. Back then, the water had seemed bluer and greener, and bigger too.

But I didn't trust my memories of the woods or the lake anymore.

Why am I here? Why did I walk all the way down here? Deep down, I already knew the answer to that – the gnawing, rotten feeling in my gut that maybe, just maybe, my sister's bloated corpse was somewhere beneath this water.

The lake had been all but forgotten. No one came here anymore, not to fish or skip rocks. At least I didn't think so. The grass and cattails were wild and tall, like no one had been here for years. Eighteen years ago, they dragged this lake, looking for a body – the missing girl from my class, Sarah Goins. Townspeople were certain this was where they would find her – her family farm was less than half a mile from here.

I had been so young, and my parents didn't tell me anything about it, but I knew about the lake, and I knew they looked for her body. Kids at school whispered her name down the hallways, her name less of a childish chant, and more like a warning whisper ... *the girl who disappeared.*

Now here I was, almost twenty years later, wondering if my sister was somewhere beneath these murky waters. *If I was a killer, I would dispose of her body right here.*

And if someone was watching her from the woods and, somehow, dragged her out of the house and hurt her, this would be an easy spot to get rid of her. But the fact that the Jeep was found parked high on the bluff threw that theory out the window. My sister had been in her Jeep, or maybe ... maybe the blood on the headrest didn't belong to her. Maybe it belonged to someone else—the person who took her. Maybe Madi fought back.

I turned around, frantic to go find Paul and the other officers. I had to tell them—they needed to drag the lake again. I had to know if my sister was beneath these murky, old waters...

As I slid through a gap in the trees and entered the woods again, I stopped dead in my tracks. There, on a thick oak tree, were mine and Paul's initials. Like some childish cliché, we had, apparently, carved the first letters of our names into a flat spot on the bark.

Moving closer, I traced the initials with my fingertips: E.A. + P.T. It was so cheesy, it almost made me blush. But then I remembered the water and my sister, and nothing seemed important besides finding out what had happened to her.

CHAPTER THIRTEEN

By the time I made it back, the officers were packing up their kits and Paul was furious with me. 'I didn't know where you'd gone.' The other officers were watching us again, playful smiles on their faces. For some reason, their cheeriness pissed me off. *My sister is missing, dammit!*

'Don't mind me, I was just doing your jobs for you!' I shouted back. Their smiles faded away, and Paul looked stricken. 'Someone was watching her from those woods.' I pointed, wildly. 'It looks like someone was sitting out there, watching my sister, all the while having a snack. You need to do DNA testing. And … you also need to drag that lake. Maybe she fought back, and whoever took her got hurt before he drove off in her Jeep. That could be the killer's blood on the headrest. And the water … there's a body of water in those woods, in case you guys didn't know.' I aimed these last words at the young officers. They probably knew nothing about those woods, but Paul did.

'Please. I need to know if she's in there,' I cried, desperate.

Paul, no longer caring what his fellow officers thought, wrapped me in his arms and pulled me close. Much to my dismay, I started sobbing into his chest.

'Do you remember that girl who disappeared when we were kids?' I mumbled.

'What?' He pushed back on my shoulders and gave me a look I couldn't define. 'Sarah Goins. How could I forget it?'

'They dragged that lake down there when she went missing. They can do it again,' I told him.

Paul nodded. 'That was when I was a kid, too, so I don't remember exactly how it went down … but I'm pretty sure they'll have to bring in specialized divers for that.'

'So, what are you saying – they won't do it?'

'They will, if it comes to that. Boys, stop loading up. We need to go down to the woods to collect more evidence.'

I stood at the kitchen window, the same window that some creep had probably watched my sister from his perch in the woods. Watching the officers disappear between the trees, all I could feel was impending doom. Was there a chance that my sister could still be alive?

I hadn't eaten all day, but I wasn't hungry. I opened and closed my sister's refrigerator, staring at Ben's drawings of *Five Nights at Freddy's* and Shelley's drawings of swirly pink and purple clouds and tiny yellow hearts. I wondered what they were doing right now. Were they worried about their mother? Shelley seemed so young and resilient, but Ben was fragile. I could imagine him right now, rocking back and forth at Starla's house, his entire routine thrown off even more than it already had been.

There was a loaf of bread and a bruised bunch of bananas. I pulled a slice off the loaf and chewed it, not tasting the food. From here, I could see shadowy figures moving through the woods – the officers were searching. Maybe, just maybe, they'd find out what really happened to Madeline.

By the time they were done, it was well past dark. The other officers didn't come back inside; they loaded up the rest of their supplies and pulled out of the driveway, one by one. Only Paul's cruiser remained.

'Do you want me to stay for a while?' Before I could tell him no, he said, 'Or, if you don't want to stay here, you can come stay at my dad's, with me. I still live off Painter's Creek. There's a couple empty beds that used to be my brothers. I could...'

'Thanks, but no. I want to stay here, in case John needs to bring the kids back for some reason, or in case my sister shows up. Did you find anything else?'

Paul shook his head and said, 'No. I bagged and tagged the can and wrapper you told me about. And I bagged some other garbage and cigarette butts, too, but most of those looked old.'

Suddenly, I felt exhausted, the strain of the last few days rushing over me. 'Will you call me tomorrow and let me know what you find out about the Jeep and fingerprints? And will you ask them to search the lake?'

'Of course.' Paul leaned forward and kissed my cheek, his lips lingering so long I felt my chest stiffen.

'Thanks,' I said awkwardly. Then I closed the door.

***

I could have watched TV or read a book, but there was no way I could focus on anything right now. My own life had become its own version of a horror novel.

Out of pure desperation, I tried to call Madeline nearly a dozen more times. Each time it went straight to voicemail. On my last try, I left a pathetic message, begging her to call me.

I had a few more missed calls from my landlord, but I couldn't call him back right now. Somehow, doing anything normal, anything at all, seemed like a betrayal to my sister. I tried to imagine what she would do if it were the other way around – me missing instead of her.

She'd demand a full-on search party. Hell, the lake would already be full of divers. My sister was kind, but she was stubborn and headstrong. If she wanted something done, it would be. Self-consciously, I fingered the thin white scars on my wrists.

Sometimes I wondered if I did it because of her. Not *because* of her – it certainly wasn't her fault – but because I felt like I was losing her. We were best friends and then we weren't – she was caught up in anything and everything that had to do with Jessica and Rhonda. I stopped being her confidant and became a nuisance to her and her friends. And then there was Paul; we were inseparable. In fact, it was because of him that I was able to deal with the growing distance between Madi and me. But then, like Madi, he dropped me like a bad habit. He stopped talking to me and started avoiding me at school right after the prom.

It hurt, losing the only two people besides my parents that I cared about. Maybe cutting my wrists was less an attempt at harming myself, and more of an attempt to win them back. But my suicide attempt only pushed them farther away; I pushed everyone away, including my parents. And in addition to all the things I already was, I became 'that girl who slit her wrists' around town. It was no wonder I didn't want to come back, there was nothing good about coming home. Bad memories, and after what happened to Madi, maybe bad people too…

I found myself back in my sister's room, sifting through her picture box. Once again, my eyes zeroed in on the tiny trading pic of Sarah Goins. *I wonder where you are.*

I flipped the picture over, surprised to find writing on the back. The letters were so small and crooked, I could barely read them. *Thank u 4 b-in my friend.*

A memory came crawling back – me, playing in the dirt with Sarah. She was a strange girl, sometimes saying and doing quirky little things in class. The other kids would laugh at her. Sometimes, even the teachers laughed at her expense.

In second grade, she sat right across from me. I could remember her chewing the tip of her glue bottle, gnawing at it like a frenzied dog chewing a bone.

'Stop that, Sarah,' I whispered. 'Stop.'

But she didn't. Her eyes were glassy as she chomped on the plastic lid. Finally, the rest of the class noticed what she was doing. Even the teacher stopped talking and stared. Laughter rolled through the room like thunder. Louder and louder, everyone laughing at her. Poor Sarah didn't even notice at first; she was focused so intently on the glue.

'Leave her alone,' I muttered.

'What did you say, Miss Ashburn?' my teacher boomed.

'I said leave her alone!' I screamed. The sheer volume of my own voice scared me that day. Suddenly, Sarah dropped the glue. It hit the floor and bounced. She looked at everyone laughing, like she'd just woke up from some sort of trance, and then she looked over at me and she smiled.

Turning the picture back over, I stared at her face again. She wasn't smiling in this photo that had probably been taken in fourth grade. By then, I had stopped talking to Sarah Goins. I didn't make fun of her, I did something worse – I pretended she didn't exist. I became an 'innocent' bystander while she was bullied mercilessly by her peers.

Once again, I remembered that chant: 'Go in! Go in!' Boys and girls would say those words, over and over, in their singsongy voices. There was a group of girls leading the chant. *The blonde in the middle was Jessica Feeler,* I just now realized. I closed my eyes, trying to remember every detail of every single face in the crowd. My sister and Rhonda were among them – they were standing on either side of Jessica, a small horde of girls and boys growing larger and larger behind them. I was standing on the other side of the playground, my lips slowing forming the words, and then I was saying them. I don't know why, but I was. Sarah ran off, devastated about her torn pictures. She looked at me as she passed by, almost like she was secretly asking: *Will you defend me again?* But I didn't.

CHAPTER FOURTEEN

I didn't wake up until nearly twelve o'clock in the afternoon. I'd slept on the couch, unable to sleep in my sister's bed. I was too heartbroken by the kids' empty beds across the hall from it.

My body was stiff and achy, the way it always got when I slept too long.

I wondered how the kids' first day of school was going. Madeline was definitely taken against her will; there's no way she would miss their first day unless she was forced to.

I thought about Ben in his new class, and I remembered, again, the articles on my sister's computer. Did kids at school pick on him the way kids used to pick on Sarah?

I hope not, I prayed, my heart filling with dread.

Quickly, I got dressed and brushed my teeth, then I called the car rental place to let them know I needed to extend my rental agreement for the Honda Civic. I didn't know where I was going exactly until I'd reached the bottom of Star Mountain.

Misti said that Starla lived across from the bingo hall. I knew the kids wouldn't be there; they were still at school. And I was hoping that John was at work today.

If I could catch Starla at home and convince her to let me

inside, maybe I could snoop around for signs that my sister had been there, or that John was hiding something.

I stared at the dark bingo hall on my right as I waited to turn left into Starla's driveway. It hadn't occurred to me until now – John and his mistress were living across the street from the place where John and Madeline's wedding reception was held. Somehow, the thought of that disturbed me.

Starla's house was an old Victorian that had to be at least a hundred years old. When Misti mentioned the location, I knew exactly where she meant because this creepy old house had caught my eye a few times as a child.

But now I could see that the house had been sectioned off into apartments. I parked between a blue Volvo and a purple Prius. At first, I didn't see the Mercedes, but then I spotted it at the end of the drive, parked beneath the shade of a flowering dogwood tree. Soft white petals covered the hood of the car. Again, I thought of my sister's wedding – the bright white flowers in her hair, the scattering of pink petals down the makeshift aisle between the doorway and altar of the bingo hall. She had never been as beautiful as she looked that day.

I walked up to the car, casually bending over to peek through the windows. Ben and Shelley's car seats were still in the back. The car's interior looked neat and pristine. *Maybe because it was recently cleaned?* I considered. A few steps away from the door, I noticed a side door to the big old house. It was labeled as S. Foster, which I assumed stood for Starla Foster.

Nervously, I tapped on the door.

I waited a few moments and then I rang the buzzer. It took a few more minutes, but then I clearly heard someone running down stairs…

When Starla opened the door, she was stunned to see me. 'Hi. Can I help you?'

'Can we talk for a few minutes?'

'Listen. I don't want to argue or answer lengthy questions about why I'm with John. Please,' she said, uneasily.

'It's not about that. I'd like to talk to you about the kids and my sister, if that's okay.' For a moment, I thought she would refuse me, but then she stepped aside, letting me in the heavy wooden door.

I was shocked to see three straight sets of stairs leading up to the third floor. 'Wow. You guys live on the top floor?'

'Yep. Carrying up groceries is a real bitch,' she complained. I followed her up the shiny wooden stairs, and then up two more sets of stairs. Starla took them two at a time. I hadn't noticed how fit she was until I was staring at her backside the whole way up. She was wearing pink yoga pants and a matching yoga top, her hair pulled up in a neat ponytail.

'How old are you?' I had to ask, as we approached the top of the stairs. There was no door to their apartment; the top of the stairs just opened up into a huge studio space. It took my breath away.

'Twenty-one.' Starla hugged herself with her arms, staring at me expectantly as I reached the top. When I was twenty-one, I was just starting college. It wasn't that long ago, really. This must have been uncomfortable for her, but who cared how she felt right then! My sister was missing.

The studio was impeccably decorated. Funky, flat couches and chairs sat in the middle of the room. There was a kitchen off to the right, with stainless steel appliances and rows of industrial brick for backsplash.

'Where did the kids sleep last night?' I tried not to sound too judgy. But I couldn't see how they would fit here.

'Over here,' Starla pointed to the opposite side of the studio. There were two large partition walls, separating a full-sized bed and a king. I assumed she and John slept in the king.

'It's really nice here,' I said. I was trying to at least act cordial. If I wanted to find out what she knew, I had to wear a friendly face for a while.

'Thank you. I took the kids to school this morning. Everything went off without a hitch.'

I was shocked to hear that she had taken them, and not John ... but, no, I wasn't. After the way he'd acted yesterday, I wasn't sure if he just wanted the kids because they were his, or if he really cared about them.

Starla was starting to look more and more uncomfortable, both of us standing at awkward angles in the middle of the living room.

'Have you ever met my sister?'

'If you're asking me if I knew he was married, I did. I used to be his secretary. I've loved him for a long time, and when I found out he was going to get divorced, that's when I told him how I felt about him.'

I doubted that whole story was true. Most men only leave when they've found a replacement. But I nodded, playing along. After all, this wasn't Starla's fault. She wasn't the one who promised to have and to hold my sister forever...

'What I meant was – when was the last time you saw her? Has she come here to try to speak with John, or shown up at his work? You said you were the secretary there.'

'Honestly, I haven't seen her in over a year. She used to come up to the office sometimes, and she and John would go out for lunch. But they seemed more distant. He called her less and less, and she never called the office for him anymore ... but, I don't work there now. John is a stickler for following rules. Interoffice relationships are forbidden there, so he had me transferred to another branch.'

'Did that make you mad?'

Starla chuckled. 'No, quite the opposite, actually. I sort of like the fact that we don't see each other all day long. It makes it more exciting when we do.' She was smiling now, her mind somewhere else ... in a place I didn't want to go.

'So, you haven't seen Madi at all?'

'No. John finally moved in a couple weeks ago. Cyndi from the station called here yesterday, just as he was walking through the door. That's how he found out she was missing. I shouldn't tell you this, but John did not get along with Madeline's father. Well, your father too.' Starla blushed, as though she'd made a mistake by saying that.

'I didn't always get along with him either,' I admitted. This seemed to surprise Starla. 'Why didn't they get along – John and my dad?'

Starla shrugged. 'I have no idea. He called him "difficult".' That sounded about right. My father could be grumpy and mean, at times.

'When he heard Madeline was missing, and that you were in town and with the kids, he got worried. He said he didn't know you well and didn't trust you. He said maybe you're a pain like your dad … anyway, he was worried that maybe you did something to Madeline. So, that's why he showed up so abruptly to get the kids.'

'I would never hurt my sister!'

'I know that. I mean, it's not like I know you or anything, but I have a sister myself. Sisters don't hurt each other like that. They might fight sometimes, but I can't see you, or anyone, wanting to cause harm to their sister. I know Madeline is technically the enemy, the ex … but she always seemed nice to me. I'm sure you're nice and trustworthy too.'

I was a little taken aback by her kindness. Unlike mine, hers seemed genuine. 'Well, thank you,' I said, awkwardly.

So, if what she was saying was true, then John suspected me just as I suspected him. *Could there possibly be someone else who wanted to hurt my sister then?*

Leaving Starla's, I wasn't sure how much information I'd gained. She made John sound innocent, and more than anything, I wanted to believe that. The thought of Ben and Shelley's dad being a complete psychopath was unbearable. And she'd mentioned John didn't get along with my dad – was that a source of tension between him and Madi?

Before I left, I asked Starla if it would be okay to come and see the kids in a day or two. Nervously, I waited for her answer. 'Of course you can,' she said, finally. I felt relieved, at least temporarily. She walked me all the way back downstairs, all three flights of them, and gave me some sort of weird half-hug on my way out.

'Oh, wait. Does John own a gun? I was just wondering ... because Officer Templeton said that he had a permit for one.'

Starla gave me a conspiratorial smile. 'Well, let's just say, he used to. Until he got involved with me. I don't believe in them, you see. I made him get rid of it.'

'Get rid of it? How does someone get rid of a gun?'

'He sold it to the pawn shop owner in Merrimont. He got four hundred bucks for that thing!'

After thanking her again, I sat in the rental car and called Paul. Yesterday he'd given me his personal cell number, so I didn't have to go through his grumpy secretary anymore.

When he answered, I filled him in on my visit with Starla. I told him about John selling his gun weeks ago to a pawn shop. 'Can that be verified?'

'Yep. I'll go down there today and talk to the owner. Any sort of gun purchase or sale will have a paper trail. If he sold it, I'll find the proof.'

I hung up and headed home. But as soon as I climbed Star Mountain, my cell phone was ringing again. It was Paul again.

'Hey,' I answered.

'I have some news. I just got off the phone with your sister's bank. Someone used her bank card this morning at Sam's.'

'What?!' I practically screamed. *This is good news,* I told myself. *This means Madi could very well still be alive and unharmed.*

'So, who used it? Do we think someone robbed her...? If so, where is she?'

'Well, most of the other officers think she's just fine. Her husband left her, her parents died … maybe she's just taking some time to herself, Emily.'

I couldn't believe he still thought that! I chose to ignore that part of what he said. 'Do we know what they purchased?'

'No. Only that they spent less than twenty dollars.'

'What sort of sense does that make? If the motive was money, wouldn't they be spending more of it? I don't know how much money my sister has, but I can promise you it's not much.'

'She didn't have much, according to her bank statements. But I still think it's more likely that it was her using the card…' Paul explained.

I groaned. 'But that still doesn't explain why her car was abandoned at the top of the bluff, and did you forget the part about the blood on her seat?'

Paul was quiet. For a moment, I thought maybe we got disconnected, or maybe he hung up on purpose. 'Emily, can I ask you something?'

What else could I say but 'yes'? 'Of course you can.'

'Has your sister ever pretended to be hurt, or played some sort of practical joke?'

'No!' But the joke part was a lie. My sister loved playing pranks … but she wouldn't play one as serious as this. *Or would she?* Doubt trickled in again as I recalled that trick she played in the kitchen with the kids when I first arrived. And when Madi was a teenager, she loved to jump out and scare me, or tell me something bad had happened to our parents just to record my reaction with her video camera. She might like to play pranks, but she would never drag this out so long … would she?

'Does she have a reason to hide, or want to get away from something?'

'I don't think so,' I replied, watching a royal blue truck fly past me. The Honda rattled and shook on the side of the mountain. 'No, not really,' I reiterated. But again, this wasn't exactly true.

Could she be trying to get back at John by making herself disappear? Could this all be a cry for attention? It was almost too mortifying to say aloud to Paul. I didn't think Madi would fake her own disappearance, but was it possible? Yes, she was definitely capable of it.

But could there be *legitimate* reasons to get away … reasons to hide? I thought back to Jessica Feeler's ominous warning on Facebook. Maybe she was threatening my sister, holding some sort of information over her head…?

As much as I wanted to defend my sister to Paul, I wasn't altogether sure of my answers. Madi *did* play pranks, and I knew she had a secret … and with everything going on with John and his new girlfriend, it made sense that she would want to get away from it all, or to get back at him somehow…

'I'll call you when I know more,' Paul said, then he hung up, without even saying goodbye.

I stared at my phone, mulling over his words. I didn't want to believe that my sister orchestrated her own disappearance, even though I knew it was possible. Jessica's words came flashing back to me: *You'd better keep your fucking mouth shut.* Did my sister know something that she wasn't supposed to?

Even more questions and doubts swirled through my mind.

123

CHAPTER FIFTEEN

A sick feeling rose in my stomach as I stared at Jessica's Facebook message again. I was back at my sister's desk, chugging a Red Bull, and working up the nerve to make some sort of response.

If Jessica knew what my sister was running from, or if she was somehow involved in her disappearance, I didn't want to say something that would screw up my chances of learning the truth.

Clicking through Jessica's pictures, I could remember the girl she used to be. Pretty, blonde, competitive. A ring leader. Definitely what I would call a mean girl. She had this way of changing the air in a room – I could 'feel' her in it with me, even if she was standing on the other side of it.

Thinking back, I could recall many eye rolls and annoyed looks coming from her direction when I was around. Rhonda was Jessica and Madeline's other sidekick in high school. She was a cute redhead, and nicer than Jessica. But she was a follower, a hanger-on, always right on my sister and Jessica's heels.

Still working up the nerve to write back to Jessica, I searched for Rhonda Sheckles on Facebook. *Everyone had a Facebook page these days, right?* But my searching only yielded one result – a lady named Rhonda Sheckles who lived in Dallas, Texas. That Rhonda Sheckles looked sixty or seventy years old.

I clicked back on the message again, staring at the strange threat from Jessica. Suddenly three tiny bubbles appeared on the screen. *Jessica was typing something right now!*

My heart raced as I waited to see what she might say. What were the odds of her writing back to my sister while I was sitting here perched, preparing to write something to her myself?

But then the bubbles disappeared. 'What the hell?'

I was about to start writing when the bubbles popped up again. And then a message came through from Jessica.

I see that you're online! I SEE YOU! You're not fooling anyone. What is your deal?

Dumbfounded, my fingers hovered above the keyboard. What was I supposed to say to that? Jessica obviously thought I was Madeline, and apparently, she, like the rest of the town, had heard about her disappearance.

I held my breath as I typed out a short reply: *Why are you so worried about me keeping my mouth shut?*

I couldn't tell if she read my message or not, and no more bubbles appeared. I glared at the screen until the message box grew blurry, then I chugged the rest of the Red Bull.

While I waited for Jessica to respond, I snooped through more of her posts and pictures, hoping to see something that would catch my eye. There weren't any pictures of her and Madeline, or of her and Rhonda. They obviously didn't hang out on a regular basis anymore. So, why the recent communication?

Finally, I walked away from the computer and walked around the house, re-checking the windows and doors. I wondered again how the kids' first day at school had gone. Were they missing their house and their mother? Were they missing me?

It was crazy how I'd spent the last eight years not knowing them, and now it had only been a day and I was missing them like crazy.

There was a tiny ding from the living room. Racing back to the computer chair, I was thrilled to see another message from

Jessica: *I just didn't want you pulling a Rhonda on me. I know depression runs in your family.*

I was even more confused now. Had Rhonda opened her mouth and told somebody something she shouldn't have?

Before I could even think of a response, there was another ding. *You're still my girl, Madi. Even if we're not as close as we once were, we'll always be summer sisters.*

I narrowed my eyes at the screen. *Summer sisters.* I could remember a time when I was Madi's 'summer sister'. When we'd massaged our bloody fingers together and made it official. Apparently, she and Jessica had done that too.

I don't know why, but that fact hurt me deeply.

But then, immediately I felt foolish. We were only kids. Of course Madeline had friends other than her little sister. After all, she was a few years older than me, and if I'd been the older one, I probably wouldn't have wanted to hang out with me either. I'd always been the one chasing Madi around, trying to get her to hang out with me the way we did when we were kids. It had nothing to do with her age and everything to do with the way she treated me when we were alone. Madi had this way of making me feel like it was just her and me, and that there was no one, and nothing, more important than being with me in that moment. When she looked at me, it was like I was the only one in the room. And when we were very young, I felt like we really knew each other, in that bone-deep way only best friends can.

Now I wondered if I wasn't the only one she made feel that way.

Jessica must have stopped typing because the bubbles were gone again. I needed to say something quickly or else risk losing her and any chance at finding out what she knew about Madi. Something that would get her to tell me what this thing was that Madi needed to shut up about...

Finally, I typed: *You're my girl too, Jessica. But I just don't*

126

think I can stay quiet. I can't keep my fucking mouth shut, as you put it.

Three bubbles appeared almost instantly. But whatever she was typing, it seemed to be taking a while…

Finally, the message came through: *Don't be stupid. Where are you? Did you go back home? If so, I'll come over, so we can talk. We haven't done that in a long time. Let's discuss this first.*

Damn. Now what? *Discuss what?*

I typed my next words out slowly, unsure. But then I clicked enter and hoped for the best. *You can't come over right now. I'm not home and my sister is staying at the house. I just had to get away for a while. Needed time to think.*

I was hoping for more, but then ten, twenty, minutes passed and Jessica didn't write back.

Madeline had a secret. But I knew that already, didn't I? She told me herself that she had something important to tell me, something she could only tell me in person. I just wished she'd done it before she took off, then maybe I could have helped her figure things out.

I'd been so caught up in myself and my own secret about losing my job, I never considered the fact that my sister might have something serious to tell me…

Disappointed, but hopeful that Madi really was just hiding out somewhere and shopping at Sam's in her spare time, I retreated to the kitchen. I opened the cabinets and saw that there was plenty of food. For the first time in days, I was feeling hungry. My stomach grumbled noisily.

I decided to go with Shelley's usual choice, even though Shelley wasn't here, and I took down a box of macaroni and cheese. Stirring the noodles with one hand, I texted Paul with the other.

Jessica Feeler knows something. I pretended to be Madeline on Facebook and she alluded to some secret she doesn't want Madi to tell, and she also mentioned Rhonda Sheckles. You need to talk to both of those ladies, ASAP.

A few minutes later, I sent another one.

Do you remember Rhonda Sheckles? Do you know if she still has family around here? I was trying to find her on Facebook, but I'm thinking she might have a married name now. Maybe she knows something?? It's worth considering, don't you think?

I was still waiting on Paul to respond when the noodles finished. I sat back down at the computer desk with my bowl of mac and cheese, and I pulled up Madeline's profile page. She only had 101 friends, which wasn't a lot, but seemed like a ton when it meant going through each and every single one, searching for someone with the first name Rhonda. Luckily, I discovered that Facebook had a search function where I could search her friends list for anyone named Rhonda. No luck. None of Madeline's friends were Rhonda Sheckles or Rhonda anyone for that matter.

Next, I moved to Jessica's page. Unfortunately, her friends list was protected. *Damn.*

I considered checking other social media sites but resorted to using Google first.

I typed in 'Rhonda Sheckles', and then 'wedding announcement', hoping I'd find something that would reveal her married name.

But instead of finding a wedding announcement, I found something else, something I hadn't expected. Rhonda Sheckles was an artist; she even had a website – *Twisted Imagery*. I clicked through the images on the welcome screen – dark, twisted paintings filled the page, living up to the site's name. Rhonda sold graphic images for digital use, and commissioned art work as well.

A memory came flooding back – Rhonda, aged nine or ten, doodling in that spiraled notebook of hers, protecting its contents with the curl of an arm. Rhonda drawing on her own body and everyone else's, too, always with that black Sharpie of hers.

Don't pull a Rhonda on me. That was what Jessica wrote. But what did Rhonda do?

I flipped through more and more pages, turning my head side to side to study the images. One in particular gave me pause – a ghostly moon-shaped face of a girl, twisted into a look of horror. It almost reminded me of a modern-day Edvard Munch's *The Scream*, only more life-like, less cartoonish.

These weren't your average pictures – they all looked dark, demented even. *Tortured.*

But despite how dark they were, I found myself drawn to them—in fact, if I could afford it, I'd hire Rhonda to make a painting for my apartment ... the apartment I probably wouldn't have in a couple of weeks, I reminded myself.

Finally, tearing my eyes away from her work, I clicked on a dropdown box at the top of the page – *Contact the Artist* was one of the choices. When I selected it, a full body image of Rhonda filled the screen. She still had that wild, red hair and sprinkling of freckles across her face and arms. She looked the same, but older and more ... artsy. She fit the mold – dark, brooding, and morose in a see-through black shawl. Her make-up was darker than she used to wear it. In fact, she reminded me of an older, more gothic version, of that girl who was working the register at Bed and More the other day.

Rhonda's bony hands were draped in unusual jewelry. My eyes immediately fell on a black and silver bird that took up most of her middle finger. I'd never seen anything like it ... or had I? It reminded me of something...

Pushing my seat back, I jogged up the stairs and into the spare bedroom. The box with the bird on it still lay limply on the floor. It was a different bird altogether, but still, I knew, beyond a shadow of a doubt, that Rhonda was the one who'd drawn the bird on the box. Another memory emerged – Rhonda, and her weird obsession with birds, especially ravens. She liked to draw them in a way that looked Edgar Allen Poe-ish. That notebook of hers was full of them. All different types of birds, with one thing in common – they were always black and frightening. She carried that notebook everywhere, I remembered, until ... Jessica made fun of her for it one day on the bus. After a while, it disappeared from my memory, along with the memory of Rhonda and her artwork.

For whatever reason, Jessica had taken the brooding, lonely Rhonda under her wing. I think Jessica saw her less like a friend, and more of a pet project, to be improved upon, and by the start of the next school year, we had all forgotten about the old Rhonda ... until now.

Rhonda had to be the person who sent that package to Madi, I decided. But what was in the box? And was it somehow related to Madi's disappearance?

I carried the box back downstairs with me, pondering what used to be inside it. Madeline, Rhonda, and Jessica had some sort of a secret. That was clear to me now. Those three. Always those three. Why hadn't I thought of this sooner?

Maybe the secret was some*thing*, something Rhonda sent to Madeline, and then Jessica found out about it? My sister wanted to show someone – who? The police, maybe? Did it have something to do with Rhonda's art? But for some reason, Jessica didn't want my sister to have it or tell anyone about it...

You'd better keep your fucking mouth shut.

I remembered Paul's words, about the simplest explanation being the right one – maybe Madi bought some artwork from Rhonda. Had I seen anything in the house that resembled Rhonda's dark, signature handiwork?

Definitely not, I decided.

Were they protecting a secret of Rhonda's? My mind was racing as I sat back down in the desk chair. I dropped the box onto the floor beside me, carelessly, and I pulled up the Google search bar again. I stared at Rhonda's face on the screen. Beneath her photo was a brief biography. *Rhonda Sheckles – now Rhonda Gray – grew up in Bare Border, Indiana. She resides in Merrimont...* Bingo. So, she might have left this town and pursued her dreams of becoming an artist, but she hadn't gone far. In this day and age, you could run a successful business from the tiniest town on earth, as long as you had an internet connection.

A quick Google search of Rhonda Gray led me to an address in Merrimont. She was less than an hour away. *Yes!* It was a minor lead, but I couldn't help feeling a glimmer of satisfaction. Maybe I was getting somewhere. Maybe I was getting closer to finding my sister. Maybe if I talked to Rhonda, she'd have some sort of insight…

A loud bang on the front door shocked me out of my daze. I gasped.

Startled, I went to answer it, thinking it was probably Paul … but when I looked out the living room window, I was floored by who I saw – Jessica Feeler was standing on my sister's front porch.

CHAPTER SIXTEEN

Oh shit. Should I lie down and play dead, or should I open the door? I knew what Madi would do – well, I *thought* I knew what she would do before I discovered how secretive she'd been lately. Madi would face Jessica head on.

Quickly, before I could change my mind, I closed down the computer screen. I didn't want Jessica to know it had been me talking to her on Facebook. But what if she already knew?! What if she was the one who took Madi?

Jessica knocked again, louder this time. There was something desperate about the way she was pounding on the front door. I had to open it. She was not going away.

'Just a second!' I yelled through the door. The curtains over the window weren't see-through, but it wouldn't be hard for her to catch a glimpse of me running around in here if she tried to peek through the side.

I went to the door and took a deep breath, then I opened it a crack.

'Yes?' I tried to feign sleepiness.

'It's Jessica Feeler. Let me in now.' Taken aback by her brashness, I opened the door and did exactly what she wanted me to do.

Jessica stepped in the living room and looked around as though she were a potential buyer or a home inspector. Her haughtiness pissed me off.

'It's late. What are you doing here, Jessica?'

'I could ask you the same thing,' she sniffed.

Confused, I said, 'What the hell does that mean?'

'It means your sister is missing and her kids are with John. Why are you still in her house?'

I cleared my throat. If it wasn't for the circumstances, I would almost find this rude conversation amusing. I'd almost forgotten how arrogant and entitled Jessica Feeler could be.

'Actually, Jessica, this is my childhood home, as much as it is Madi's. I came here to visit right before she disappeared. I was taking care of Ben and Shelley, but then their dad came and got them for the night.' I don't know why I said it like that – like John was bringing them back tomorrow, or something.

Jessica's face softened, but I wasn't buying her act. 'What do you want Jessica? Have you heard from my sister?'

For a moment, I thought she might tell me about the 'contact' they'd just had on Facebook, but then she surprised me by saying, 'Nope. I hardly ever talk to Madeline anymore. But I'm still concerned. I was hoping maybe you had some news.'

Every fiber of my being wanted to scream the word 'liar' in her face. What was she trying to hide?

'No news besides what you've probably already heard. Paul Templeton is working the case. They found her Jeep parked near the bluff and there was some blood on the headrest. Probably not enough blood to kill her, but it's worrisome, nevertheless. So, you don't know where she is or why she might have run off?'

Jessica's eyes narrowed. 'Like I said, we don't talk much anymore.' Despite the summer heat, Jessica was wearing a light leather jacket. *Did she drive a motorcycle now?* I wondered. The thought of her preppy ass on a motorcycle, her now-thinning blonde hair a-flying, was almost enough to make me laugh out loud.

'I'm parched. Can I get a drink of water?' Jessica asked. We were still standing in the doorway. I was trying to keep her away from the computer, but even so, the screen was off. Unless she was so rude that she plopped down and helped herself to it, she wouldn't see anything I'd been doing online.

'Sure,' I answered, although I wasn't that crazy about the idea of letting her even farther into the house. *What if she's a killer?* a tiny voice screamed in my ear.

I led the way through the dining room and into the kitchen. Jessica hung back. What was she looking for? Did she not believe 'Madeline' when she said she wasn't home?

'The kitchen's in here.' I stuck my head into the dining room, where Jessica was still looking around suspiciously. 'Is everything okay? You're acting strangely,' I blurted out.

'I'm fine. Just worried about my friend,' she said nonchalantly, stepping into the kitchen.

I took a glass down from the cupboard and filled it up with tap water. When I handed it to Jessica, her hand was shaking so badly that she nearly dropped it.

There were blue-black circles beneath her eyes, and I realized that time hadn't been kind to Jessica. She had aged, considerably, since the last time I saw her. Maybe it was due to the stress over whatever secret she'd been hiding...

Jessica took a few small sips from the cup, then sat it down on the table. 'Thanks for that. Well, please let me know if you find out anything else. I hope Madi is okay.'

'Me too.' I stared into Jessica's eyes, trying to peel back her layers, one by one.

'I need to get back home to my husband.' Jessica turned as though she were going to leave, but then stopped dramatically. 'Do you mind if I look for something in the family room? I left a tape here a while back and I was hoping to get it back.' This entire moment felt planned to me, as though Jessica were just acting out a scene she'd practiced on the way over.

'Okay,' I said, dragging out the word.

I followed Jessica as she walked through the kitchen and toward the living room, staying on her heels. If she was looking for something, I wanted to know what it was exactly.

'All of the movies are on the shelves by the books.' I stood in the doorway of the family room, my arms crossed over my chest, watching. 'When you say "tape", are we talking about VHS? I didn't know anyone actually watched those things anymore.'

Jessica stood at the shelf, running her fingers across the rows of DVDs. She pulled out a few of them, checking for a second row of movies behind them, I guess. 'Yeah, it was a tape of my wedding ceremony. I brought it over here to show her and then I forgot to take it back home with me.'

'I thought you said you guys didn't talk anymore.'

Jessica's hand stilled on one of the DVDs. For a second, I wondered if she would respond to that.

'We don't, not really. It was a long time ago that I brought it over. It's been years.'

'Then how come you want it now?'

Jessica turned around and looked at me, her eyes searching. She was probably wondering if I knew something I shouldn't. Or maybe she already knew I was pretending to be Madi on Facebook...

'Honestly, I forgot she had it. But then I heard she was missing, and it reminded me of the time I came over and we watched it together. We used to be such good friends.'

I almost said: *Wouldn't a good friend have been at your wedding?* But I held my tongue.

'I don't see any tapes,' I told her, coming over to stand beside her. Jessica's face looked pale, almost sickly, as I hovered over her.

'Is there anywhere else she might keep her movies? Maybe

in her bedroom or upstairs?' There wasn't a chance in hell that I was letting Jessica Feeler snoop around my missing sister's house.

'No, there isn't. I hate to admit this, but I've snooped through almost everything already, in the hopes of finding some sort of clue about where she went. I haven't seen even one VHS tape. But I promise that I'll call you if I do find it.' Actually, I wasn't lying. I hadn't seen any tapes laying around. Who in the hell still owned VHS tapes anyway?

I started walking back toward the kitchen, hoping Jessica would take the hint. When she didn't move, I said, 'I'm sorry to rush you out, but I really need to get back to sleep. I have to go down to the sheriff's office tomorrow. They want to ask me more questions, and they want me to take a look at the Jeep and confirm it belonged to Madi.' This was a lie and it sort of surprised me how easily it rolled off my tongue. *It's okay to lie to a liar, especially when that liar is Jessica Feeler.*

'I understand. I'll let you get some rest,' Jessica said, reluctantly. Back at the front door, she perked up again, using her false charm to throw me off her game. 'If you need anything, anything at all, please don't hesitate to get a hold of me. I can come right over if you do. It was really good to see you, Emily...'

'Sure thing. Although I don't think I have your number.'

Jessica went out the door and was walking down the front porch steps.

'Oh, no worries, I can write it down for you. Just let me grab a scrap of paper...' she stopped, shuffling her purse open.

'That's okay. I'll track you down on Facebook again if I need you.' I slammed the front door, giggling as I pressed my forehead against it. I'm not sure why I said it – I think I just enjoyed knowing that comment would make her squirm. If she didn't know that it was me on the other end of Madi's messenger, she probably suspected it now.

Oh well. That bitch was hiding something. And unless she was just using the tape as an excuse to search for something else, I knew that I needed to find this mystery tape.

I peeked through the curtains, watching Jessica's blue mini-van pull out of the driveway. I didn't know what she was hiding, but the first thing I'd do in the morning was call and tell Paul.

I fell back onto the living room couch and that was when I noticed the box from Rhonda on the floor, still laying limply on its side. *Did Jessica see the box just now?* I'd completely forgotten about it and left it laying out...

I guess it didn't matter if she did. What was Jessica Feeler going to do to me? If she wanted to kill me, she would have tried it just now. And if she was the person who tried to hurt my sister, then why was she nosing around, asking questions...?

I lay back on the couch, resting my head on the stiff armrest. I was too tired to get up and seek out a pillow. I needed to rest – tomorrow, I had a VHS tape to search for.

CHAPTER SEVENTEEN

My cell phone vibrated against my belly, stirring me awake. My eyes still glued with sleep, I answered it without checking to see who it was.

'Hello,' I whispered. My throat felt scratchy, like I'd been screaming in my sleep.

'Emily, is that you? It's Starla.'

I slowly pulled myself up from my sister's couch, my abdominal muscles clenching from the strain. 'What's up?' I managed, clearing my throat.

'It's Ben. Something happened at school. Can you come over?'

I was already up on my feet, yanking my pants up over my hips. I was still wearing my T-shirt from last night.

Out the door within seconds, I roared down the windy mountain for the second day in a row. My mind was racing as I drove to Starla's – *what had happened to Ben?* Starla didn't give me any details over the phone, but it didn't sound good.

I pulled up and parked beside her Mercedes again. On the other side of her car was a big white truck. Was John here too?

I got my answer when the door to the apartment sprung open. John emerged, stopping in his tracks when he saw me. 'I have to go back to work, but Ben's upstairs. He really wants to see you.'

John didn't look happy about it, but he held the door for me as I raced up the three sets of stairs, moving much faster than yesterday.

'Ben?' He was sitting on the couch next to Starla, his eyes red and raw from crying. 'Oh, honey. What happened?'

I sat down on his other side and took his hand in mine. 'What happened?' I asked again.

'What happened?' Ben repeated. I rubbed his back as he rocked back and forth on the couch.

'Some boys on the bus were making fun of him. He punched one of them square in the nose and now his parents are threatening to sue. The principal threatened expulsion if it happens again…'

Ben was becoming more and more agitated as she talked. I held up a hand for Starla to stop, and then gently, I pulled him onto my lap. He was so small for an eight-year-old, barely weighing more than Shelley.

'It's okay, Ben. I'm here. We're here,' I corrected, not sure how I felt about including Starla in this equation.

Ben's head popped up, his piercing brown eyes focusing on me for the first time. 'Where is my mother?'

I wouldn't swear to it, but I thought I heard Starla gulp.

'I don't know, but I'm going to find her.' I'd been saying that so much lately that it made me feel like a phony.

Ben didn't look any less worried, but he did stop rocking back and forth.

'Why was he riding the bus? Doesn't Madeline usually drive him to school? He needs routine. His condition – well, he relies on it.'

Starla sighed. 'John thought it would be a good idea for him. He said that the best way to overcome a fear was to face it head on.'

'But what happens when that fear is realized? Now he'll never want to ride the bus again.' It came out sounding harsher than I wanted it to.

Starla shrugged, chewing on her thumbnail. 'What happened

139

with the kids, Ben?' she asked him. 'I haven't been able to get him to calm down long enough to tell me,' she explained.

'Go on, Ben,' I encouraged.

'They were making fun of *Five Nights at Freddy's*. I was drawing a picture of Chica in my notebook and one of them took it from me and tore it up.' My heart lurched. The cruel chants on the playground rang through my head, and the fluttering of photo paper falling like snow on the playground flashed before my eyes ... Sarah's eyes as she silently pleaded with me to be her friend, her protector...

'Oh, Ben. I'm so sorry.'

'It's okay. I can draw another one. It's just ... I got so mad. Sometimes I just can't control it...'

'I know, honey.' I pulled him into another hug. 'But no matter what, you can't put your hands on someone else. Not unless they hurt you first.'

'But they did hurt me. They hurt my feelings. And sometimes, that feels worse.'

He was so right. 'I know, Ben, I know. But if you get mad and hit them, then you're letting them win. Don't let them turn you into the bad guy. Don't be the bad guy, Ben...'

Ben's eyes grew wide, understanding twinkling somewhere in there. 'Okay, I won't. If I sit there and act good, then I win?'

'Yes. You win, baby.'

'Can I go home with you?' Ben asked, his face hopeful.

I wasn't sure how to answer him, but thankfully, I didn't have to. Starla said, 'Your daddy wants you and your sister to stay here for a while. But maybe, if your dad says it's okay, you can go over and visit with your Aunt Emily this weekend. Would that be okay?' She directed the last question to me.

My chest filled with relief. 'Absolutely. I would love that.'

I gave Ben another hug and then Starla walked me back downstairs. 'You're so good with him. With kids, in general. I'm surprised you don't have any of your own.'

I'd never considered myself 'good with kids', especially because I'd hardly ever been around any. But even so, I hated it when people said this – that maybe I would change my mind, or my favorite line of all: 'Just wait and see, you'll have your own someday…' I didn't think I ever would. But one thing was clear, I loved my niece and nephew in a way I'd never loved anyone. I wanted to protect them, and I never wanted to be that distant aunt from South Carolina again.

'Thanks for calling me, Starla. Please call me if you need help with anything else. And tell Shelley that I love and miss her too. I hope preschool is going well?'

'It's going great,' Starla said, with a smile. I climbed back behind the wheel of the Civic. I wasn't sure how my sister would feel about me fraternizing with the 'enemy' but I felt like I was doing the best I could under the circumstances. And honestly, Starla didn't seem so bad.

Taking a moment to check my other missed calls and texts, I saw that Paul had left a message last night and this morning. Instead of listening to them, I went ahead and called him.

Paul didn't say hello when he answered; he immediately launched into, 'I was so worried about you. Why didn't you call me back?'

'Paul, I'm fine. And by the way, I can take care of myself. I've been doing it for a long time. Now what can you tell me about my sister?'

He sighed. 'I'm just worried about you, Emily. You're back and I can't help wanting to protect you. Is that so bad?'

I squeezed my eyes shut, holding my breath.

Words fluttered into my memories. *Let me protect you. Let me love you, Emily,* I remembered the teenage-version of Paul, whispering those words in my ear while we made out. *Promises he couldn't keep, even then.*

'Emily, are you still there?'

'I'm here,' I breathed. 'Please just tell me what you've found out about Madi.'

141

'There's been no more card activity, but I'm trying to get some footage from the security cameras at Sam's. If we could see who was using that card, it would answer a lot of questions. Also, I confirmed what Starla told you about John. He sold his 9-millimeter handgun at the pawn shop last month.'

'Well, that's good news, I guess. I got something for you too … I got a late-night visit from Jessica Feeler last night. Apparently, she's searching for a tape.'

'As in VHS?'

'Yep. She didn't come right out and say it, but she showed up, pretending that she needed to look around my sister's house for a wedding tape. I don't buy it. And there's something else. Rhonda Sheckles might be involved. Well, her last name is Gray now.'

'Yeah, I see her around sometimes. She doesn't live too far outside of town,' Paul mulled.

I wanted to tell him that I already knew that, but I didn't want him to know where I was headed next – I was going to go see Rhonda myself and ask some questions before Paul, or the other officers, spooked her.

Paul said he had to go but promised to follow up on Jessica Feeler today. 'Maybe we can search for that tape together tonight,' he suggested. *Was he inviting himself over?*

His words fluttered back again. *Let me love you, Emily.*

I tried. I really did. And he hurt me, badly.

'I'll bring pizza,' he offered.

I don't know why, but I said yes. Hanging up the phone, my stomach was doing somersaults. I'd almost forgotten how it felt – this rush of excitement, this hopefulness in my veins…

But I also couldn't forget how it felt when the thrilling ride jerked to a halt and my heart got ripped from its chest. Again, I thought back to prom night – one of my lowest moments.

Paul Templeton would break my heart again if I let him. The question is: would I?

150

CHAPTER EIGHTEEN

I plugged Rhonda's address into the Civic's GPS, then I rolled the windows down and turned the radio up. I wasn't sure if Rhonda would be home, or what I would say to her if she was. But I had a feeling that she was the only one, besides Jessica, who might know where my sister had gone.

Did Rhonda know anything about this tape Jessica alluded to? She might think I was crazy for just showing up at her house.

Hell, she might not even remember me – those girls never paid any attention to me. To them, I would always be Madi's annoying little sister, nothing more, nothing less.

The town of Bare Border passed by in a drowsy cloud of sunshine, and the busier streets of Merrimont emerged. I tried to remember everything I knew about Rhonda, but besides the art thing, I couldn't think of much. She'd followed Jessica around with puppy dog eyes, always eager to please her. But that description could have fit Madi, too. Did I have that same puppy dog look in my eyes when I begged my sister to play with me?

A shudder ran through me. *Please let my sister be okay.* I recited those words again and again as I took a sharp turn on Linden Lane. Rhonda's house was the last house on the left, and instantly, I felt a chill as I parked next to the curb in front of it.

Linden Lane was deserted but it was a weekday afternoon, after all. Most people were at work by now. At least those who were lucky enough to still have jobs. I pushed back embarrassing memories of my job at the paper.

I approached the fence, my keys gripped in my hand as I stared up at the odd A-frame that belonged to Rhonda Sheckles Gray.

A child's tire swing shivered back and forth in the breeze as I lifted the latch on the metal gate and walked inside. The yard was tidy, but there was this grayness to it – something depressing. *Something stale.*

Following the crooked stone path up to her door, I tried to figure out what to say. I hadn't seen Rhonda in more than a decade...

But before I could even plan it out, I was wrenching open Rhonda's screen and knocking on her black front door. There was a window next to the door and as soon as I knocked, the curtains rustled. I leaned over, trying to see if Rhonda was peering out, when a big black dog mashed its snout against the glass and started barking crazily.

The dog ran back and forth in the window, its face appearing and then reappearing between the curtains. Well, if she didn't know someone was here before, she did now. I knocked again, tentatively.

But no one came. Finally, I turned to go, but then the barks grew louder. They almost sounded desperate, like the animal was in pain.

The dog raced back and forth in front of the window again.

If Rhonda wasn't home, it wouldn't hurt to snoop around a little bit, would it?

I glanced over my left and right shoulders to make sure no one was watching, and then I tiptoed across her flower garden, until I was standing right beneath the window.

I tapped on the glass again, and the dog's movements became

144

even more frantic. He was howling now, like some sort of wild, strangled plea that set my teeth on edge.

The curtains were knocked off-center by his movements, and there was a gap on the far-left side that might be enough for me to see inside...

Looking around again, to make sure no one was watching, I then pressed my face up to the gap in the curtains. The dog pressed its wet snotty nose right to mine.

'Hey, you. Where's Rhonda?' I purred. The dog jumped around wildly again, and this time, I saw someone standing behind him in a living room area.

What the hell? I squinted through the vitreous glass and what I saw confused me. There were legs and bare feet, but they seemed to be dangling in mid-air.

'Oh, no.' The glare on the window shifted, and suddenly I could see who the legs belonged to. A mess of curly red hair on a cold white face. A thick knotty rope twisted like a necklace around Rhonda's throat...

'No!' I screamed, banging my hands on the glass as though it weren't already too late to save her.

CHAPTER NINETEEN

My mind whirring with possibilities, I yanked on the front door first and then ran around to the back of the house. Shockingly, the knob twisted easily in my hand; it was unlocked. The back door opened into a rundown laundry room. There were shoe skid marks on the walls and a mess of paint cans on the floor, next to a washer and dryer. I stepped around them, cautiously.

I was inside Rhonda's house. Suddenly I realized that the dog was no longer barking. Who knew if the dog was even nice?! He might bite … but I needed to save Rhonda.

Crossing through a kitchen and dining room, I made my way toward what I knew was the front of the house. The house was dark and sunless, even though it was the middle of the afternoon.

All the shades were drawn. *And with good reason*, I realized, as I stepped into Rhonda's living room.

Rhonda Sheckles Gray was beyond saving. She looked even deader from here than she did from behind the glass. She was hanging so high I could barely touch her feet if I'd wanted to, but from here, I could see that her skin was a dull bluish-gray.

The dog, who had been so frantic only minutes ago, now lay sullenly on the floor beneath her. Its head drooped to the floor, its expression sullen. He understood that his owner was dead. *He's mourning her*, I realized.

'I'm so sorry, buddy.' I knelt beside the dog, which looked like a Gordon Setter, and began scratching behind his ears and around his silver collar. I wasn't a coroner, but I ventured a guess that Rhonda had been dead for at least a few days. The poor dog probably hadn't eaten.

'What happened, buddy?'

I had to call the police immediately. But, suddenly, I realized that I had an opportunity here – I needed to search quickly before I called them. If Rhonda had this tape Jessica was looking for, or something that seemed suspicious … I had a limited amount of time to find it.

I glanced up at Rhonda one last time, and for some unknown reason, I reached out and touched her foot. It was as stiff as a rock, but not as cold as I expected. My touch must have triggered the rope, because she swayed a bit. I jumped back, almost afraid the rope would snap, and Rhonda's lifeless body would come barreling down on me…

I cringed at the creaking sound of the rope straining against rafters. My stomach was doing somersaults as I waited for the rope to still.

The dog was staring up at her, an almost hopeful look on his face.

'I'm so sorry, buddy. Can you show me where your food bowl is?'

The dog got up slowly from the floor as though the simple act of straightening his legs was painful. He wandered past me toward the kitchen. I followed him, watching as he nudged a glass bowl on the floor with his nose.

It took me a few minutes to find his food inside a bag underneath the sink. I filled the dog's bowl with a heaping portion of the dry food and then I filled up another small bowl with tap water from the sink. He ate and drank hungrily, while I wandered off through the house, looking for any sort of connection to Madi.

The first place I checked was the living room. Rhonda had a small collection of DVDs and CDs. Nothing suspect, and definitely no VHS tapes, from what I could see. I sifted through cupboards and drawers, my hands shaky. Unsure what I was looking for, and feeling like a total creep…

A sudden thought sent a shiver up my spine – what if Rhonda's husband or child came home? It would be hard to explain why I was inside the house, snooping around while Rhonda hung lifelessly from the rafters.

But Rhonda had been dead for a while. Either her husband and child hadn't been here in a few days or they moved out, otherwise they would have discovered her body by now.

This thought was confirmed when I went upstairs. The bedroom closet was filled with women's clothing and a small amount of men's. There were a lot of empty hangers on the left side of the closet.

The bed was unmade, sheets and blankets tangled up wildly on the floor. I drifted in and out of two other bedrooms – one must have been her daughter's room because it was filled with ballerinas and super heroes. But like the father's side of the closet, hers was mostly empty too. The other bedroom looked to be some sort of guest room. It was the only bedroom that contained a made bed and it was in pristine condition. My search was becoming fruitless, until I came across a small door at the end of the second-floor hallway. I'd assumed it was a linen closet, but when I opened it I found a narrow old staircase leading up to an attic space.

Nervously, I tiptoed up the creaky stairs. It was at least twenty degrees warmer up here and I felt the strange sensation that I was the one being strangled, or suffocated, as I entered the open attic space.

This was obviously Rhonda's art studio. There were easels

holding unfinished canvas paintings. At least they looked unfinished...

I crept closer inside, looking at the splotchy black paintings. One looked mostly done – half of a woman's face. She had wild black hair and one hooded eye; strangely, she looked just like Rhonda.

Suddenly, I couldn't wait to get back outside and suck in fresh breaths of air. I turned to go, and that's when I saw a short bookcase leaning against one side of the wall. From here, I could see that it was mostly full of books. As I moved closer, I realized that most of them were art textbooks or books about specific artists, but there on the middle shelf, between a book on Van Gogh and a guide on acrylic painting, were three VHS tapes secured in those rainbow plastic sleeves that tapes used to be stored in.

I slid them off the shelf, my nose tickling with dust, and I glanced at the paper labels stuck to the sides. There were no words, only dates: 1990, 1987, and 1982. Hurriedly, I ran back down the stairs and slipped back through the back door. There was no one outside, no one had any idea that poor Rhonda Sheckles was hanging dead inside...

Quickly, I popped the trunk on the Honda and tossed the tapes inside. I went back inside the house and sat on the floor next to Rhonda's dog while I dialed 911 to report her death.

CHAPTER TWENTY

It was Paul who came, along with two other officers. The other two pulled up in Merrimont cruisers.

I was sitting on Rhonda's front porch, my knees tucked up to my chest like a protective shell, her dog mashed up against my outer thigh.

Despite the balmy August heat, I was freezing, and my teeth chattered together noisily.

Paul was the first to reach me. He gave me a strange nod and went straight for the door. He pulled out some strange-looking crowbar, probably to wrench the door apart with.

'It's already unlocked,' I told him, getting up on my feet. The dog stood up too, and I rested my hand on his soft, fuzzy head.

'Stay out here, ma'am,' one of the officers told me as they crowded in behind Paul.

But I didn't listen. I moved to the doorway behind them. From here, they could clearly see it was a suicide. If it wasn't suicide, it was perfectly staged to look like one.

The rope was still attached to the rafters. A ladder sideways on the floor nearby. The ceilings were so tall, she obviously would have had to climb to the top of the ladder to tie the rope, and then swing out from it.

'How the hell are we going to get her down?' one of the officers, a large balding man, muttered to his partner.

'Paul, you guys should investigate this like a homicide. With my sister missing, this might not be what it looks like...' I tried to tell them.

'Get back, lady!' Another officer, a tall man with thinning brown hair, approached me. He stood in front of the doorway, blocking my view. But it wasn't like I needed to see her again – that dull, lifeless look in her eyes would forever be etched on my brain.

'I'll talk to her,' Paul said, pushing the officer aside. 'I need to get some tools out of my cruiser anyway.'

I followed him down the skinny sidewalk, my heart racing. Rhonda's dog came nipping at my heels. 'What do you think this means, Paul? Are we sure she killed herself?'

Paul stopped at the gate and turned around to look at me. 'I'm positive she did this to herself.' He reached for me then, and I let myself sink into his chest. The buttons on his uniform were scratchy, but he smelled and felt so good. Rhonda's cold dead eyes flashed before me again and I shuddered, pulling away from him.

'How are you so sure?' I asked.

'This isn't the first time we've been out here. Rhonda has threatened suicide half a dozen times. Her husband called several weeks ago, and we had to get a judge to order a seventy-two-hour hold on her at the hospital. Third floor, that's where they keep the mentally unstable. She was threatening to shoot herself then, but I guess she got out of the hospital, and this time, nobody could stop her.'

The street had finally come to life, neighbors drifting out of their houses and nervously approaching the fence.

'Please stay back, ma'am,' Paul warned one of the women who was closest. She was an elderly woman, with honey-colored skin and hair. She kept leaning against the gate, despite his warning.

'Did she do it this time?' the woman crooned.

Paul stuck his hand out. 'Ma'am—'

151

'I'll call the husband. I know his number, if that will help? He and little Jenny moved out a few days ago. They just couldn't take it anymore, I don't guess,' she told us.

'If you could write that number down for me, that would be most helpful,' Paul told her. He took his hat off and rubbed the back of his head, looking exhausted.

The woman turned away, inching along the main sidewalk back to her house. The thought of her walking all the way home and back to get a piece of paper made me feel bad, and plus, I wanted to speak with her.

'I have a pad of paper in my car. Want to come with me and you can write it down over there?' I pointed toward the rented Civic. She nodded and waddled back toward me.

'I'm going back inside. Are we still on for pizza?' Paul asked, as the neighbor and I started toward my car.

I glanced back, giving him a perplexed look. It worried me a little; that he could seem so cool and calm in this moment, and that there was actually some portion of his brain still thinking about what was for dinner tonight.

Reluctantly, I nodded.

'By the way,' I told Paul, drifting back over to him so the neighbors wouldn't hear, 'my prints are all over the place in there. I snooped around some.'

'Dammit, Emily. That wasn't smart!' he shout-whispered. 'But we're pretty sure this was just a suicide, so you should be okay … this time.'

'See you tonight,' I said, aware of Rhonda's neighbors' watchful stares from the sidewalk. I walked over to the elderly neighbor, who was now standing by my car.

'How do you know Rhonda, dear?' she asked as I leaned into the backseat to retrieve a pad of paper. This lady reminded me of Mr Tennors – she was one of those nosy neighbors that probably knew everyone's story on this block.

'We used to be friends at school. Well, she was my sister's

friend. I'm a few years younger than Rhonda. Can I ask you something?'

The woman took the pad from my hands and said, 'Sure thing.' She had a tiny knit purse attached to her waist. She dug around inside it, taking out a small pencil.

While she wrote Rhonda's husband's number down, I got my cell phone off the passenger's seat and pulled up Madi's Facebook page. 'Have you seen this woman around here lately?' I showed her a picture of Madi.

She cocked her head to the side, then said, 'No, I haven't. Rhonda doesn't get many visitors, to be honest, unless it's the cops or an ambulance. She's an artist, you know. Bat shit crazy.' She twirled her finger around her ear, reminding me of Shelley the other day.

'Are you sure you haven't seen her?' I pressed.

But the woman shook her head again. 'No, I'm sorry, but I haven't.' So, my sister and Rhonda didn't hang out anymore – so why the recent box in the mail? There must have been some sort of communication between them, why else would Rhonda send her a package?

My mind drifted back to the videotapes with the dates on them. They could be nothing or … they could be one of the tapes Jessica Feeler was searching for.

'Why do you think she wanted to kill herself?' I asked the woman.

She shrugged. 'Like I said, she's never seemed right to me.' She finished writing down the number and then ripped it out. I thanked her and then ran it back up to the door and handed it to one of the officers. Rhonda's dog trotted back and forth beside me.

'I can take Roxie there,' the woman pointed at the dog. 'We're old friends, aren't we dear? I'll make sure she gets back to Rhonda's husband safely.'

'Okay,' I said, reluctantly. I leaned down and planted my lips on Roxie's soft black scalp. She licked my cheek and then I watched her and Rhonda's neighbor make their way slowly across the street. I wondered how Rhonda's husband and daughter would react to her brutal death. I could only hope the daughter was too young to understand it fully.

Determined to get out of here before they arrived, I walked back up to the front door to make sure there was nothing else Paul needed from me. From here, I could see him with what looked like a pair of hedge trimmers in his hand. He was balancing on the top rung of the ladder, hovering above Rhonda's body and preparing to cut her down.

Her hair had drifted over her face now and those lifeless eyes were gone. Nevertheless, I shivered again. I was glad not to see that horrified expression, but somehow the covered face was worse. For some reason, it reminded me of that creepy image on her website – the wide-open mouth, and twisted expression ... and that hideous half-face on the easel in the attic upstairs...

'Move on,' the tall officer moved to the door, barking at me again. He was eager to run me off, apparently. When the officer shouted at me, Paul's eyes jerked down to meet mine, and for a moment, the ladder wobbled beneath him dangerously.

I whisked around and made my way back out to the car. The crowd had thickened, the elderly woman, with Roxie by her side, leading the crowd. *That will be Jessica Feeler when she's an old woman,* I realized. *Always the leader of the pack.*

Climbing back behind the wheel, I had to wait a few moments for my hands to steady before I put the car in gear.

I barely remembered driving back. The city streets of Merrimont blew by, eventually dissolving and evolving into Bare Border.

One thing kept swimming around in my brain, making lap after lap. *Three women knew a secret of some kind.* One of them was missing and one of them was dead. Maybe it was time to focus my attention on that third woman. *Jessica Feeler.*

I just hoped these tapes held some sort of clue that could help me find my sister.

CHAPTER TWENTY-ONE

The first thing I did when I got back home, was sneak the tapes out of the trunk. I stuffed them down the front and back of my pants, in case anyone was watching.

I'd wracked my brain – where would I get a VCR? But then I remembered Shelley's old-fashioned, boxy TV set – the one with Tinkerbell on it. It had a DVD/VCR combo built inside it, thankfully.

As I entered the Bare Border Inn, I was met with deafening silence. The place felt like a tomb and it'd taken on this weird sort of damp-dishcloth smell.

The postal box from Rhonda Sheckles still lay on its side next to the computer desk. I picked it up and peered inside. I even stuck my nose inside it and sniffed.

I wasn't certain what she'd sent, but one thing was obvious – it was big enough to fit a VHS tape. What if Rhonda had found a tape of something – something that would harm Jessica in some way? Then maybe she sent the tape to my sister, and that was why Jessica was threatening her…? But then how did Rhonda get these tapes back?

I closed the door behind me in Shelley's room and stuck the first tape I grabbed into the VCR. I knew right away it wasn't anything related to Madi. These were homemade movies – a red-headed woman and a dark-haired man, celebrating Christmas with their tiny rosy-cheeked, red-haired baby girl. These must be Rhonda's parents' home movies.

I watched for a while, marveling at how different everything looked in the Eighties. I wondered if Rhonda's parents were still alive and how they would handle the death of their only child...

I fast forwarded through the tape, but in order to see what was going on, I had to do it slowly. After hours' worth of Christmas and Thanksgiving and birthday footage, the tape finally came to an end. My hopes, by now, were dashed as I stuck in the second, and finally the third, VHS tapes. All three tapes were from Rhonda's childhood. Seeing her as a kid, so alive, so unknowing of what the future would hold, was almost like watching a horror movie.

Feeling guilty for stealing the tapes in the first place, I stacked them up on Shelley's dresser, silently promising Rhonda that I would send them back – anonymously, of course – to her family. Now that she was gone, they would want this footage of her.

So, Rhonda didn't have any weird tapes at her house – at least none that I could find. So, the only place left to look was right here under my own nose.

I started searching in Madi's room. Up until now, I'd tried to be respectful of my sister's things. But this time, I tossed all her clothes out of the drawers. Then I pulled the drawers all the way out and took them off their hinges. I could remember hiding some of my journals and joints inside my dresser when I was younger. I could also remember hiding my razor blade inside there...

But there were no tapes tucked away inside it. Next, I pulled everything out of her closet. I checked through her papers, dumped out old purses, and stuck my hands inside the lint-filled pockets of her jackets and pants that were hanging on wire hangers.

Her mattress! It was an obvious place, but one I hadn't thought of until now. Too bad I hadn't thought to check under Rhonda's mattresses while I was there. I lifted the top mattress and then the box spring, and then I got down on my hands and knees and peered beneath the bed itself. I even tore apart her bathroom.

I stuck my nose inside Kleenex boxes and jugs, anyplace that could be used to conceal *anything*. The kitchen search took a while. I looked through cereal boxes and removed all the pots and pans from the lower cabinets. *Nothing.*

By the time I'd gone through every little nook and cranny on the bottom floor of the house, it looked like my sister had been robbed. It would take me days to clean up this mess, but what if my sister didn't have days...? She needed me to find her now. Rhonda was dead, and although it appeared to be a suicide, how could I be sure of that? *What if Madi turns up dead next?* I feared.

Shelley and Ben needed their mother.

Upstairs seemed like a good hiding place. It was a rarely used space, and the kids said themselves that they never came up here. In the smaller upstairs bedrooms, I flipped through the pages of books and sifted through the old toy bins. Where would I hide a tape if I had one? Where would I hide *anything* around here...? This was starting to feel like a big waste of time.

I took a seat in my dad's old armchair, feeling exasperated. My thoughts kept drifting to Rhonda Sheckles. Why did she hang herself?

But why does anyone commit suicide? a nasty voice inside me replied.

Because they want to.

Because there's always this tiny part of us – this part that wants to give up and die. Or maybe that's just me. Usually, people can overcome it ... but sometimes that grimy little side of ourselves wins. Maybe Rhonda let hers win.

My thoughts drifted down through the floorboards, to the room beneath this one ... my duffel bag still down there on the floor in my mom's old sewing room. I hadn't put away my clothes. Buried deep, in the bottom of the bag, was a bottle of tiny white pills that the doctor had prescribed me. I'd gone to see her after I lost my job at the paper. I thought I had mono or something: always tired, low mood, no appetite ... then the doctor told me I was depressed. I wish I could say that I laughed, but I knew in my heart, it was true. I'd always been depressed, and losing my job had brought me to my lowest low...

Right then, I promised myself that I would start taking the pills. *As soon as I get downstairs*, I decided. *I don't want to wait until it gets this bad ... I don't want to pull a Rhonda Sheckles.*

Suddenly, I realized what Jessica must have meant. *Was she worried my sister would commit suicide?* According to Paul, Rhonda had made half a dozen attempts to take her own life over the years. Did Jessica and my sister know that? Was Jessica worried my sister might try that too...?

Or what if ... what if Jessica already knew that Rhonda had hung herself? What if Jessica beat me there ... maybe she saw Rhonda hanging from the rafters first. Or maybe she was even responsible for her death. Suddenly, Jessica Feeler seemed a lot more sinister. What was she hiding? This had to be about more than some silly video tape...

My chest cramped, my stomach roiling as I tried to imagine what I would do, what those kids would do, if Madi took her own life. Surely, Madi wouldn't 'pull a Rhonda Sheckles', as Jessica had implied. *Would she?*

I got up slowly, feeling helpless. I stared at the blue-black stitching on my dad's old chair. For the first time in a long time, I wished my dad was here. Despite all his flaws, he always knew how to fix things. He always knew what to do when nobody else did.

I traced the edges of the chair with my eyes, trying to remember exactly how it used to look with my dad sitting in it...

That's when I realized – the chair didn't look as old as I would have expected. He'd had that chair maybe twenty, twenty-five years ago. How did it look so pristine?

I ran my hands over the fabric. Had my sister had it re-upholstered? On my knees now, I ran my hands all over the chair, along the bottom ... there was something – something with weight to it – in the apron of the chair. I pressed my face to the carpet, peeking underneath.

Yes. The bottom was sagging. Something was in the chair.

Did my sister sew something in the bottom when she had it reupholstered?

I hated to tear up a piece of furniture that belonged to my dad, but I was desperate. Bounding downstairs, I found a box cutter in my sister's junk drawer. I had to cut the chair open, but first, I set the box cutter down and went to get my pills.

Swallowing one of the tiny pills without water, I instantly felt better. There was no way it worked that fast, but I appreciated the placebo effect. Maybe I could get my life under control, after all. I didn't want to let myself reach the point Rhonda got to, where she saw no other option than to end her life.

I went back to retrieve the box cutter and I carried it upstairs.

Carefully, I made a long slit in the bottom of the chair. I slid my fingers into the opening and right away, they brushed against something plastic. The slit wasn't big enough, so I had to make another gash in the other direction, widening the hole.

Finally, I was able to get my entire hand inside the chair. I pulled out a black VHS tape.

CHAPTER TWENTY-TWO

The tape had a white sticky label on it, like the kind they used to put on jumbo packs of blank tapes. My mom used to tape shows all the time: *General Hospital, The Ricki Lake Show,* etc.

There was nothing written on this label. Nothing to distinguish it from any other blank tape in the universe. What if there was nothing on it?

But there had to be – nobody goes to this sort of trouble just to hide an old blank tape.

I was nervous to watch it, but what choice did I have? If I was lucky, it would solve the mystery once and for all about my sister's whereabouts. Or at least give me an idea as to why she felt compelled to leave...

Shelley's room was darker than it had been earlier, just a pale sliver of sunlight sneaking in through the curtains. I closed them tight, cloaking the room in complete blackness. I slid the tape into the VCR and turned the TV back on. But just as I was about to hit play and sit down to watch it on Shelley's bed, there was a loud knock on the front door.

I jumped, knocking over toys and trinkets on the dresser and I leapt for the television. I punched the off button and tiptoed into the living room. The knocking grew louder and louder. *Was Jessica back again?*

'It's me, Emily,' Paul called through the door. Letting out a sigh of relief, I unfastened the deadbolt and opened the door.

'You okay?' He gave me a once over, his eyes questioning. 'You look exhausted.'

'I am. This whole thing has been so stressful. Rhonda's face was so awful … and Ben got in a fight today. I need to find my sister, Paul. I need to know what happened to her.'

'Is Ben okay?' Paul's face wrinkled up with concern.

'He's fine now. Starla and hopefully John are going to let them come stay with me this weekend. Unless Madi comes back before then. That's what I'm hoping for anyway…'

'Were you searching for that tape?' Paul looked around at the scattering of toys and papers on the floor.

I'd nearly forgotten that I told him about the VHS tape Jessica was looking for.

'I did. But I didn't find it.' I wasn't sure why I was lying to him. I probably just wanted to see the tape for myself before I showed it to anyone else. This was Paul, and despite the fact that he had hurt me in the past, I trusted him. But Paul the person was different than Paul the cop – if the tape contained something about my sister that was illegal, he'd be compelled to report it. Wouldn't he?

'Well, I can help you look. I'm a cop after all. I know how to find things,' Paul offered.

My voice shook as I said, 'No, seriously. That's okay. I don't want to search anymore right now.'

'You could sit down and take a break while I look. Come on, let me help.'

Panicked, I blurted out the first thing I could think of, 'I thought you were bringing pizza.'

Paul chuckled. 'I was going to, but I thought: why not take you out for pizza instead?'

'Sounds good. Just let me slip on my shoes and we'll go right now.' Going out on a date – was it a date? – with Paul Templeton was a bad idea. And the last thing I should be doing while my sister was missing, and Rhonda was dead, was hanging out, eating pizza like any other normal night. But I wanted to get Paul out of the house and away from that tape. I didn't want him, or anyone else, to see it before I had a chance to look at it.

I grabbed my purse and practically shoved him out the door. 'I'm starving.'

'Apparently,' he said, laughing. He opened the door of his cruiser for me.

'I've never ridden in a cop car before.' I slid my seatbelt on, looking around. His floorboards and console were neat. This wasn't the Paul I knew, the one with beer cans littering the floor of his dad's truck and the pile of poorly graded schoolwork tossed in the backseat.

He got behind the wheel, giving me a sideways smile. 'Well, that's a good sign, I guess.'

As we crunched our way down the driveway, I watched the house in the rearview mirror. There was this part of me that felt guilty for not telling Paul about the tape. And another part was worried that Jessica might break into the house and steal the tape right out of the VCR while I was gone…

That's ridiculous, I told myself. But then … my sister must have been worried about someone taking it or finding out she had it. Why else would she have hidden it as well as she did?

It was possible that the tape contained home videos of our own, or something unrelated to her disappearance, just like the tapes I found at Rhonda's, but again, why would you hide something like that unless it contained something important?

***

For a weekday night, Rosita's was unusually crowded. It seemed strange – people out eating, socializing, all the while Rhonda's family was coping with her tragic death.

Paul and I had to wait a few minutes before we were seated. The waitress was tall and lean, with black hair that reached all the way down to her bottom. As she led us to a quiet booth in the back, I stole a glance at Paul. For someone who had just been to the scene of a suicide, he looked remarkably calm.

I slid into the booth first, watching Paul as he took the seat across from me. He was so handsome when he was younger. Most men from my childhood had gotten larger, hairier, and older-looking – which was what happened when you get old, I guess – but somehow, Paul looked even better. The crinkles around his eyes and mouth suited him. Even the soft spray of gray at his temples was attractive, to me. I tried to imagine myself letting go, letting him back in my life ... the thought made me nervous, but not all together uneasy. He was different now, more mature ... a better version of himself, perhaps?

We ordered sodas and a large pizza with everything on it. My stomached grumbled noisily. Once again, I had gone all day without eating. Even still, it felt wrong to eat and act normal with everything going on.

'How are you doing?' he asked. He reached across the table, the tips of his fingers brushing against my own. When he was a teenager, he spent most of his free time – when he wasn't partying or getting into trouble – working on cars in his dad's garage. No matter how often he showered, he always had this grime embedded in his nails and skin, and he usually smelled of it, too. But over time, I'd grown accustomed to his smell, enjoying the scent as he passed by me in the hall. I expected him to move away, or to become a mechanic ... but a cop? That was something that never crossed my mind.

'You okay?' He teased the tips of my fingers with his own, staring deeply at me from across the table.

I shrugged. *How to answer that question?* 'Well, Madeline is still missing, and I found a dead body today, so I'm doing as well as can be expected, I guess. I'm holding up. I just keep thinking my phone will ring out of the blue or I'll pull up to find her Jeep parked in the driveway, like she never left in the first place...'

'One of the other detectives doesn't buy the whole leaving town theory.'

My stomach curled. 'Oh? What does that mean?'

'He thinks someone hit Madeline over the head outside and then made her drive up to the bluff. She was hurt, but not bad enough to incapacitate her. Maybe they had a gun, maybe not. But somehow, they forced her to drive up to the bluff. They took her card and used it at Sam's – maybe because they didn't have the money for whatever it was they needed, or maybe they just did that to throw us off, make us think she skipped town on her own. Sam's isn't very far from Bare Border. If they were from out of town, they would have gotten farther away than that ... I'm thinking they used the card on purpose to make us think she's still alive, and that it was somebody local. But then again, some of the other guys think she just took off...'

A small moan escaped from my lips just as the waitress came strolling back up. I pressed my lips together, fighting back tears, as she sat down my drink and a straw.

'I'm sorry, Emily. I'm not saying she's dead, or she won't come back. Maybe they just wanted us to think she jumped from the bluff...? Maybe they're holding her somewhere. But why – that's the real question. We have to figure out *why.*'

My thoughts drifted back to Rhonda Sheckles – her freckled legs dangling in the air, her body swaying limply like a scarecrow in the wind. 'Is it possible that my sister jumped? Her body wasn't at the bottom, but what about animals...?' The thought of my sister trying to kill herself was inconceivable. Madi, who always denied feeling depressed, and never admitted weakness ... but how much can you really know someone? *Maybe this thing with*

John sent her over the edge? Shaking my head, I still couldn't believe. Madi wouldn't do that to herself, to those kids...

Paul took a sip of his Coke and slammed it back down. 'I don't think so. There was no blood at the bottom. We found nothing – no body parts, no ground that had been disturbed, no items that belonged to your sister...'

'Oh my god.' The color drained from my face as I realized something crucial I'd forgotten. 'You said my sister's keys were still in the ignition of the Jeep?'

'They were. Why?'

'Because the person who took her could have a key to the house. Even if the house key was still on the chain, they could have made a copy...'

Suddenly, I was grateful that John had taken the kids away from my sister's house ... unless he was the one who took her.

'I need to go home.' My mind was on the tape again. If the person who took Madi had a key, they could easily go inside and take the tape. The tape had to be the key to everything. I needed it to be – because, other than that, I had nothing to go on. And if they could get inside, they could get to me...

'There were a lot of keys on that key ring, probably to your sister's work and the house ... but you're right. We should have thought of that sooner.' Paul clenched and unclenched his fists, veins bulging from his forearms.

I was standing up, yanking a wad of ones from my pocket. Just then, the perky waitress returned, balancing the pizza on one hand. 'Is everything okay?' she asked.

'We need that pizza to go,' Paul said. The minutes ticked by as he paid for the food and the waitress loaded the fresh, hot pizza into a cardboard box for us to take home. Any appetite I'd had earlier was gone now.

Paul drove quickly, which made me relieved, until I realized we were going the wrong direction.

'I'm stopping off to get a new lock kit. I'll change them for

165

you when we get back, if that will make you feel better. I know it will make me feel better.' I didn't want to wait any longer – my mind was focused on protecting some blank tape that could very easily be something meaningless – but it *would* make me feel better if he changed the locks.

I waited in the cruiser while he ran inside Home Depot. After he got back in the car, we rode in mostly silence.

'We should probably tell John that we're changing the locks. After all, it's still his house,' Paul said.

I groaned. I hadn't even thought of that.

'But right now, my only concern is your safety, and finding your sister of course.'

'Thank you,' I whispered as I stared out the window, willing the hot wet tears not to come.

'Did you see Rhonda's husband and daughter today?' I asked, still unable to wipe her face from my memory.

When he nodded, I asked, 'How did they take the news?'

Paul's face turned grim. 'The husband handled it considerably well. I think he'd been expecting it for a while. But the little girl was hysterical … she had to be sedated. The poor thing couldn't be much older than Shelley…'

I was sorry I'd asked. My stomach churned and ached as I tried to wrap my brain around their pain. I only hoped that Shelley and Ben didn't have to endure that, too…

166

CHAPTER TWENTY-THREE

Paul changed the locks on the front, back, and side doors. He worked quickly and methodically, like he'd done this a thousand times.

'My mom used to kick my dad out of the house all the time. I'd change the locks for her and then he'd show up again, drunk off his ass, pounding on the door all hours of the night. One time, he just punched his fists through the glass…'

I never went to Paul's house as a kid, but I'd met his parents a few times. His mom was a quiet mouse of a woman, whereas Mr Templeton was loud and boisterous. A memory of him shouting profanities at a baseball game swirled through my mind. And everyone in town knew about his drinking problem. He got arrested often, and when Paul started getting in trouble as a teenager, nobody was surprised.

'My mom always took him back,' he said, sadly.

'Did she pass away?' I remembered him mentioning that he lived with his father still, but he hadn't mentioned his mom.

'Yes. Never drank or smoked a day in her life, and she's the one who gets cancer. Go fucking figure.'

'I'm sorry, Paul. How is your dad?'

'Still drinking. But not as mean as he used to be. I think he lost the fight in him when Mom passed away.'

'Do you still keep in touch with your brothers?' Paul had two older brothers, if I remembered correctly.

Paul shrugged. 'They don't come visit much, but we still talk on Facebook. Occasionally, one of them calls. They're both married with kids now. Jimmy lives in Arizona and Martin lives in Utah.'

'I miss my mom. I miss dad too, but we never did get along either,' I said, quietly.

Paul gave me a sad smile. 'Want to eat this pizza? I'm so hungry.'

I laughed. Paul was always hungry, at least that's how he used to be when we were kids. I could remember him eating every bit of food off his lunch tray and then turning around to finish mine.

'Yeah. Want to eat out here? It's a nice night.' We were still outside, standing on the front porch. The summer sun dipped down low behind the trees. The locks were changed, and even though I was still worried, I felt considerably calmer now. Nobody had broken in. The tape was still in the VCR waiting to be watched…

The box of pizza was laying on the old porch swing and Paul pulled me off a slice, handing it to me on a paper napkin. It was cold, but nothing had ever tasted better. Between the two of us, we ate nearly the entire pizza.

'I didn't realize how hungry I was. I haven't been eating much since Madi left. It just seems wrong, doing normal everyday things while she's missing.'

'I know. But you have to take care of yourself. Your sister wouldn't want you to suffer in her absence.' Paul placed both hands on my cheeks, forcing me to stare into his eyes. I tried to pull away, but he gripped me tighter. My heart pounded like a hammer in my chest.

His hands felt warm, like fuzzy gloves on a snowy day. I had the biggest urge to kiss him just then … to let everything else fall away, at least temporarily. To forget we weren't who we used to be, that he was someone new, a perfect date for once in my life…

As though he heard my thoughts, Paul leaned forward, pressing his lips on mine. His kiss was soft, tender … like butterfly wings on my tongue.

When he pulled back, I didn't want the kiss to end. If this were a normal day, and about fifteen years earlier, I'd gladly invite him in. But things had changed, there was no denying that. And I needed to watch that tape, alone.

'Do you want me to stay here with you?' he offered, reading my mind once more. I rubbed at my cheeks and neck, still flushed from that kiss … but the moment was over. Reality set in – I needed to view that tape by myself, needed to see what sort of help it could offer in the search for my sister.

'Thanks for offering, but no. I'll be fine, I promise. Thank you for changing the locks, and for dinner … thank you for the kiss.' I blushed at that last part, glancing down at my feet.

When I looked back at Paul, he was grinning. He leaned in and kissed me again, a tiny peck on the cheek. 'Keep your phone nearby and call me if you need me, promise?'

'Promise.'

'Maybe we can meet for breakfast tomorrow? Hopefully I'll know more details of the case by then. Also, I was on my way to see Jessica Feeler when I found out about Rhonda Sheckles, so I'll have to try again tomorrow.'

I nodded, my stomach turning as he climbed back inside his police car and left. I didn't go back inside at first; instead I sat back down on the porch swing, wishing I could just be happy about hanging out with Paul again. Wasn't this what I wanted, all those years ago? Could we go back to the way things used to be?

But even if Madi showed up, and everything turned out okay, I still had to go back home, I still was without a job. Even without all this additional craziness, my life was at its lowest point. And even Paul Templeton, with his boyish charm, couldn't fix my life. Only I could do that. When I was young, I thought I could tie up my dreams in other people and interests – Madi, Paul, my parents, writing – but in reality, those people and things were just parts of me. There had to be a bigger picture in all this…

I drifted back inside the house, careful to lock the door behind me. Paul had given me the new keys and I laid them on the kitchen table.

There were a couple pieces of pizza left, so I stuck the box in the fridge, then stared out the kitchen window. The sun slowly melted behind the trees and I shivered. Darkness was coming. But it wasn't the dark that scared me – it was who was out there in it.

I wandered back to Shelley's bedroom. It was completely dark as I took the TV remote in my hand and sat down on her tiny bed. The floor of her room was still scattered with toys and discarded clothes. A porcelain doll stared back at me from the corner, its eyes glassy and menacing, reminding me of Rhonda's dead blank stare and bloated lips…

Even the tiny toy cars and trains seemed evil. Nothing felt right anymore. *But it never did in this town, did it?*

I turned the TV on and pressed play on the VCR.

A white snowy screen appeared and then the loud hissing sound of static bellowed through the tiny speakers. Cringing, I turned the volume down as fast as I could with the remote.

The snowy screen popped off and a black screen appeared. I stood up from the bed and moved to get a closer look.

'It's on,' a girl's voice suddenly said through the speakers. The screen was still dark, and I pressed my face closer to the screen, trying to see through the darkness…

And then suddenly, the screen jumped; someone was walking around with a handheld video camera of some kind. The view became clearer and I immediately knew the video was taken from inside this house. I recognized my father's armchair as it blurred by, and the coat rack in the corner … the white front door appeared, and then it swung open.

'What do you guys want?' said a playful voice. I finally recognized the sing-song, childish voice – *my sister was the one holding the camera.*

Jessica Feeler and Rhonda Sheckles were standing on the front porch – the younger versions of them. They looked so much younger than I remembered, Rhonda with her babyish freckles and Jessica with all that make-up. She looked like a little girl playing dress-up.

They were both smiling into the camera. Jessica struck a pose on the porch and Rhonda blew kisses. 'Are you going to let us in or what?' Jessica snapped, dropping her pose as she lost interest in the camera fast.

The screen bounced around and then went black again. *Was that it?* I wondered, feeling baffled.

I sat back down on Shelley's bed, watching. Waiting.

'I told you she was here,' someone whispered, causing the hairs on the back of my neck to stand on end. The screen was still black, but I could hear the sound of my sister's bell-like voice. I clutched Shelley's thin bedspread as I watched.

'Where?' another voice asked. That one sounded like Rhonda talking, but I couldn't be sure. The screen stayed black for several minutes. Time ticked by and I wondered if the video was over.

But then suddenly, Ben's room came into focus on the screen. Only it wasn't Ben's room, of course. Rather, it was my sister's old bedroom. My sister panned around the room with her camera, passing by the Debbie Gibson poster and her walls lined with Perfect Attendance awards. I could hear her breathing on the other end, raspy and urgent.

'Here we go guys, episode forty-two,' my sister's voice said from behind the camera. And just like that, a memory came rushing back to me … my sister, the prankster. She went through this phase where she wanted to be a TV host. She liked to play pranks on her episodes, barging in on me in the bathroom once and making me scream. And then there were the times she hid in the closet, times she filmed my reaction to some lie she'd made up...

The camera popped back on, still panning around my sister's room. She stopped when she got to the bed. I gasped. Sarah Goins was sitting on the edge of the mattress, her hands tucked neatly in her lap.

I shuddered at the sight of her; it was like seeing a ghost, or being a ghost myself...

Sarah was smiling, but it was a nervous sort of grin. 'Why are you taping me?' she asked, her voice so small and mouse-like. She was small – probably eleven or twelve – and not much bigger than Ben was now. Even when she was nearing her teenage years, she looked and acted so much younger than she really was...

'I can't believe you stood up to Jessica. I don't think anyone's ever called her a bitch before. Well, at least not to her face,' my sister said. I couldn't see Madi's face, only Sarah's reaction to her.

The corners of her lips curled up in satisfaction. 'She's a bully, Madi. I'm glad you finally realized it, too.'

'Guess what? I have a surprise for you,' my sister said. I kept waiting for my sister to turn the camera toward herself, so I could see it was her. *What the hell was she playing at with Sarah?*

'What is it?' Sarah asked, her smile fading completely.

The camera panned over to the closet on the wall. It was closed.

'Us, that's who!' Rhonda and Jessica leapt from the closet, startling even me. They were cackling, obviously pleased with themselves. The camera panned back around to Sarah sitting on the bed. Her eyes were wide, but she didn't look scared. More like, annoyed.

'I thought you weren't friends with them anymore, Madi. They're mean.' Sarah stuck her chin out, staring into the camera lens at my sister, her face defiant. The question was obviously directed at Madeline, but my sister said nothing in response.

'You really think she would be friends with you? That anyone would want to be your friend? You're fucking crazy.' Jessica popped into view. She was standing in front of Sarah now, blocking my view of the girl.

Jessica, with her hands on her hips, towering over the younger girl – she was your quintessential bully. My teeth clenched in anger as I watched her. *Were they going to beat Sarah up?*

Rhonda appeared at the right of the screen, coming over to stand right next to Jessica. There was a small white pillow in her hand. I recognized that pillow; it was one of the silky-smooth couch pillows my mom used to make.

Oh god. My eyes watered as I forced myself to keep watching.

'You shouldn't have called Jessica a bitch,' Rhonda snapped. Suddenly she leapt toward Sarah, knocking her back on the bed. I cried out, jumping up to my feet.

'No!' I screamed as I watched, in horror, as Jessica held Sarah down by her shoulders. I couldn't see Sarah's face, but it was obvious that she was struggling to get Jessica off her.

Then Rhonda leaned over the struggling girl and shoved the pillow down over her face. There was heavy, muffled breathing; Madeline huffing and puffing, the camera shivering and shaking in her hands.

'Okay, guys! You scared her! That's enough,' I heard Madi say, her voice babyish and her confidence fading.

Sarah's stick thin arms and legs kicked out wildly, fighting to get the bigger girls off her.

'Please don't,' I whispered. 'Please…'

As though she could hear me, Rhonda released the pillow and stepped back. I let out a sigh of relief. *Thank god.*

Sarah was trying to sit up, but Jessica was still holding her down. 'Put the pillow back on her face,' Jessica commanded Rhonda.

'Guys, that's enough.' Madi said. Her voice was frightened, fueled by adrenaline. I didn't think smothering Sarah Goins was what she'd had in mind for a prank.

'Do it now!' Jessica screamed at Rhonda. Sarah's arms and legs were flailing, fighting against the bigger girl.

'Don't,' I whispered, as Rhonda stepped back toward the bed. She looked back at the camera for a moment, the pillow held out in front of her like a shield.

'Don't,' I heard Madi whisper, her voice cracking. 'That's enough … please…'

Rhonda shoved the pillow back over Sarah's face. Her flails became wilder, more frantic. And then her limbs stopped moving completely.

Jessica let go of her arms and then disappeared from the screen. Rhonda glanced back at the camera again, right into the lens, then she removed the pillow from Sarah Goins' face.

Madi was panting behind the camera, a strange gurgled sound I'd never heard her make. She zoomed in on Sarah's face. She was like a doll, still and dreamy as though she'd simply just fallen asleep on my sister's bed. Like Goldilocks, she was taking a nap after dining on my sister's porridge…

'Madeline?' a tiny voice rung out through the speakers.

'Oh, shit,' Madeline hissed. The camera crashed to the floor.

'Madi, are you okay?' I could still hear the voice.

'Cover her up before you open the door!' Rhonda hissed.

'God, your sister is so annoying,' Jessica muttered.

It's me.

It's me, standing at the door while they'd just finished killing Sarah Goins.

The camera was laying sideways, my only view a distorted shot of the closet. But then I heard the creak of a door opening and two pink Nikes filled the screen.

'Madi, do you want to play cards with me?' I recognized my own desperate, child-like voice.

'No, I don't. Get out of here, Emily! Get the hell away from me!' I couldn't see anything but a side view of my own shoes and youthful legs, but somehow, I could suddenly remember that moment. Her words had stung. They'd hurt me more than anything.

My sister must have seen the hurt look on my face. 'Listen. We'll play later. Me, Jessica, and Rhonda have to go down to the woods now.'

'Can I come?' the young-me pleaded.

'Not this time. We have to be alone … to work on a school project,' Madeline explained.

The feet disappeared, the view of the closet reappearing when my feet stop blocking the screen. I heard the click of the door closing behind the young version of me. I was probably going back to my own room, to sulk.

'Let's carry Sarah out of here. Madi, you guard your sister's door, then meet us down in the woods. We can't wait much longer. Your mom and dad will be coming home soon.'

I don't know what Madeline said next because the camera shuffled around again, and then suddenly, Madeline's fourteen-year old face filled the screen. She looked directly into the camera, her eyes dark and hollow, boring into mine … and then the screen went black again.

175

CHAPTER TWENTY-FOUR

I waited for what felt like hours, for something else to happen. Finally, I got up and fast forwarded to the end of the tape, almost expecting to see another shot of them burying the body somewhere or killing some other innocent girl.

There was a click and then the tape ejected itself from the VCR, the finality of it deafening, and all too real.

I sat back down on Shelley's bed, clutching the gruesome tape in my hands while my whole body shook uncontrollably. A loud rumble of thunder outside nearly sent me into cardiac arrest. I got back up, flipping on Shelley's lights and then the lights in the hall. I couldn't spend time in the dark anymore. In fact, I wanted to wash away the grimy image of that video that was forever burned into my brain...

My head was throbbing as I stumbled into my sister's bathroom, searching for that bottle of Ibuprofen. Another clap of thunder rang out. *Was that outside or in my head?*

There were only four pills left in the bottle. Tossing the bottle back, I tried to swallow all four, but then I choked and sputtered, suddenly unable to breathe. Like Sarah, my breath was being taken from me...

I clutched at my throat, panicking, but then the pills

dislodged and suddenly, I was okay. Greedily, I drank water from the tap.

When I was done, I stared at myself in the mirror. My nose, my lips – they were mirror images of Madeline's. *How could someone who looked just like me and grew up in the same house as me, participate in something so evil?* She knew they were planning a prank on Sarah. I don't think she knew Jessica and Rhonda would kill her, but she should have done more to stop it ... *why didn't she tell the police, or our parents?*

I thought about my words to Ben the other day, about Madi and I sharing the same blood. How could I share anything with the same person who participated in that heinous act?!

But I remembered her shaky voice as she held the video recorder, she'd sounded so scared, so shocked ... and I had to remember she was only a child herself at the time. *What would I have done differently?* I wondered. I'd like to think I would have fought them off, encouraged Rhonda not to be pressured into helping, that I would have screamed for help...

But even now, I could remember that tension Jessica carried around. She set the tone of a room when she walked inside it. She was scary and mean, and no one ever stood up to her. *Including me.*

Madi didn't hold the pillow over Sarah's face, but she might as well have. She was an accomplice in someone's *murder.* Madi obviously lured Sarah over to the house after school – what did she tell her? That they could finally be friends? She tricked her into coming, and then when the prank got out of hand, she did nothing to stop it.

Remembering the look of hope on Sarah's face when she passed out those pictures in elementary school, I could only imagine how happy she was when my sister asked her to come over.

The taste of stomach acid filled the back of my throat. I ran for the toilet, heaving, but nothing came out.

Eventually, I wandered out of the bathroom, found my way to Ben's room, and stared at his bed. It wasn't far off from where my sister's bed used to be – and the place where Sarah Goins was murdered. How could she let Ben sleep in here after what they did?

I tried to think back to that time frame, after Sarah went 'missing' and I had my head injury … that was around the same time my sister became more distant, and then eventually, she moved her room upstairs for the last few years that she lived here. That was when we became less close, summer sisters no more.

Was this the secret she wanted to tell me? If so, why did she wait so long to confess?

'I've never believed in ghosts,' I said out loud, to the empty room. 'But if you're in here, Sarah, I'm so sorry for what happened to you. For what they did. I wish I could go back and rewind the tape – if I'd have come home just a few seconds sooner, maybe they would have stopped … maybe you would have lived.'

Suddenly, the lights in the room flickered, and then they flickered again. Rain pounded against the rooftop and thunder roared. I walked through the empty house from my childhood, my eyes glazed over as I pictured Sarah's flailing limbs as she took her final breaths… Suddenly, I didn't feel so bad about Rhonda's death. No wonder she'd killed herself – who could live with that sort of secret? Jessica had wanted Sarah dead and as usual, she'd made Rhonda do her dirty work. No wonder Rhonda was always depressed … living with that sort of guilt couldn't be easy.

Thunder boomed again and again, rocking the house to its core. I found myself in the middle of the kitchen, my brain pounding against my skull, the world rocking around me as the lights flickered again.

I glared out the kitchen window, into the darkness of the night and into the middle of a storm – a real one and a metaphorical one. My sister was involved in a murder.

The trees of the forest were swaying back and forth, a dangerous quality to the way they were leaning. Thunder clapped and then a bolt of lightning struck the sky, lighting up the entire backyard. For a brief second, I saw a moon white face peering out at me through the trees. *Sarah Goins is out there, watching me!* Haunting our lives forever ... and who could blame her if she did?

Was I going crazy?

But then another bolt of lightning struck the sky, and I saw the haunted face again.

Only it wasn't Sarah's face peeking out through the trees – it was Jessica Feeler's.

CHAPTER TWENTY-FIVE

I should have been frightened. I should have run for my cell phone and called the police, called Paul...

But for some reason, all I felt was hot white rage surging through me like lightning in my veins. I threw open the back door and stepped out into the raging storm. 'Jessica!' I screamed her name into the wind.

I wasn't wearing shoes, but I ran toward the woods anyway, broken branches slicing the tops of my toes and sharp, pointy rocks digging into my soles.

I ran right toward the spot where I'd seen her from the window. 'Jessica! Come here!' I screamed again. For a second, I thought she was gone, or that I had been seeing things after all...

But then I spotted her – she was running toward the beaten main path, her silhouette floating through the trees.

Still screaming her name, I turned back and ran toward the path. I was younger and faster than she was, and when I reached the open mouth of the woods, I saw her panting at the top of the slope.

'You evil bitch!' I kicked her as hard as I could with my foot, and watched, in shock, as she tumbled headfirst down the muddy slope. I skidded down behind her and reached the bottom just as she was struggling to pull herself back to her feet.

'What are you doing?' she shouted. Her hands were up, a pleading gesture. 'Please don't hurt me,' she said, her eyes wide and frightened.

'Hurt *you*? What do you think I'm going to do – smother you with a pillow?!'

Jessica's face contorted and even though it was dark, I could see that she had turned several shades paler.

The rain was unrelenting, pouring down in sheets, making it hard to catch my breath.

'Why are you spying on my sister's house? Were you planning to kill me too?'

'Of course not!' Jessica shouted, her eyes wild. 'I would never do that.'

I laughed. It echoed through the trees, sounding wild and maniacal.

'I saw the tape, Jessica. I know what you did. And I know damned well what you're capable of. You're just a pathetic bully. A nasty, evil bully! You always have been...'

'You mean you saw what your sister did, too, right? I guess you don't think she was a bully too?'

My face sagged. 'I know what my sister did. I also know that Rhonda sent her the tape before she killed herself, and that my sister wanted to come forward, but you told her to keep her mouth shut. Did you shut her up yourself? Did you kill my sister too?'

The rain was so heavy, I could barely see her expression, but I could tell she was shaking her head in the dark. More lightning crashed, and I could see the evil glint in her eyes.

'First of all, Rhonda didn't send the tape. Your sister did. I don't know why she felt so guilty all of a sudden, but she did. We kept that secret buried for so long ... and then out of the blue, she grows a fucking conscience. Rhonda called me, she was out of her mind, drunk and crazy as always ... but I didn't think she'd kill herself over it. I thought I could talk Madi out of coming forward. And I wondered what happened to the tape after Madi sent it but now, I guess I know. Rhonda must have sent it back to your sister before she killed herself.'

'Where is she, Jessica?'

'I told you! I really don't know!'

'I don't mean my sister. I mean Sarah. What did you do with the body?'

Jessica was bent forward at the knees now, rubbing her two bloody shins. 'We threw her in Moon Lake,' she muttered.

'Impossible! They already searched the lake for her body.'

'Yes, they did. I don't know how we got so lucky, honestly. Maybe the fish devoured her, or maybe she's hung up down there, somewhere so deep, they couldn't find her. But trust me, she is in there – I tossed her in there myself. I watched her body sink beneath the water. I waved goodbye from the shore...'

'Why were you so damn mean to that girl? What did she ever do to you?'

For the first time, Jessica's eyes turned glassy. Her mouth sagged and then she said, 'I don't know. She was an easy target, I guess. She made me feel better about being me. I know I was a bully, okay? I hate myself for what I did. When I replay it in my mind ... well, I just don't know who that girl back there was. I'm not that person anymore. I'm nothing like that now.'

'I find that hard to believe.'

'So, what now? Are you going to turn us in? Your own sister? For all we know, she went off and killed herself too!'

'You are damned right I'm turning you in. Sarah's mother deserves to know the truth. You're a mother now, Jessica – how would you feel if someone did that to your precious Chelsi, huh?'

And just like that I knew why my sister had suddenly felt so guilty. Her own son, Ben, always getting picked on and bullied for being different, for being strange ... she couldn't live with the secret of what they'd done to Sarah anymore.

'You think I don't feel bad about what I did? There's not a day that goes by that I don't think about it ... but I'm not the one who held the pillow over her face.'

I couldn't help it, I laughed. 'Did you forget my sister was taping you? It was you who pressured Rhonda to smother her. It was you who held her down, so she couldn't move. Don't forget, I went to school with you. I know how mean you were. And yeah, maybe you've changed ... but I bet there's a lot of you that's still the same. That mean girl is still in there, just waiting to come out. I'm going to the police, so what are you going to do to try and stop me?'

I stepped forward, only inches from her face.

'Nothing. All I can do is beg you, just like I begged your sister ... what difference would it make, anyhow? Sarah Goins is dead. Her mother thinks she ran away. Isn't that better than knowing the truth? What will happen to her mother if she learns the truth? What will happen to my children if I go to jail? Emily – think about what will happen to Ben and Shelley if Madeline goes to jail. They will always be tainted by what their mother did.'

I shook my head, considering her words. There was this deep, dark part of me – the part that loved my sister and my niece and my nephew – that wanted to agree. *Let it go.*

But that was what I'd done all those years ago when I saw Sarah getting picked on – I let it go. I kept on walking. I ignored it. And now that poor girl was dead. If I had been her friend, defended her ... could I have changed the course of time? Could I have prevented her death? That thought hit me like a bolt of lightning and I rocked back on my heels.

I tried to imagine a group of bullies doing the same thing to Ben. Or even to Shelley. A ball of rage fueled inside me. I imagined myself smothering Jessica or beating her until she died. I had enough anger inside me to do it...

'Did you hit me over the head in the woods? Was that you? Everyone said I fell that summer, but that was around the same time...'

Jessica's eyes widened. 'No, of course not. Although your sister thought it was me. I tried to scare her. When we took the body down to the woods, she was still freaking out. I warned her that I would hurt you if she went to the cops or told her parents. After you got hurt and she thought it was me … well, I sort of let her believe it. But it couldn't have been me; Rhonda and I went straight home after dumping her. You must have followed behind an hour or so later, because that's when it happened…I don't know how you fell, and to be honest, we were all so worried about them finding Sarah's body, that none of us spent too much time thinking about your head injury, except Madi. I saw no harm in letting her think it was me. I wanted her to be scared of me. If she feared something happening to you, she'd stay quiet. And for a while, she was, but I promise, it wasn't me.'

I stared into her eyes, trying to figure out how much of what she was saying was true…

'Get out of here before I do something I'll regret,' I told her. She looked stunned, still frozen in place. The rain was slowing; we were both soaking wet. My teeth chattered, and I could hear hers chattering too.

'Go!' I pointed toward the mouth of the woods. Then Jessica took off up the hill, struggling to run up it.

'And Jessica? Don't let me catch you snooping around my sister's house again!' I called after her.

If she heard me, she didn't turn around. Slowly, I climbed the slippery hill. From the edge of the forest, I watched Jessica's dark figure cut across Mr Tennors' field and head for the main road.

I didn't take my eyes off her until she melted into the inky blackness of the night.

CHAPTER TWENTY-SIX

The last thing I would have expected to do was fall asleep. But when I came back inside my sister's house, I was freezing. It was the sort of chill that burned and ached, and made my brain grow fuzzy.

I stripped out of my soaking wet clothes and let them fall in a pile on the kitchen floor. There was a stack of blankets upstairs and I carried them all back down, slipping and sliding with my wet feet on the staircase. I wrapped one blanket after another around myself, then collapsed onto the couch.

I didn't know if it was because of the trauma I'd endured, or if it was the anti-depressant I'd taken earlier, but I fell asleep within seconds of lying down on the couch.

I dreamt of Ben – thrust down in the backseat of the bus as boys took turns holding their backpacks over his face. Pushing and shoving, I tried to reach him, but the aisle was clogged with screaming children – no, not screaming; they were chanting something. At first, I thought it was, 'Go in! Go in! Go in!' But then I realized they were saying, 'Kill him, kill him, kill him, kill him…' I screamed until my throat filled with tiny needles, but all I could do was watch his little feet and legs kicking wildly as he struggled to take his last breath…

Gasping, I sat up straight on my sister's couch. I felt like I was being smothered as I rolled and jerked, trying to untangle myself from the heavy blankets, until eventually, I landed face flat on the floor. I was feverish, my head and body burning up as I stripped the remaining blankets off my naked, sweating body.

In the bathroom, I ran cold water in the tub, and then added a little hot. I climbed in, the water engulfing me like a silky cocoon. I let myself sink deeper and deeper, until my entire body and face were immersed.

Poor Sarah Goins.

She didn't deserve to die. Her only mistake was being different and trusting my sister – trusting that someone actually wanted to be her friend.

I didn't know how long I lay there, but time slipped away from me. I fell asleep again, half of my face pressed against the back of the tub.

Finally, I got out and wrapped myself in the biggest, softest towel I could find on the linen shelf. I didn't want to see, touch, or even think about that VHS tape again. The horror it contained would never leave me. It was embedded on my soul, making this grimy imprint on my subconscious. There were some things you couldn't un-see.

I forced myself to go get it anyway. With the tape in my hand, I carried it into my father's old office. I stuck it in a large, yellow envelope and wrote 'Paul Templeton' on the back. Wrapping tape around and around it, I tried to seal it so tight, as though I could despool the terror burned on its magnetic tape...

I needed to take this down to the station right now, but there was still something holding me back. What was it?

I wanted to talk to my sister. I wanted to ask her why.

I tried to imagine Ben and Shelley's faces when they found out the truth about their mother.

I went back to my sister's closet and got the box of pictures out.

The pictures of the three of them – the murderers. I couldn't even look at them. I pulled out the school photo of Sarah Goins instead and squeezed it hard in my hand.

Before I could change my mind, I got changed into some clothes and walked out the front door. I needed to go see Paul at the station, to tell him everything I knew … but instead I crossed the field and kept going – heading for the Goins Farm.

CHAPTER TWENTY-SEVEN

The field was like quicksand, my borrowed boots sinking further and further into the mud as I tried to reach the Goins Farm. Sarah's picture was still hidden away in my palm. I could feel it there, burning a hole straight through me.

A dense layer of fog clung to the air, making it impossible to see the farm in the distance, or much of anything in front of me. Dark clouds loomed overhead; I wondered if another brutal storm was brewing.

Sarah deserved a storm, the kind that rips and roars, tearing Bare Border apart. All this time, she was lying at the bottom of Moon Lake at the hands of my sister and her friends.

Orange-yellow lights split through the fog, and finally, I could see the brown and white farmhouse where Sarah Goins used to live. We had lived only a short walk away from each other, but I'd never even once considered going over to visit her when she was alive. God forbid the kids at school find out that I was friends with her. I was a coward. My cheeks burned with shame.

A bright red barn set back in the distance. There were only a couple dim lights glowing inside the farm house. I didn't know what I was going to say. It was very possible that I might admit the truth, right then and there, standing on Sarah's front porch.

I didn't give myself long enough to plan it out, I just knocked on the door.

It was early. I hadn't bothered to check the time before I left. My best guess was that it was seven or eight in the morning. An unexpected house-call this early was rude, but I felt compelled to see Sarah's mother. Her name was Mindy, that I remembered. But, honestly, I'd rarely ever seen her. I could remember her coming up to school to pick up Sarah a few times. She was an eccentric woman, wearing shawls in summer, her fingers and neck adorned with strange, antique jewelry.

The door opened an inch. An elderly woman with shocking silver-white hair stared out at me. Mindy Goins looked different than I remembered – sadder. Her eyes were raccoon-ish, her face drooping down in a perpetual frown. She gazed at me, wordlessly.

'Um, hi. I'm Emily Ashburn. I used to live across the field.' My own voice sounded strange and strained, like it belonged to somebody else.

'Yes. I recognize you.' Mindy looked suspicious, her lips pursed and her eyes narrow. After what I found out last night, I couldn't say I blamed her.

'May I come inside for a minute?' I was ready for her to tell me no, ready to turn around and go away, to forget everything I knew … but she opened the door and motioned me inside.

The farm house had a wet smell to it – like something moldy was growing inside. There were newspapers spread out on the kitchen table as though some sort of arts and craft project was about to begin. The countertops were littered with rancid packs of rice, and next to the sink, I spotted a rotting bag of green potatoes.

I followed Sarah's mother into a sitting room with two mismatched chairs and a shabby loveseat. *This was where Sarah grew up.*

The walls were covered in photographs – some of them were of Mindy and a man, presumably Sarah's father, but most were

189

of Sarah herself. I could feel her eyes watching me, accusing me, as I passed her by. I gripped her picture tighter in my hand. *I'm so sorry, Sarah.*

Mindy sat down in one of the chairs and I took the other, clearing my throat. 'I was going through my sister's things and I found this picture of your daughter.' I handed her the now crumpled picture I'd been holding. She stared at it for so long, I wondered if she would ever take it.

Finally, she plucked it from my hand.

'We went to school together.'

'Yes, I know. She told me you were one of her friends.' Mindy gave me a look I couldn't define – wistful, maybe. *She didn't believe Sarah when she told her we were friends. Maybe, deep down, even Sarah knew the truth—I was too big of a coward to be her friend.*

'She was a good person,' I said abruptly, shifting uncomfortably in my seat. I tried not to look at the pictures on the wall, but my eyes were drawn to them. Sarah perched on a stout, gray pony. Sarah in her underwear, draped in her mother's pearls and wearing high heels. Sarah in a pair of stonewashed overalls, holding up a fish. Sarah, as a baby, clutched in the arms of a smiling, mustached man – her father, perhaps.

'I remember this photo. She got this taken at school,' Mindy said. When I looked over at her, she was cupping the photo in her hands, lovingly. 'She was so happy that year because she gave out a bunch of these to her friends.'

'I remember that, too,' I said, softly.

'Only nobody gave her any pictures in return.' Mindy's face had hardened into a stiff mask. I wasn't sure what to say.

'I'm so sorry about Sarah, Mrs Goins. I really am. I'm sure you miss her terribly.'

Mindy had a far off look in her eye. 'I like to imagine that she ran away. It isn't so hard to believe, was it? I mean, after all, she was too good for this town. Nobody understood her or accepted her. They laughed at her expense. I like to think that she's some-where else – some big city where she fits in. She just wanted to make friends. She wanted that more than anything...'

My heart filled with sorrow, and I felt the guilt of what I already knew rolling through me. *Maybe she would be better off if she never knew what really happened to her daughter...*

'Did you find your sister yet?'

I looked up, startled by the change in topic. Apparently, even Mindy Goins knew about Madeline's disappearance.

'No. I have no clue where she is either. I wish I did...'

'I'm sure her children miss her deeply,' Mindy said.

'Did you know my sister well?' I asked. Mindy shook her head.

'Not really. Not well, anyways. Until ... well, I saw your sister at one of my grief groups in Merrimont. I've been going for years, so when she walked in, I was surprised. I'd recognize her anywhere – she always looked like a little yellow angel, out there playing in the sun by the field.'

'What was my sister doing there? I mean, did she say?'

'Well, the loss of her mother and father affected her deeply. And her son – your nephew – he's autistic, isn't he? She told the group about it, so I went up to her after class. I don't think she even knew who I was, though we've been neighbors most of our lives. I told her that my Sarah was the same way. She struggled with the same sort of issues Ben does; she was special needs. Only, back then, they didn't really know how to diagnose it as well, you see.'

My stomach fluttered. This was why. My sister felt guilty. Ben reminded her of Sarah. She probably sent the tape to Rhonda, hoping she would agree to come forward too. But Rhonda was already unstable, and that sent her over the edge, so she killed herself.

Something inside me was breaking. I couldn't imagine losing a child I loved, like Mindy had. It was hard enough being apart from my niece and nephew these last couple days. Being a mother, and losing a child like that, not knowing what happened to them ... it was presumably so much worse than anything I'd ever had to endure in my life.

I also couldn't imagine how difficult it was to live with the guilt of what my sister had done. She deserved to feel it, but damn, it must have hurt.

If it didn't hurt, then my sister was a complete sociopath. The possibility of that scared me more than anything ... but then I remembered the tremor in her voice, the way she tried to stop Jessica and Rhonda. *Why couldn't she have tried harder, dammit!*

'I just wanted to come by and give you the picture, Mrs Goins. I didn't realize you had so many already...' I stood up from the chair, looking around the room at the shrine one more time.

'You keep it, dear. She would have wanted you to have it.'

'Thank you,' I said, and I had to fight back tears as I took the picture back.

As though I were in a dream, I drifted through the sitting room and into the kitchen, eager to catch my breath outside.

Mindy shuffled behind, walking me to the door. My shin banged against something hard and I caught myself on the doorframe. I stared down at a twelve-pack of cokes by my feet. *RC Cola, a brand from another life...*

'I hope they find your sister's body soon. I would hate for it to stay missing forever, like my Sarah's.' Stunned, I looked back at Mrs Goins. I was shocked by her statement, but even more shocked when I realized she was pointing a gun in my face.

CHAPTER TWENTY-EIGHT

'What are you doing?' I stammered, but I knew perfectly well.

'I know you weren't the one who killed Sarah, but I can't have you snooping around, taunting me with your pictures, and pretending you don't know what your sister did.'

The barrel of the gun looked like a deep black pit waiting to consume me.

'Walk. And do it slowly. Out to the barn now, please.'

'But why? Why are you doing this?' Shuffling my feet, I was trying to put off the inevitable.

'You know why. Your sister killed my Sarah.'

'When did you find out?'

'When she told me.' Mindy jabbed the back of my head with the metal barrel of the gun, and I lurched forward out the door. 'Now don't try to scream or I'll blow that pretty little head of yours right off.' My heart jumped, the panicked beat of it pounding in both my ears. *She's going to kill me*, I realized.

I kept my mouth shut as I crossed the yard, Mindy breathing down my neck the whole way.

'I'm sorry about Sarah. I really am. I only found out the truth about her death last night.'

'Uh huh. Just keep moving and shut up.'

The door to the barn was closed. Mindy moved around me, and I watched as she unbolted the heavy barn doors. *I should just lunge at her, try to grab for the gun...*

But the doors swung open; I'd missed my chance, for now.

Mindy closed the doors back behind us, shrouding us both in the dark musty tomb that was the Goins barn. It smelled like horses, cow manure, and hay. There was also the smell of mildew – it was so strong I could taste it in my mouth.

All the stalls were empty. The farm was no longer a farm, just a ghost of a place that used to house animals and crops...

'Did you kill my sister? I understand why you did it. Believe me, I really do. I can't imagine how you're feeling, but really, I didn't know. I had no idea what those girls did...'

Mindy froze. 'Girls? What girls?'

I stiffened, unsure how much she knew. Had she seen the tape? She said that Madeline told her, but I couldn't see Madeline doing that...

'Did Madeline tell you she killed Sarah?'

Mindy shoved me forward and I stumbled over loose hay on the barn floor. This place smelled of *death*.

'Yes. She came over about a week ago. We'd sort of become friends from our time in that grief group together. She said she had something to tell me and then she admitted to killing my Sarah. Just like that! She didn't give me the details, all she said was that her body was in Moon Lake and she was going to turn herself in. I was shocked. After all these years, I never thought I'd know the truth. She begged my forgiveness and told me that as soon as you got to town to watch over her kids, she was going to go to the police and tell them what she did. I think she wanted to be punished for her crime, and your sister felt like she was being punished by God – all of Ben's troubles, and then him getting picked on at school ... she needed to repent. She wanted to do her time for the crime, so to speak.'

'But she didn't turn herself in. She disappeared.'

'Exactly.'

'Did you kill her? Did you kill my sister?' I asked her again.

'Not yet. Jail is too good for her. Death is too good for her. I want to make her suffer before she dies. My Sarah didn't get to choose her fate so why should your sister get to choose hers? The world doesn't work that way.'

A flash of hope exploded inside me. *Madi's alive!*

'Oh, Mindy. Please don't do this. Let Madeline go to the police. Let her do the right thing. Do you have her? Have you been holding her here?'

'The right thing! The right thing! The right thing would have been to let my daughter live to grow old.'

'So, it was you? Watching her from the woods. How did you take her from the house?' I was stalling now, my eyes jerking around the circumference of the barn – looking for weapons, or better yet, an alternative way out.

Mindy Goins threw back her head and cackled like a madwoman. 'I called her and told her I had to talk to her. She came outside, and I had the gun. For someone who committed murder, your sister is really dumb. She thought I was going to let her get away with it. Such a moron! I was going to just throw her off at the bluff, but like I said, that would have been too easy, too good for her. I wanted to make sure she suffered.'

'But you don't want to be a murderer too, do you? You're not evil, you wouldn't…' But my words were falling on deaf ears.

'Punishing your sister is the right thing, missy. And what better way to do it than to hurt you? I wonder how she'll feel when she sees you die. And after that, I'll bring in Ben and Shelley. I'll make her watch me kill them next.'

CHAPTER TWENTY-NINE

Mindy Goins pushed me further inside the barn. She pointed toward the last stall on the left. *What was she going to do to me?*

'Please.' I gave Mindy one last, pleading look before walking into the stall. I nearly stumbled over a cold white figure on the floor. *Madeline!*

'Madi!' I fell to the ground beside her and started trying to shake her.

'Enjoy visiting with your sister before I kill her.' I'm not sure which one of us she was talking to – maybe both of us – but then she slammed the stall door closed and there was a rattling sound on the other side. She was locking us inside.

'Madeline.' I shook my sister as hard as I could without hurting her. She was lying in a fetal position, her eyes closed ... but then suddenly, her eyelids lifted. She stared at me, her expression at first unseeing, and then perplexed.

'What are you doing here?' she croaked. I was shocked to see that her lips were bloody and cracked. She was wearing loose-fitting pajamas – the same pajamas she had on days ago when she disappeared. It looked like she'd lost thirty pounds already, but how was that possible?

Her shoulders jutted out at strange angles, her collarbones

stretched taut beneath her thin skin. Even her cheekbones were protruding, like an extra from *The Walking Dead.*

'Has she been starving you?' I was shocked beyond belief. I held my sister's head in my hands, stroking her hair. Strands and strands of her dirty blonde hair fell away with my fingers.

'I don't blame her,' Madeline croaked. 'I killed her daughter for god's sake.'

'But you didn't, Madi! Jessica did, she orchestrated all of it! Why isn't she going after Jessica?'

My sister closed her eyes again and flinched, as though blinking – and thinking – were painful tasks.

'I didn't tell her. I decided that I was just going to turn myself in, but I didn't want Mindy to see it on the news. I felt like I owed her that, at least. She deserved to know the truth. I thought I had time to … to get everything in order. But then she showed up and forced me into the car at gunpoint. She hit me over the head and made me drive…' Madeline choked and sputtered, her tears were waterless.

'I thought she was going to push me over the edge. And just when I thought I couldn't be any more scared than I already was, she said if I screamed or made a move, she'd kill Shelley and Ben.' Madeline's voice cracked as she mentioned her children's names. She began sobbing, but still no tears were coming out, maybe because she was too dehydrated to cry.

'Does she have them? Please tell me she didn't take them too.'

'John's got them. They're okay for now, Madeline. She didn't take me either. I found the tape. I came here to talk to her. I had no idea what I was walking into. She's old. She may have a gun, but together, we're stronger. We can fight her.'

'Can you blame her? If someone did to Ben what we did to Sarah, I'd hurt them even worse than this. You better believe I would…'

I didn't know what to say to that – I couldn't disagree – so I kept rubbing my sister's crumpled hair, looking around the stall for a way out. 'If we scream loud enough, someone will hear us. The walls on this barn aren't soundproof.'

Madeline let out what was either a cough or a chuckle. 'If you try it, she'll shock you with a cow prod, just wait and see.' Gently, she lifted the edges of her nightshirt. Gasping, I stared in disbelief at the red burn marks on my sister's sunken stomach. The strange burns were leaking pus and I now realized that they were the cause of the sickly smell in the barn. My sister had a life-threatening infection, not to mention she was starved and dehydrated.

'I'm so sorry, Madeline. She can't do this to us!'

'Monsters beget monsters…' At least that's what it sounded like she said as she closed her eyes again.

'Madi?' I tried to shake her again, but she was asleep. Nervously, I checked for a pulse. It was thready, but it was there – thank god.

Slowly, I slid her head off my lap and onto the dirty floor of the stall. I stood up, trying to stay quiet, and peek through the gaps in the wooden door.

'Mindy, are you there? I need to tell you something.'

My sister might have wanted to act all righteous and not bring Jessica into it, but I wasn't that nice. Maybe if I told Mindy about Jessica's role in the murder and mentioned the tape, she would leave the farm to either go hunt down Jessica, or at least to verify my story with the tape. If I knew she was going to be away, I could find a way out of this barn…

But Mindy didn't answer me, and I couldn't see her through the slats. Did she go back inside?

I remembered what my sister said about screaming and the cattle prod. Oh well. I'd let her shock me, if it meant I could tell her about Jessica first.

I opened my mouth and released a blood-curdling scream.

My throat was raw, but I still couldn't hear her coming. If she let me go on much longer, someone might possibly hear me. I took a deep breath and screamed again, waking up my sister beside me.

Madeline clutched my ankle, digging her nails in deep, a terrified look on her face. 'Please, don't do this,' she whispered.

But then I heard the door to the barn slide open. *She's back.* I backed up in the stall, terrified but preparing myself for what was to come.

'Before you shock me, I need you to know that someone else was involved! Two other girls! Rhonda Sheckles and Jessica Feeler. Madi just filmed what they did. She even tried to stop them! She didn't kill your daughter, Mindy. If you want to torture someone, then you better go get Jessica! I have proof. There's a tape at my sister's house, I can show you where it is...'

There was a loud popping noise that set my ears on fire. *Was that a gunshot?*

'Emily!' The voice didn't belong to Mindy Goins.

Oh my god. 'Paul! Is that you? We're in here. The last stall!'

I ran up to the stall door and peered through the slats. Suddenly, Paul's face appeared, and it had never looked as beautiful as it did in that moment.

'Oh, thank goodness you're here. Please, let us out! Madeline's in here.'

'Just a minute,' Paul said. I heard rattling sounds again. 'I'll have to come back. I have to find the key, or something to cut this lock off with.'

'No, don't go! Please!' But his feet pounded against the floor of the barn and I heard the screech of the barn door open and close.

I bent down and shook my sister again. She was drifting in and out of consciousness.

She's dying. I finally found my sister alive, and she's going to die on me anyways...

Paul had been gone so long, it felt like an eternity. But then I heard the screech of the barn door again. I was half expecting

Mindy's horrifying face to reappear through the slats, but I was relieved when I heard the jangling of keys and saw Paul's liquid blue eyes through the stall door.

The door flew open and he grabbed me into his arms. I'd never been happier to let him hold me.

'Where is she? Where's Mindy Goins?' I shouted.

'Dead,' Paul said, simply. He was holding me up in his arms, and finally, he sat me down on my feet. I ran back into the stall to comfort Madeline as Paul barked into his radio, calling for an ambulance. Sirens rang out in the distance, the sound of them like a beautiful symphony.

CHAPTER THIRTY

I never thought the click and whir of hospital machines could be so comforting. The doctors had Madeline on an IV – she was getting fluids and antibiotics to treat the infection.

'It will be a few days before she starts to look and feel better. She's in a great deal of shock. She's lucky you found her when you did,' the doctor told me.

Paul was standing at the door of the hospital room and he looked like he was guarding the door, with his uniform and gun belt. 'You can come in, Paul,' I told him.

He came and stood next to me, waiting for the doctor to leave the room. 'When will you tell the children?' he asked me.

'They already know their mom is okay. I called Starla from the back of the ambulance. But I told her not to bring them yet. I don't want them to see her like this. Not yet, anyways.'

'Do they know…?'

I shook my head. 'I just told them Mommy was very sick and had to be treated in the hospital. But I promised them that I would take care of her, and that they could come see her in a few days when the doctor said she was better.'

'I'm so glad you're okay,' Paul said, his eyes still scrunched up with worry.

'How did you know I was there?'

'Well, we were supposed to go out to breakfast, right? When you didn't answer the door, I realized your front door was unlocked. After I'd just changed the locks, I knew you wouldn't leave it unlocked unless something was very wrong. Just as I was walking through the house, Albert Tennors came to your door. He said you were trucking across the field toward Goins Farm. He was watching you the whole time from his window.'

'Of course he was. And for once, I'm glad of it.'

'So, I went over there to ask her if she had seen you. She said she hadn't, but then I heard the most god-awful scream coming from the barn. When I started walking toward it, she pulled out a gun on me. I dived for it, but it went off. She took a bullet to the brain. I didn't want to kill her, Emily. I really didn't. But she gave me no other choice…'

Regardless of what Mindy Goins did to my sister, I couldn't help feeling sorry for her. That woman had every right to be angry.

'We need to talk.'

'About what?' Paul asked, scratching his head.

'We'll have to go to my house. I need to show you something.'

**

It felt wrong, leaving my sister all alone after I'd just found her, but I needed to show Paul the tape. I needed him to know the truth about my sister's crime, and about what Jessica and Rhonda did all those years ago to Sarah Goins. The last thing I wanted to do was watch that tape again, but he had to see it for himself.

He asked me what was going on the whole ride back to my sister's house, but I stayed quiet. Just as we were pulling up, he said, 'I heard a little bit of what you were saying when I came into the barn. You said something about your sister and another girl killing someone?'

'I'm sorry to make you watch this, but you need to see it for yourself.'

I took his hand and led him into Shelley's room. I told him to take a seat while I went to unpackage the tape. I rewound the tape and then we sat, side by side, on the bed. Again, I watched my sister as she stumbled through the house with the camera. Jessica and Rhonda were standing at the front door...

'What is this?' Paul asked, perplexed.

I let out a deep whoosh of air. 'Just keep watching, please. But prepare yourself.'

This time, I stayed quiet as I watched Jessica and Rhonda suffocate Sarah Goins. Paul stayed quiet too, but I watched his face. I'd never seen him look so drained of color. After the final scene when I came into the room, I got up and turned it off.

Before I could say anything, Paul blurted out: 'Your sister didn't kill Sarah Goins.'

'I know she didn't. But she taped it for Christ's sake! Who does that? She was scared, and she told them to stop, but it was like she was frozen. She should have done something, called the cops or at least told Mom and Dad! She's kept this secret for almost twenty years, Paul. That's why Mindy Goins did what she did.'

Paul's eyes were glued to the blank screen, looking past me. 'It finally all makes sense.'

'What does?' I threw up my hands in exasperation. None of this made any sense to me. What Jessica did to Sarah Goins was unspeakable. Rhonda was pressured, and my sister stood by, but still, they were guilty too. In a way, we all were...

For the second time, Paul said, 'Your sister didn't kill Sarah Goins.'

'What are you talking about, Paul?'

He coughed into his hand, then his eyes met mine, staring at me intently. 'She didn't kill Sarah. Neither did Jessica nor Rhonda. And I know this because I'm the one who did it.'

CHAPTER THIRTY-ONE

I took a step back, my backside jarring against the dresser. 'What the hell does that mean, Paul? That's not funny, at all.'

He stood up from the bed. 'Let me explain.'

Goosebumps were sprouting on my arms and legs as I tried to back up further. He took two steps toward me, then stopped when he realized how scared I was.

'If you watch the video back, you'll see it. Rhonda didn't hold that pillow over her face long enough to suffocate her. Sarah was playing possum. And she was pretty smart to do it too.'

'Are you saying she played dead?'

'She did.'

'But I saw her arms flailing around like a fish out of water. And then she stopped breathing.'

Paul sighed. 'She stopped *moving*. That doesn't mean she stopped breathing. And I promise you she didn't.'

But I saw her face. *She hadn't looked dead, more like a doll sleeping...*

'You didn't see them checking her pulse, did you?' No, I hadn't. But still...

'You said you killed her.' I stuck out my chin defiantly.

'I did. Well, I didn't exactly kill her...But I did it all to protect you.'

'To protect *me*?' I screamed. 'What sort of sense does that make?'

'They must have carried her somewhere into the woods, and then she got up again...' Paul said, more to himself than me. He was on his feet now, pacing around Shelley's bedroom.

'Jessica admitted to me that they threw her in Moon Lake. They watched her body go under the water,' I told him.

'Well, she came back up. Trust me.' Paul stopped pacing, his stare intense again.

'But how do you know that, Paul? How?!'

'You remember how we used to meet down by our tree? The one with our initials on it?'

I nodded, remembering how good it felt to see it again the other day. I'd nearly forgotten about it.

'I was cutting across the field, the way I always did...I was coming to see you. We had to sneak, remember? Your dad hated my guts and we weren't even thirteen yet. That day, I was going to surprise you. You were walking down to the woods, maybe looking for your sister, or ... yeah, I think you were trying to find Madi and her friends in the woods.'

'Okay. And...?' I pressed.

'Well, I saw you before you saw me. I liked watching you. You were cutting through the trees, following the creek down to our spot. And that's when I saw Sarah Goins. She had her back pressed against our tree. She was wet – soaking wet – like she'd just gone for a good long swim. I didn't know her very well at all. All I knew was that she was the girl everyone liked to make fun of.'

My head tilted to the side, listening intently as I tried to figure out where he was going with this...

'You were walking straight toward the place she was hiding. I just figured she didn't see you coming, but then I saw she was holding something in her hand. It was a rock, Emily. A big, pointy ass rock. I tried to yell for you, but it was too late. Just as you approached the tree, she whipped the rock out from behind her

205

and slammed it down over your head. You hit the ground so hard. I took off running, but by that point, she was beating you with it and you were flailing around on the ground, stunned. She slammed it down on the back of your head so many times, I thought for sure you were dead.'

Without realizing it, I was rubbing the scar on my scalp. *Could this really be true?*

The *red, red, red* of my memories, the sharp hot pain as I crashed over and over again ... only it wasn't a fall that caused my injury. It was Sarah. Did she really go missing on the same day as my injury? I'd been in the hospital and when I got out ... news of my accident was overshadowed by bigger news: Sarah Goins had gone missing. The timing made sense. But why would Sarah do that to me...?

Oh god...

'What did you do, Paul?'

'At the time, I didn't know why she was hitting you. I thought she was just going crazy. But now, I realize that either she saw you coming and mistook you for Madi, or maybe she just wanted to hurt *someone* after those girls had tried to kill her ... and that someone was you. I didn't know. I didn't know what they did, Emily, I swear...' Paul was rubbing his face with his hands, trying to erase the memory.

'What happened, Paul? I need to know.'

'I grabbed her arms from behind and yanked her back. She was shocked to see me, and still trying to escape my arms so she could hurt you...When I looked over and saw you on the ground, all that blood gushing out of you ... I thought for sure you were dead. I wrapped my hands around that little girl's neck. And I squeezed. I was shouting at her, asking her why she did that...'

'But my sister found me.' This image of Paul, strangling a little girl to death, was too horrifying to imagine. I tried to picture his big hands around her tiny neck...

'Madi found you. I heard her shouting for you just as I took my hands off Sarah. I saw what I'd done, and I could hear your sister coming. I knew someone would find you then, but I thought you were already dead and maybe they would think I killed you both. I lifted Sarah from the ground and I ran. I hid behind the closest bush, the one just past our tree. I held that girl in my arms until your sister ran back up the hill to get your mom. Emily, she was still *alive*. I swear she had a *pulse*. I was so scared. Everyone in town knew my dad was a mean drunk, and I thought they'd blame me for your attack and for Sarah's ... so, I left her there, disoriented, and took off across the field.'

'But no one ever found her. Where is her body, Paul? It's not in the lake, and somebody would have found it by now in the woods...'

'That's the weird thing. I sat at home, waiting for the cops to come. I was so sure she'd tell them I grabbed her neck ... but when they didn't show, I went back out to look for her. It was dark then, but I looked everywhere. I even went to her house and tried to look through the windows. It was like she'd just vanished into thin air. And when I heard she was missing, I was sort of relieved. But then I also thought ... I thought that maybe I'd killed her after all.' He was sobbing into his hands now, his words barely audible.

'Then where the hell did she go? This doesn't make sense. We still don't know where Sarah Goins is.'

'I do,' Paul choked. He buried his face in his hands. 'A few years later, I was drinking with my friends. They parked at the side of Star Mountain and dared me to hang from the edge. I was so stupid – I always was – and I did it. I climbed down the side, but I slipped a bit ... and hanging there by one arm, I looked down and that's when I saw her. She's laying at the bottom of Star Mountain, Emily. She's been there all this time. And that's why I stood you up for prom. I couldn't show my face at a school dance after finding Sarah like that. I hid inside for weeks after, her cold, dead face popping up every time I closed my fucking eyes! And that's why I left school shortly after, too. My past was coming back to haunt me, and I just knew that someday they'd find her ... but they never did. No one ever found out.'

A dam inside me broke apart just then. *Everyone I love has a secret. Secrets I wish I never knew...*

Monsters beget monsters. They tried to kill Sarah Goins, and so she tried to kill me. Her mother tried to kill Madi. Paul almost killed Sarah trying to protect me, and he succeeded in killing her mother. It was all too much to take in right now...

'I couldn't even look at you afterwards. I thought I could move past what I did, I thought I could ... but when I saw your face, all I could think about was Sarah's face, and how it looked when I was choking her. I used to have these dreams, and sometimes I still have them. She's always in them. And being around you, well, it always made it worse. That's why I broke up with you back then. I kept trying to come back. I wanted to take you to prom ... but then I would freak out again. I would think about that girl, and how she'd never get to go to prom, or grow old. I went into law enforcement to make up for what I did. I thought if I could help people, do the right thing ... maybe I could make up for it. I thought I was protecting you, and I was, but I know I'm responsible for her death. I don't know if she jumped from Star Mountain, or was just so disoriented that she fell...'

Paul slid to the floor on his knees, taking me down with him.

I don't know how long we stayed there. It might have been hours, or it could have been days.

My sister was safe, and now I knew the truth about my accident and what happened to Sarah Goins ... but somehow, I couldn't help feeling more scared than I ever had. How could I ever trust my sister or Paul again?

208

EPILOGUE

'What does everyone want for dinner?' Madeline asks.

'Mac and cheese,' Shelley and I say in unison. Ben giggles and says the words 'mac and cheese' eight times.

We're all sitting at the dining room table – Madeline, me, Shelley, and Ben. It's Madeline's first day back in the house, and the place has never felt more alive. Ben and Shelley are happy to have her back, Ben especially; he's been bouncing off the walls all day, waiting for her arrival.

'Sit down and let me make it, you silly woman,' I insist. I stand up and get the pot down from the cabinets, while my sister sits back down next to Ben. She looks as though she's gained ten pounds, but her eyes are different – they still look dark and hollow, like a piece of her happiness has been stripped away forever.

Next month my sister goes to trial for her role in the attempted murder of Sarah Goins. The judge let her out on a low bond, but Jessica Feeler wasn't so lucky. She's being held on a 250,000-dollar cash bond. Even if her family could afford to get her out, I'm not sure they'd want to. The people of Bare Border will never look at her the same way. They will never look at Madeline the same way either.

Footage of the horrific tape has been making its rounds on the internet – so far, pieces of the horrible incident have been played on news channels and talk shows. The complete video is available on YouTube.

As for Paul, he has been temporarily placed on suspension from the police force.

Both his and my sister's lawyers think they'll be let off the hook since they were children at the time of Sarah's death. Paul hurt Sarah defending me, and my sister was just an accessory, at least that's the defense's argument.

But I'll never look at my sister the exact same way. I don't think the media, or anyone in this town, will either. She'll wear it like a scar, the same way I carry the scar of her actions on the back of my head. I wish I could have talked to Sarah, reasoned with her. If she'd gone to the police, those girls would have been locked up, including Madi. Maybe … or maybe not. Maybe everyone would have called her crazy, just like they always did.

Sarah Goins – for the first time – has been raised to saint status. Her picture is displayed in almost every store window in this town. 'Justice for Sarah' is what the signs in people's yards and the ribbons in their windows say.

Now I look at that photo of her, the one torn to shreds by Jessica Feeler, and I think about how much she would love knowing that everyone in town wanted one of her pictures, that she was finally the hero of her own story…

Tomorrow we're putting the inn up for sale. There are parts of it that I will miss, the parts of my childhood that were good. But memories don't live in walls – they live inside the people who dwell there. For the most part, I'm happy about the move. I think it's time to go.

There's a small bungalow on Painter's Creek that will be perfect for the kids. The trees on the property are young, their rings of memory not tainted yet – at least I hope not. It will be a good place for a fresh start, and to make new memories, hopefully good ones.

Madeline made me promise that I would stay in Bare Border, although I didn't need much convincing. I've fallen in love with my niece and nephew, and I want to stay close by. I promised Madeline that if she was found guilty, I would take care of the children in her place. John has been playing a more active role in their lives, but with his work schedule and recent break-up with Starla, he won't be able to keep them all the time.

I'm scared for my sister – scared about what will happen to her in prison if she goes – but I'm confident that I can take care of the kids in her absence.

We'll make it work.

As far as Paul is concerned ... there's still this version of me walking around this town that loves him. But I'm not that girl anymore. And frankly, he's not the boy he once was either. We've agreed to take it slow, and for now, that's good enough for me.

I didn't think I would find any sort of work in Bare Border. But when the news finally broke about the twenty-year-old mystery and my sister's kidnapping, I realized that there hadn't been a local paper in Bare Border for almost fifty years.

I'm taking over the news in Bare Border, starting out slow. I've never run a paper before, but I know how to write, and after all the snooping around I did when my sister went missing, I feel pretty good about my investigative skills.

You'd think there wouldn't be much news to share in this tiny town, but every day there's something. Today I had a meeting with the manager at Bed and More. They're talking about going on strike, in an attempt to become unionized. I'm going to interview the employees and tell the world about their grievances.

I don't know if small town news is my 'calling' or not, but I'm enjoying the art of writing again. I enjoy telling stories, especially the ones that are founded in truth. My sister asked me the other day if I'm going to write a book about Sarah Goins' death. I told her no, but I've already been outlining chapters. I think it will be hard to write about something so personal and close to home, but somebody needs to tell Sarah's story. Someone needs to make sure her memory lives on…

I didn't see her body. But I heard that when they pulled her out of the water, she was pristine – like a sleeping, timeless, porcelain doll. I only wish her mother could have been there to see it. To see her Sarah that way, young forever, might have offered her some sort of closure. Or maybe not. Maybe the Sarah she had imagined – the one who ran away to find a better life – was better than the truth. Sometimes the truth is scary.

There was another piece to the puzzle that I never knew until recently: all those years ago, Sarah's mother had found a soggy wet note on her bed: *This town will be better off without me.* Her mother and the police assumed she ran away, but as we know now, the true meaning of the note was more sinister than that. She must have returned home after beating me over the head and Paul's attack, written the letter, and then went to Star Mountain and jumped. I can't imagine what was going through her head in that moment…

This town will be better off without me.

She couldn't have been more wrong about that.

They said it was a miracle. *But how can being found dead at the bottom of Star Mountain be a miracle?* Nevertheless, they said it was virtually impossible, the way she fell…

Six thousand feet down from the cliff was a small, naturally formed, body of water. The water down there was freezing.

The fall wasn't a straight drop. There were jagged rocks and jutting cliffs all the way down … and at the very bottom, mostly rocks. If you drop from that high up, those rocks will slice through your body like butter – a body that jumped from that far should have been smashed to pieces at the bottom, after being torn up by rocks all the way down…

But Sarah's body didn't.

The cops said that no matter how they tried to reenact it, they couldn't figure out how Sarah Goins fell six thousand feet and landed so far away, undamaged, in that small lake. For the second time in one day, Sarah found herself face up in a body of water. Only this time, she never climbed out of it.

But like an angel, she'd lain there, splayed out in the icy cold water. Waiting. Watching. Wanting to be found. *This town will be better off without me.* That's what she thought that day, and we were all to blame for that. In the end, she took her own life. This fact will probably help Paul, Madi, and Jessica escape blame. But I know – and hopefully, they do too – that we are all to blame.

I know that Sarah tried to kill me. I know there's a part of me that should be mad. But just like with Madeline and Paul, my feelings for Sarah are mixed. *Monsters beget monsters.* I choose to remember her the way she was – a sweet, misunderstood girl who wanted to make friends. I just wish we could have been friends.

If I'd have been more courageous and kinder, we might have been.

What happened to Sarah has changed my life, but it has changed *me* too. When I think about Ben – and other kids like him – who are misunderstood and often mistreated, I think about the adults they eventually become. We never know what demons plague our classmates, neighbors, friends, and families. We never know what others are capable of, or how bullying will impact their lives.

Not being a bully is not enough. We have to stand up and defend others when they can't defend themselves. I hope that the next time I'm given the chance, I'll be one of those defenders.

Keep reading for an exclusive look at
Carissa's next gripping thriller...

Without a Trace

I don't believe in ghosts. But standing here now, with the tips of my toes tingling with heat, and my eyes stinging, not from the fire but from me, forcing myself to keep them open, never blinking, I can't help wondering if she'll come back and haunt me for this. Her limbs twist at uneasy angles. Her skin splits apart and dissolves. Her hair and clothes fall away, like feathers caught in a dust storm. And her face...it almost looks plastic, quivering and bending in the amber glow of the flames. It's as though she never breathed life in the first place. This is not how I imagined it—I thought it would be quicker. I thought she would scream more. Fight more. But it's almost like she's resolute, like she's telling me it's okay...that she forgives me for what I must do.

CHAPTER ONE

The Mother

NOVA

I shivered as I stepped off the front porch and followed the well-beaten path down to the shady tree line. It was early, the sun playing peek-a-boo through the trees, and little wet kisses of dew were sprinkled around the yard like watery pockets of glitter. Such a peaceful morning, like the promise of a brand-new day. A *beautiful* day, in fact.

It was a rental property, but still, it felt like mine. Like the perfect place to raise my daughter.

Suddenly, the wind whipped through the trees, shocking the breath from my chest. It reminded me of what I already knew—*looks can be deceiving.*

Clouds bubbled up in the sky, the morning sun dissolving away like a figment of my imagination. As a flurry of cold air rushed around me and through me, I pulled my jacket tight against my chest and glanced back at our new house. It was a small log cabin, like something you'd see at a state park or campground. But the size was perfect for the two of us, and unlike my husband, I liked the coziness and simplicity of a single-family home.

Lily would be waking up any second now, and I didn't want her to be afraid in our empty, new house.

How can I raise a daughter who is strong and brave when I'm so damn scared all the time?

I took one last look at the trees, at the once-soothing sunrise. Branches morphed into bony claws. They reached for me, gnarly and twisted, eager to pierce through my ragged flesh like broken bones...

Whipping around, I raced back toward the house. A low moan escaped from between my teeth as the house swayed from side to side, like one of those carnival mirrors. The distance between the front door and the tree line suddenly stretched, for what looked like miles...

My sneakers were squishy on the cool, wet grass, and as I slipped and slid across the yard, I imagined the mud was quicksand, sucking me deep down into the earth, consuming me whole...

Once inside, I locked the door and pressed my back against it, sucking in long, craggy breaths until they evened out. It only took a few minutes to still my thumping heart.

That's better. Well done, Nova, I commended myself. Each time I panicked, it was taking fewer and fewer minutes to calm back down.

Hell, maybe after a few weeks of being here, I won't have panic attacks at all.

Fumbling for a light switch in the kitchen, I stubbed my toe on Lily's tiny *Cars* suitcase. It was still lying in the middle of the kitchen floor, next to my duffel bag, where we'd tossed our luggage last night.

In the light of day, our new kitchen looked different than it did last night. White paint on the cupboards looked yellowish and worn. The sink was rusty, and a slow drip of water *ping ping pinged* in the basin below. Looking around, I tried to imagine this kitchen as our own—baking cookies for Lily while she sat on the edge of the counter, kicking the backs of her heels against the cupboards below. Normally, I would make her get down because Martin didn't like that.

But now Lily and I can do whatever we want.

And a rundown, drippy kitchen was better than any sort of kitchen we might share with Martin.

A scarred wooden table with four chairs was set in the kitchen. There were other modest furnishings, too—a chair in the living room, beds and dressers in both bedrooms—which was one reason I chose this place. It was the perfect getaway spot, out in the middle of nowhere, and we didn't need to bring much to get started.

The refrigerator and cabinets were still empty and in need of a good scrubbing. We'd grabbed some fast food on the way to West Virginia, but I hadn't wanted to stop at the grocery store yet.

All I wanted to do was get us here.

But now that we were, I'd have to spend the weekend making it as homey and comfortable as possible for Lily.

We're doing this. We're starting over. This is our home now.

For months, *years*, I'd imagined this moment. But then, it had just been a fantasy, a twisted version of hyper-reality. I never really thought I would leave. Even the night before we left, I'd expected myself to back out. To freeze. To panic and collapse in the middle of the street after loading our cases. But I didn't. And it wasn't until we were almost a hundred miles outside of Granton that I knew it was really happening...that we were leaving Martin for good.

My duffel bag lay sprawled open on the floor beside the table, from where I'd taken out my pajamas last night. We were so tired when we got here, to the point of delirium. It had taken nearly ten hours to reach Northfolk, the rising hills and winding curves of West Virginia making me skittery and afraid. I couldn't stop checking the rearview mirror and my heart was thrumming in my ears the entire drive. During the daytime, it hadn't been so bad. But at night, I'd imagined every pair of headlights were the angry, glowing orbs of Martin's truck, chasing us up the wild, mountain roads...

Lily had handled the move so well, believing me when I told her that we were going on an adventure. With her mousy brown hair and cornflower blue eyes, she looked just like Martin. But, luckily, she hadn't inherited his meanness, or his wild mood swings.

Lily was, by all accounts, a normal four-year-old year girl. But that wouldn't have lasted long, not while living with Martin. Eventually, his violence would have moved onto her, seeping into her pores and saturating her life with his poison.

She was innocent, so seemingly unaware, yet she'd already learned to fear her father and his unpredictable ways. And the way Martin looked at her...his eyes searching, evaluating her every move, it made me uneasy.

I'm taking her away from her dad. What kind of mother does that?

Emotions played tug-of-war inside me—I felt guilty for stripping her of her fatherly influence, but I was relieved—exuberant, even—to give her a fresh, safe start in life. During the drive to Northfolk, I'd been so focused on getting away, that the guilt hadn't had time to settle in yet. And last night, I'd been too tired to stay up worrying. But now...now all those worries came rushing back at once.

What will I tell her when she's older? Surely, she will remember Martin. Will I tell her why we left? How much memory can a four-year-old retain?

"I m-made the right decision," I told myself, firmly, for the hundredth time this morning.

Pressing my face against the window pane, my eyes scanned the backyard. From behind a layer of murky glass, the branches no longer seemed murderous or threatening. Even the clouds were wimpy, less dark. It was ironic, really. After years of feeling

222

claustrophobic, shut inside the house with Martin, now it was the outdoors that overwhelmed me.

Everything overwhelms me.

Again, my thought from earlier came crawling back: *how can I raise my daughter to be a stronger, better version of me when I'm so scared of the world and the men that live in it?*

Clutching the necklace at my throat, my fingers curled around the dainty silver cross that Martin had given me on our anniversary. The holy symbol should have brought me comfort, but all I could think about were his hands pressed against my throat, the crossbars digging sharply into my flesh as I struggled for a tiny bit of air…

Tenderly, I reached back and unclasped it. It seemed wrong to throw it away, but then again, I couldn't keep it. It hadn't protected me when I'd needed it to, and expelling Martin's memory from our lives was my top priority now. Before I could change my mind, I carried the lightweight pendant over to the waste basket and tossed it inside.

I didn't put on makeup this morning. There was no rushing around to make Martin's breakfast, or to see him off to work.

No slamming doors or missing shoes or screaming.

No angry fists pummeling my body.

Most mornings, the air felt suffocating and dense. I'd wake up panting, a surge of panic hammering through my bloodstream and lifting me from bed. I was always afraid I'd oversleep, and sometimes I did. If Martin was late for work or didn't have the things he needed in the mornings, he blamed it on me. And worst of all, he seemed to enjoy punishing me for my mistakes.

He must have been so angry when he realized we were gone. We didn't take much when we left, just Lily's suitcase and my bag. But he must have known immediately.

The first thing he probably did was call my cell phone, and from there, it wouldn't have taken him long to find where I'd left it—on the nightstand next to our bed.

He can't reach us here.

There was no note. No paper trails. I'd saved up small amounts of cash over the past year, so there wouldn't be any need for ATM withdrawals. I had enough money to last us for a while, until I could figure out how to get some more.

Pinching my eyes closed, I couldn't shake the image of his seething blue eyes, the angry caterpillar brows furrowing in anger.

He's probably mad enough to kill me right now. To kill us both.

I could almost his taste his rage from six hundred miles away. It tickled the back of my throat and burned the edges of my tongue.

Fear. I can taste that, too.

The fear I'd felt earlier was rushing back. My old friend Panic seized my chest, like a boulder pressing down on my belly, making every breath tight and controlled.

He might find us. What will I do if he does?

As I passed through the hallway, fingertips grazing the unfamiliar walls of the cabin, I thought I heard a muffled grunt coming from behind Lily's closed bedroom door.

Nonono. He's not in there. I'm only imagining he is.

I'd imagined his voice last night, too, before I fell asleep. The angry, breathy snores that he made while he slept. My body so accustomed to sleeping next to his, I'd lain against the edge of the mattress, curled into a tight little ball, despite all the extra space.

"One, t-two, th-three…" I counted out loud.

I read somewhere that counting helps alleviate anxiety. My lips silently formed the words, but the clenching in my chest remained. Suddenly, I was hurtling back to our house in Tennessee. Fear slithered in through the logs. Martin's anger dissolving and sinking down through the rafters…

"F-four, f-five, six…" My skin tickled and crawled, my stutter rearing its head again, becoming worse, the way it always did when I sensed a confrontation coming. As I moved through the hallway, I fought the urge to look back over my shoulder.

Martin is not standing behind me. He's not! I chastised myself.

The hallway tilted and swayed, then slowly, the buttery yellow paint dissolved. I wasn't back home in Tennessee; I was in our new house, faraway from Martin.

Safe.

"A-are you a-awake yet, Bunny?" My stumbled words a mere whisper through the heavy door.

Bunny. It was a nickname given to her by Martin, and I'd have to remember to stop using it. It would only serve as a reminder of him, and Lily wouldn't need any of those, now that he was out of our lives for good.

Closing my eyes and taking a deep breath, I nudged the bedroom door open. Soft sunlight streamed in through moth-eaten curtains above the bed. There was no Martin.

See? Nothing to be afraid of.

Lily, so tiny, was curled up beneath the blankets in a ball, unmoving. Like me, she was always trying to make herself smaller and unseen…

Lily had never been a good sleeper. She was prone to nightmares, but last night, she'd slept all the way through. Reaching across the bed, I slid the curtains back, welcoming more light into the room. The bright white heat was soothing, like a warm cloth across my face. I released a long stream of breath, relieved.

"Rise and shine, B—" I stopped myself from using the nickname again, squeezing my lips together. There were so many bad habits to break, and this was only just one of them…

I prodded the soft little lump in the middle of the bed. But Lily didn't move a muscle.

Finally, I rolled the covers back, imagining her sweet morning smile and sleepy doe-like eyes.

I know they say you should always love your children no matter what, and I do, but for some reason, my heart just soars when I see her doughy cheeks every morning. She is always at her sweetest when she first wakes up.

225

"Lily?"

A strange wisp of gray-white hair poked out from beneath the blanket. I stared at it, my mind not comprehending the strange bit of fur.

Tentatively, I rolled the covers down. Button-eyes stared back at me, black and menacing.

It was a toy rabbit, but not like the ones Lily used to keep on her bed in Tennessee. This bunny looked ugly and old, its limp arms and legs adorned with black, plastic claws.

I poked at the strange stuffed toy, shaken.

"B-bunny? Where are you?" I grasped the corner of the blanket in one hand, then yanked it the rest of the way off.

Lily wasn't in her bed.

A deep guttural scream pierced the morning air.

CHAPTER TWO

The Cop

ELLIE

It started with a phone call, buzzing on the bathroom sink as I painted my eyes with charcoal liner.

"Makeup? Is that wise?" My mother was leaning on the doorframe, watching me get ready for work. Even though she retired from teaching five years ago, she still got dressed up like she was going to work each morning. Today she was wearing a creamy, salmon-colored pantsuit with brown pumps and a string of pearls.

"Just stop, mom." I rolled my eyes, dusted off my right palm, then took the call. It was Sergeant DelGrande, so loud and brash my mom could probably hear his words clear as day, even if she hadn't been standing right by my side.

I mumbled 'yes' a few times, adjusting my thick brown ponytail in the mirror as I balanced the phone between my shoulder and cheek. I hung up and tucked the phone in my back pocket.

"What was that about?" my mother clucked, pretending she hadn't heard.

"Nothing to worry over. See you at dinner." I kissed her on the cheek then hurried out the front door.

227

"Be safe," she added as I left, almost too quiet for me to hear.

As I climbed in my cruiser and buckled my seatbelt, she was perched like an eagle behind the curtains, keeping watch as I reversed down the driveway.

Most parents would be proud of their twenty-eight-year-old daughter who was just starting out in the police force, but Barbara James wasn't your usual mother. She was Catholic and came from a strict family, and she had tried to raise me much the same way.

When I told her I was taking the law enforcement entrance exam, she had laughed. But when I passed the test and entered the police academy, that laughter had turned to tears.

Not only was she worried because the job was dangerous, but she was also concerned about my reputation. *What will people in the parish think when they find out you want to be a cop?* she'd asked.

First off, I didn't give a damn about my mother's parish. Part of me relished the thought of their gaping faces when they learned about my new job.

Secondly, I'd reminded her that I didn't *want* to be a cop. *I am a cop now*, I'd told her. And there was nothing Barbara James, or anyone else in Northfolk, including the parish, could do about it.

I'd always been fascinated by people. I wanted to help them. *Understand them.* And as corny as it sounds, I wanted to make a difference in the world. At first, I'd considered psychology or social work. But what better way to make a difference than to help the one group of people that no one gives a damn about? The *incarcerated*.

But Eddyville Penitentiary was hours away, and it paid more to be a cop than a corrections officer. It started out as a small dream, but once I'd entered the academy, it became an obsession. An obsession that, once upon a time, stretched beyond being a small-town cop in my tiny town of Northfolk...

But my views on helping and understanding criminals were

looked down upon by my peers, and I was reminded at the academy, more than once, that it was my job to help the *community*, not the criminals who muck it up. I understood their point of view, but I was idealistic—couldn't I help the community *and* try to make a difference in people's lives? Was it really impossible to do both?

Northfolk was a close-knit mountain town, comprised of less than five thousand people. Nevertheless, it was riddled with poverty and with that came heavy drug problems, specifically heroin and meth. Besides drug crimes, sometimes I had to cite people for shooting off unregistered guns or riding ATVs on private property. Domestic disturbances and petty thefts occurred occasionally, too, but they were the exception, not the norm.

I'd only had one serious incident since joining the force, but it was enough to change all those well-thought-out plans I'd previously made. Four weeks into my new job, I'd been called to the scene of a domestic disturbance. I didn't recognize the red-faced, frazzled woman who opened the door, but I did recognize her husband. A well-known cop, Ezra Clark, was accused of assaulting his wife. I had no choice but to call it in...and to arrest him. But what happened next...well, let's just say that Ezra didn't take too kindly to a new, young, female cop trying to take him into custody. He was angry and drunk, and although the scuffle between us only lasted a few seconds, the results had caused long-term effects. Possibly, *lifetime* effects. Memories of that day came floating back...the pounding pop when I fired my own gun, the burning smell of gunpowder in my nose. On my lips...

Would I ever be able to forget that day? And most importantly, would my colleagues and the residents of Northfolk...?

Sergeant DelGrande's instructions circled back through my mind. He'd asked me to go directly to 8418 Sycamore Street, where a woman had called in, claiming that her ex-husband had stolen her child right out of bed. It sounded like a domestic disturbance, but I wasn't familiar with the address. It was near the old Appleton farm, but no one lived out there besides the Appletons, as far as I knew.

As I pulled down the gravel drive to the property, I was instantly met by a running woman. Thick black hair swept across her face, a silky pink robe blowing back like a cape in the wind. I closed my eyes, fighting back images of Mandy Clark opening the door that day...if I let myself think about it long enough, I could still remember the smoky smell of Officer Clark's flesh as I pulled the trigger...

The events of that day were still such a blur. One minute, I was sliding the cuffs on his wrists, and the next, it was me being slammed against the hood of my cruiser. *You think you're tough, don't you? You don't know shit, rookie.* He let me go, but then he did the unthinkable: he reached for my gun. Afterwards, my fellow officers would claim that Ezra was probably just teasing, trying to show me I was ill-prepared as a new cop...but he was wrong about that. When he reached so did I...and moments later, one of us was lying dead on the ground...

Cautiously, I parked and emerged from my patrol car. While most of my male colleagues would have itched their fingers over their guns at the sight of a hysterical person, my instinct was to go to her, to calm her down. She was clearly distraught, her cheeks streaked with tears, her skin blotchy. I couldn't shake off images of Mandy Clark's distraught face, her battered skin stretched over her face like a ghoulish mask...

"Sh-she's gone," the robed woman choked out the words, all the while fighting with the hair around her face. "M-my Lily's gone."

The wind howled, blistery cold for September, causing me to stumble a bit with the heavy belt weighing down my mid-section. I shook off my whirling thoughts about that day with Ezra Clark and tried to focus. "Ma'am, let's go inside and talk. Would that be okay?"

She hesitated, giving me the once over as though I were a stranger asking to use her phone. Her eyes were wild, shell-shocked. Maybe she knows who I am. Maybe she knows I shot a colleague, I thought. But that's ridiculous, I chastised myself, immediately. This woman was new to Northfolk; she couldn't possibly know about the Clark incident.

"I'm here to help. You called *us*," I gently reminded her.

Shakily, she led the way inside. The cabin was sparsely furnished, a small arm chair and rug in the center of the living room. Everything looked worn but clean, and not recently used. There was no TV, no pictures or personal effects.

"How long have you lived here?" Awkwardly, I tried to adjust my belt, then took out a notebook and pen from my back pocket. The pages were blank, which for some reason, made me feel embarrassed.

"I just moved in yesterday. Me and my daughter, Lily. She's f-four."

"And your name?"

"Nova Nesbitt." The words were like whispers, strained.

"And your ex-husband, how long have you two been divorced?"

Nova shifted from foot to foot, chewing on a stray piece of hair and looking around the room with those wide, wild eyes. "Well, we're not. I mean, I-I only just left him y-yesterday."

I clicked the bottom of my pen, open and closed. It was a nervous habit.

"Does he live in Northfolk, too?"

"No. He's b-back in G-Granton, Tennessee. I can g-give you the address though."

After I scribbled his name, address, and phone number down, I closed my pad. "Ma'am, if you're not legally divorced and you both share custody of the girl, then it's not a crime for her to be with her father."

Nova was pacing now, her skimpy undergarments exposed as the robe shifted back and forth across her thighs. She was a tall woman, but painfully thin. I thought about that expression, the one about a stiff breath of wind blowing someone away.

She stopped moving, her face twisting with desperation as her eyes searched mine. "L-listen, you d-don't understand. He was abusive. He *is* abusive. That's w-why we left. I d-don't know how he knew we w-were here...he must have followed me! And w-while I was asleep, that bastard t-took my daughter. She's in d-danger. You have to b-believe me. Her life depends on it! He will hurt her to get to me, m-mark my w-words." It was painful watching her mouth twist and struggle to form the words.

"Do you have a restraining order against him?" Part of me was secretly glad he wasn't here. The thought of getting directly involved in another domestic dispute made me more uneasy than I'd like to admit.

Even though she was looking right at me, it seemed like Nova was seeing straight through me now. Her eyes turned smoggy and lost.

She mashed her hands down on her hips, and muttering under her breath, she said something about a piece of paper being unable to keep someone safe.

I could see her point but having a legal document that prevented her husband from taking the girl would have made my job much easier.

"Have you tried calling him?" I asked, unsure what my next move should be here. I had been so confident when I'd started this job—maybe too confident—but lately, I couldn't shake the feeling that I was like a little kid playing dress-up in my cop's uniform. After the incident with Ezra Clark, none of my colleagues trusted me or wanted to work with me...and lately, I'd found that I was struggling to trust myself...

Domestic situations were always tricky, and sometimes the parents used their kids as pawns, or weapons, to hurt each other. Was that what was going on here?

Nova shook her head. "I-I haven't c-called him." She reached for the arm of the sofa, stumbling to catch herself from collapsing to the floor below.

I kept my eyes on her as I flipped through a couple blank pages in my notebook. Still gripping the couch arm for dear life, she closed her eyes. She was muttering under her breath, counting, I think...

I was close enough to smell her breath and I noticed it was hot and stale. But I caught a whiff of something else, too. Alcohol crossed my mind, but this smelled more minty, possibly like mouthwash. Did she wash out her mouth with mouthwash before I came?

That didn't seem like something a distraught woman would do, I thought. But looking at Nova Nesbitt, there was no question in my mind: this woman was freaking out. She seemed scared. Skittish.

Scanning her face again, I looked for signs of drug use. Although heroin was the main drug of choice in these parts, I'd been around a lot of meth users, too.

She was acting strange, but her pupils were normal-sized. She didn't appear to be on drugs, but then again, it wasn't always easy to tell.

"He's d-dangerous," she repeated, rocking back and forth on her heels. "Very dangerous."

"Can I see where Lily was sleeping?"

Without answering, Nova drifted down a shadowy hallway, dragging her robe along like a bridal train. Cautiously, I followed behind, looking for anything out of order. We passed a master bedroom and bathroom. Both looked empty and pristine.

When we entered the child's room, I immediately noted that it was neat but bare, like the rest of the house. There was only a twin-sized bed and dresser in the room. The bed unmade, there was a creamy blue blanket folded neatly at the foot of it.

"Found this." Nova held up a strange, stuffed toy. I took it, turning it over and back in my hands. It was odd, unlike any sort of stuffed animal I'd played with as a girl. A rabbit, and a down-right ugly one at that, with eerie button eyes and worn out brown fur. It had plastic black claws on its hands and feet and two jagged white teeth protruded from the bunny's mouth. There were a few pieces of gray string protruding from its head. It almost looked… cruel.

"Is this your daughter's toy?" I set the creepy rabbit back down.

Nova was pacing beside the child's bed. She stopped and threw up her hands in disgust. "No! Why aren't you listening? I found it! My husband…he calls Lily his 'little bunny'. I think he left this here to taunt me. He's dangerous! Please, you have to take me seriously!" In Nova's angry outburst, the stutter had all but disappeared.

The hairs on the back of my neck stood on end as I stared at the forlorn toy. *Little Bunny*. What a creepy thing to leave behind if he was the one who took her, I thought. Suddenly, this seemed less like a custody dispute, and more like a kidnapping…but the last time I got involved in a domestic squabble, a man had ended up dead. And my nickname by my colleagues—"Cop Killer"—ensued.

"I'm going to take a look around the rest of the house. That okay?"

"Yes! That's why I called you, isn't it?" Nova huffed. She walked out of the room, mumbling to herself again.

As I walked around the side of the bed, looking more closely at the room, I couldn't help but be reminded of playing hide and seek with my cousins and friends when I was a kid. Could Lily be hiding somewhere?

It was possible that the husband took her, but I hadn't seen any signs of struggle or forced entry. How did he sneak the girl out?

The window behind the bed was locked tight. I peeked beneath the bed. The wood floors were clean, no dust or debris underneath. Next, I checked out the closet and drawers. I was surprised to find them full. A neat row of children's clothes hung from the rack. Removing a pale-yellow dress, I was surprised to find it still

234

had tags attached. I sifted through the other outfits too—everything looked brand new.

"Ms. Nesbitt?" When I stuck my head out of the bedroom, I was surprised to find her standing right there in the hall. As we came nose to nose, I jumped and made an embarrassing squeaking sound.

"F-find anything?" She gnawed on her nails, shifting from foot to foot, reminding me of a toddler waiting to pee.

"Did you buy new clothes for Lily?"

"Oh. Yes," Nova said, nodding. "We d-didn't have time to pack m-much."

I nodded, then resumed searching. The first two drawers were full of underwear and socks and the bottom drawer contained books and toys. Again, all looked brand new. Some were even wrapped in their packaging still.

Something about this whole thing felt off. I could understand having to buy new things when moving, but new *everything*? It seemed highly unusual.

Next, I walked through all the other rooms, checking for broken or unlocked windows. I opened closets and looked beneath the few furnishings inside the house.

A new thought was shifting around in my mind. "Lily wouldn't wander outside on her own, would she? New house, new place. Maybe she went off to explore?" Images of dead, floating kids in ponds fluttered through my brain. And miniature, mangled bodies by the side of the road, the bent-back limbs protruding…

I'd never seen any of those things in real life, but I'd seen plenty of ghastly images while studying at the academy. Some of the men in my class liked to "shock" me with them, sticking them in my locker and desk drawers during training. I was one of only two women in my class, and behind our backs, they liked to call us "the pretty one" and "the ugly one". I think I would have preferred the latter.

"No, she wouldn't. I s-sat on her bed, r-reading to her until she fell asleep. And I ch-checked on her a few times before I w-went to bed last night. I was w-worried. I looked around outside b-before I called, but I-I know h-he took her…"

"How do you think your ex got in the house, if he didn't have a key?" We were standing in the kitchen now. I stared at the child's suitcase on the floor. It was decorated with smiley red cars, the one from that Pixar movie but I couldn't remember the name of it. Not having a child myself, I suddenly felt unsure how to help this woman. My mother would know what to do and where to look, I thought. Instantly, I pushed that thought aside, feeling childish and incompetent.

What I should do is call one of the officers back at the station, but they all hated my guts and didn't trust me…

I stared at the suitcase on the floor. Nova had time to hang up new clothes, but didn't unload the suitcase, I noted. It was one more minor detail that made me think something was off…

Nova chewed on her bottom lip and it looked like she was fighting back tears. "I don't know. Maybe M-Martin picked the lock. He c-can be pretty clever when he w-wants to be."

"Do me a favor. Call him now, and I'll go take a look outside. Okay?"

Nova gave me a nervous nod, then opened one of the kitchen drawers. She took out a cheap flip phone and started dialing.

"He w-won't recognize this number. I left my cell behind when we m-moved. This was just a pr-prepaid ph-phone I p-picked up," she explained, pressing the phone to her ear.

Even though I'd said I was going outside to check, I stood still, watching her place the call. Please let the husband pick up the phone and say he has the girl, I hoped.

What if someone from Northfolk took this child? That thought made me queasy. The last thing I needed was another run-in with a bad dude in Northfolk. But if someone from here did

236

this…then I had to do something to help this woman and her child.

Internally, I quivered at the thought. Why couldn't some other officer have taken this call? I wondered, exasperated.

"P-prick!" Nova snapped the phone back shut.

"You didn't leave a message," I pointed out.

"He never ch-checks his m-messages," Nova explained, placing the phone on the kitchen counter.

I took my own cell out, dialing the number I'd written down in my notebook. After three rings, the phone went to an automated voicemail box.

"Martin Nesbitt, this is Officer Ellie James with the Northfolk police department. I need to speak with you right away. It's urgent. Call me back at this number, please."

I started for the front door, eager to check outside, but then I stopped in the entranceway. I stared down at a pair of women's running shoes. They were muddy. "Your daughter's shoes. Where are they?"

Nova's eyes widened as her gaze followed mine. "Sh-she h-had sparkly orange sn-sneakers on when we got h-here yesterday." Her eyes went fuzzy, her lips curling with anger. "If she put her shoes on, then she must have gone with him w-willingly! But w-why would she do that?"

"Ma'am, I'm not sure. Hopefully, your husband will call back soon and clear this whole thing up. But for now, I'm going to check outside and then contact my sergeant about your daughter. Can you get some pictures together for me? If we issue an Amber Alert, I'll need the most up-to-date photo you got…"

But Nova was shaking her head back and forth, her skin turning paler by the minute. "I don't have one. N-not even one ph-photo…" she breathed.

"I know you guys just moved here, but how about a pic on your cell phone?"

But Nova kept shaking her head. "I can't believe it. I d-don't even have one picture of my little girl. How insane is th-that?" She looked spacey now, and once again, I wondered if she might be using drugs.

"Don't worry, ma'am. We'll get one. Maybe from a family member, or friend? Or if you could just pull up one of your albums on Facebook or Instagram…that will work, too."

"No," Nova said, firmly, her eyes zeroing in on mine.

"No?"

How could this woman not have any pictures of her own daughter? It seemed completely unfeasible, but if she really was afraid of her husband maybe she did leave everything behind…

"I wasn't allowed to have a Facebook profile. I-I don't even know what I-Instagram is, honestly. M-Martin was j-jealous. Controlling. He's d-dangerous, I told you…"

Yes. He was *dangerous.* That was about the only thing she'd made clear so far. I couldn't shake the feeling that there was something else—something she *wasn't* telling me.

"Family or friends with pictures…?"

"I don't really have any family. And any fr-friends I had…w-well, that was w-way before I married M-Martin."

Surely, she had pictures at her house in Tennessee, I considered. But Tennessee was a day's drive away, and I needed something now.

"What about pre-school or daycare? Any photos on file they could fax over to my office?"

Nova cleared her throat. "Lily isn't in pr-preschool yet. M-Martin wanted me to homeschool her. Can you believe that? Homeschool! M-Me! I don't even b-believe in that crap…" she snapped, looking angry again. Her arms hung loosely at her sides, but she was shaking. As helpless as she seemed, I honestly felt the same.

"Keep trying to call him, okay? And this time leave a message," I urged, heading out to the front yard.

I walked around the front and back of the property. There was a backdrop of woods behind the house, but the trees were thin and sparse, so it was easy to see through the wooded space. I called out, "Lily!", but instantly felt silly as my own voice bounced back in my face.

It was eerily quiet out here. And as I walked around the entire house and yard space, I saw no signs of a child. My stomach churned. Something feels so wrong about this...

After going around three times and circling through the woods, I combed the ground in front of the house.

If Lily was hiding, she would surely have come out by now.

No pictures. Only new clothes and toys. It was like a child hadn't even been here, I thought, spinning around in circles. I closed my eyes and pictured my niece, Chelsea. Her room was like a landmine of toys, my sister's house a jungle gym of playthings. But Nova's house was scrubbed clean, not a toy or stray article of clothing in sight.

But she did say they just moved here, I reminded myself.

There was a blue Celica parked at the side of the house, which I assumed belonged to Nova. I peered in through the passenger window. There was no little girl hiding inside.

And no car seat in the vehicle either, I noted. How did she get Lily here without a car seat?

No toys or clutter in the backseat. Nothing. Almost like the child doesn't even exist, I thought, curiously.

My eyes floated across the field to the Appleton Farm. If I remembered correctly, Clara Appleton owned all this land. She was probably the one renting out the house to Nova.

Maybe the neighbor saw something...anything that could help me find this faceless child...

239

CHAPTER THREE

The Neighbor

CLARA

Cradling a cup of coffee in my hands, I watched Officer Ellie James through the dining room window as she stood in front of the cabin next door.

I heard Nova Nesbitt scream this morning. But still, I did nothing to help her.

My new tenant had sent me the first month's rent and a security deposit last month, and she had arrived just yesterday as planned. It was late when she got in, much too late in my opinion, but maybe she got lost or turned around on her drive into town.

I'd been tempted to go over and talk to her, to introduce myself, but I'd refrained. Landlords are known for being nosy. I didn't want to be like that. But it did feel strange having a neighbor again. With my oldest daughter in Texas, I'd grown accustomed to the quiet and lonesome life on the farm. Knowing that another human being was only a few strides away was a strange, yet welcome, feeling.

Last night, I'd watched the lights in the cabin pop off and on, wondering what Nova was up to. And then this morning, I'd been awake, toasting bread like I did every morning, when the jarring scream had ripped the air.

And now the police are here...

As the owner of the property, I probably should have gone over there and seen if something was wrong. That would have been the normal thing to do. Any sort of terrible thing could have happened related to the house—a fallen fan, a rusty nail...

But the last thing I wanted was contact with the police.

Hot coffee sloshed out the sides of my cup, dribbling between my fingers and down my arm. My mind drifted across the field to the old rickety barn at the back of the property. It used to house cattle and horses, back when Andy was here. But now it was empty. Well, except for one thing...

My hands shook uncontrollably until I lost my grip on the mug completely. It hit the floor with a dull thud just as I saw the young officer crossing the field straight toward my house. I wrung my now empty hands together, trying to steady the tremors.

The milky brown stain at my feet spread out like a halo around the unbroken mug. It reminded me of blood. Dark, thick, unrelenting blood...

Smoothing my favorite flannel shirt, I took a deep breath then went to the front door to meet her. Why does she want to talk to me?

I opened the door before she could knock, forcing a smile as I did. I recognized Officer Ellie James—she was the spitting image of her mother, Barbara. Barb and my late mother, Carol, used to hang around when they were younger. But I doubted that Officer James knew that fact or cared about it.

"How can I help you, officer?" I croaked, then grimaced at my own voice. After a decade of not smoking, I'd recently started up again. And it was obvious from the scratchy tone of my voice. I tried to swallow the lump that was forming in my throat, but it felt like a fishbone was lodged in my windpipe. Probably cancer from the cigarettes already, I lamented.

"You own the cabin next door, is that right, ma'am?"

Surprisingly, Officer James looked more nervous than I felt. She was young, and pretty, too, with a soft, freckled face. But she was wearing too much makeup, in my opinion, the lines of her eyeliner drawn out in a way that reminded me of an Egyptian princess.

"I do," I said, clearing my throat. "Everything alright over there?"

"When did Nova and Lily move in?" she asked, dodging my question.

"They came in late last night. From Tennessee. Quite a drive, you know? I was asleep. But I heard the car door, and I saw the lights go on over there."

"Did you see anything else? A child outside? Any other cars on the property?" Officer James held a small notebook in one hand, and with her other hand, she flicked her pen open and closed.

A sudden memory fluttered through my mind, then dissolved.

"Um, yeah, I did. Woke up around one in the morning, I guess it was. A second car was out there. Thought it might be her boyfriend, or someone helping her move. Not my business, you know? But I did think it was a little late for visitors…"

"What sort of make and model was this second car?" Officer James looked alert now, and she started writing something in that notebook of hers.

"I couldn't say. Too dark. Aren't any flood lights out there, you know? And the porch light wasn't on either. I heard the car pull in and the door slamming shut. Never saw a child. I guess it might have been a truck I saw…"

"Did you see anyone get out of this truck? This is important, ma'am."

I closed my eyes, thinking. "I only looked out there for a second. Didn't want to look like a peeping tom. I think they were wearing a hood. Like a hoodie sweatshirt. And they were carrying something. Maybe she was carrying her daughter in her arms. Not sure though. Why? Something happened?"

"Your new tenant's daughter is missing. Please, if you see anything, or think of anything else, call me." She snapped her notebook shut then dug around for a business card. "Oh, and we may need to come back and search your property. All this land, if it comes down to it. Right now, we're still waiting to hear from the husband."

I tried to keep a straight face as I nodded obediently, but my throat felt like it was closing up completely. Despite feeling like I couldn't breathe, I was itching for a cigarette.

Officer James added, "Most likely, the husband took her. They recently split up. Divorces are so messy..." The young officer bit her lip, as though she'd said too much, then handed me a stiff business card.

"I will call you if I do. Thanks." I closed the door, letting out a long whoosh of breath.

I listened to the sound of the patrol car pulling out as I straightened up the kitchen. Cleaning was one thing I liked to do when I got nervous. Smoking was another.

Back in the kitchen, I gathered up the mug, discovering that a small chunk of ceramic had come loose. I threw it away, then went into my bedroom to search for some sort of carpet cleaner. Anything to take my mind off smoking, and the jarring police visit.

The stain would be hard to get out. Usually, I was careful, rarely needing cleaners to fix my mistakes.

I stopped for a moment to smooth out the edges of my bedspread, my fingers trembling. My pack of Camels was tucked away in my bedside drawer, within reach.

But instead, I picked up one of the stuffed bunnies my husband made for me, squeezing it tightly to my chest.

Acknowledgements

Writing is a lonely endeavor. Two years ago, I was sitting in the woods by myself, sulking, when the plot for *My Sister is Missing* emerged, seemingly out of nowhere. You see, I'd been working on this other book for a long time, and after years of indie publishing, I couldn't seem to hit the mark. I went down to the woods to clear my mind and try to conjure up a plan for how to revise my current manuscript. As I gazed through a gap in the trees, I realized that I had a direct, creepy view into my own kitchen. I could see my family from the woods, but they couldn't see me. I tried to imagine what it would look like, watching my own family – my own life – from this hidden view in the woods. I got so creeped out, that I took off running back inside. An hour later, I was sitting at the kitchen table, feverishly writing a brand-new story. I wrote it faster than any book I've ever written, and the characters just wouldn't let me quit until I finished telling their story. That story eventually evolved into *My Sister is Missing*.

Now, I said that writing is lonely. And it is. But once the story was finished, the script completely flipped – taking this story on my computer and turning it into a real book was a group project, and I couldn't have done it without the following people:

I am eternally grateful to my agent, Katie Shea Boutillier. She believed in this book from the very beginning and made me feel like a 'real' writer for the first time in my life. Even though she believes in my writing, she never goes easy on me. Her ideas and critiques are invaluable, and this book wouldn't be what it is today without her insight and guidance at every turn.

My editor, Charlotte Ledger – Charlotte probably doesn't know this, but I secretly admired her and her clients for many years before she ever saw this book. When I found out that she loved the book and wanted to acquire it, it was one of the best days of my entire life. I tried to play it cool and calm, but inside, my heart was exploding with joy. This story evolved into the book it is today because of Charlotte's incredible insight into this story. She helped me take it to the next level, and it was like a thousand tiny light bulbs lit up when she gave me her feedback.

I also want to thank Emily Ruston and Dushi Horti for their invaluable editorial work on this book, and the entire Harper and Killer Reads team for making me instantly feel at home. They provided me with a beautiful cover and made this process so enjoyable for me.

A huge thanks to my first reader, and dear friend, Chelsi Davis. She always tells it like it is, and she believed in this book so much that it gave me the confidence to keep going. Thank you, Chelsi! And I'm so sorry that you always have to read the roughest, rawest versions of my books.

To my sister, Vicki, and my mother, Lana – thank you for believing in me and encouraging me to keep going even when the process felt impossible and draining.

To Shannon, Dexter, Tristian, and Violet – every book I ever write will be for you all. You all believe in me more than I believe in myself, and have inspired so many of my stories. As long as you all like my books, then I'm set for life.

Lastly, thank you to my dear readers – I appreciate you taking a chance on this book and me! If not for you, I couldn't write, so thank you from the bottom of my heart for reading this book.

KILLER
READS

DISCOVER THE BEST
IN CRIME AND THRILLER

Follow us on social media to get to know the team behind the books, enter exclusive giveaways, learn about the latest competitions, hear from our authors, and lots more:

/KillerReads    **/KillerReads**